"Wh
mande
"I'm
about
manners to boot.

She snorted. "I know more than any five hands about our own horseflesh," she asserted.

"Then prob'ly you've got awfully dumb hands working here. And anyway, this one isn't *your* horseflesh. It's mine, and I'm the only one as has to be pleased, which I am, for I know what I'm doing. Which is more than I can say for you."

"That's quite a mouthful for a damned kitchen hey-boy."

"Which means you know good and well who I am an' knew it when you asked."

She ignored his logic and stepped close to the horse. She ran a practiced hand over the near flank and down the hip line. Rather than comment on the quality that could be found there, though, she faced forward and pointed a finger toward the neck. "If you don't call that ugly, you're even blinder than you look," she said bluntly. Again she snorted. "My guess is you thought you had you a world-beater in this old snide and didn't cut him until it was too late. Now you've got a cresty old stag that won't ever be worth anything, and you're too damn stubborn to admit it."

Hart pursed his lips to hide the shadow of a smile that was tickling the corners of his mouth. "This here's a mare horse."

"A . . . mare?"

"Uh huh. And an awful poor prospect for being called a stag."

Charter Westerns by Frank Roderus

JOURNEY TO UTAH
OLD KYLE'S BOY
THE NAME IS HART

THE NAME IS HART

FRANK RODERUS

CHARTER BOOKS, NEW YORK

All characters in this book are fictitious.
Any resemblance to actual persons, living or dead,
is purely coincidental.

THE NAME IS HART

A Charter Book / published by arrangement with
the author

PRINTING HISTORY
Ace edition published 1979
Charter edition / October 1986

All rights reserved.
Copyright © 1979 by Frank Roderus.
This book may not be reproduced in whole or in part,
by mimeograph or any other means, without permission.
For information address: The Berkley Publishing Group,
200 Madison Avenue, New York, New York 10016.

ISBN: 0-441-56021-0

Charter Books are published by The Berkley Publishing Group,
200 Madison Avenue, New York, New York 10016.
PRINTED IN THE UNITED STATES OF AMERICA

For Arnold and Janice Goble

1

"A riding job?" the gray-haired man asked. "With eyes like yours? The hell you say. There's no way you could see well enough to rope or to spot hiding strays. Huh-uh. Don't try to tell me you can, for I know better."

"I won't try to tell you a damn thing except I can do the work. I can't see to rope as well as some, mister, and maybe I can't spot your strays. But I'm as good a flanker as ever you saw, and I can do anything there is to be done with a horse and maybe go a little ways more."

The taller, younger man showed no anger. This was an old story to him, one he had heard repeated often. With one exception his appearance was normal, even superior. His features were well formed and handsome, jaw square and firm, a nose that might have been lifted straight from an imitation Greek urn, mouth thin lipped but generously molded. His hair was brown and lightly curling. His limbs were straight and heavy with long, pliant muscles. He was trim and looked extremely fit, at his prime in his late twenties or early thirties. Only his eyes presented a jarring note.

They were pale brown and flecked with gold. They might even have been what a woman would find attractive save for one thing. They were not still long enough to be really seen. His eyes were constantly in rapid, almost violent motion, darting and weaving and stuttering in motion. They gave a vaguely felt impression of being overly rounded and a much more strongly felt impression that they were defective. That, at least, was correct.

"What happened to you, anyway?" the middle-aged rancher asked bluntly. It made it all the worse that Hart knew the man would never have considered asking so direct and personal a question of anyone else, on any more normal subject.

"None of your damned business, mister," Hart flared. He could feel the sudden heat exploding in his belly like a tossed-down glass of whiskey and spreading upward into his throat. "I came here looking for a job of work, mister. If I wanta make confession I'll go find a priest. Now either hire me or don't, but keep your mouth shut on matters that ain't your affair."

The rancher recoiled, physically backing off a short half step. "I didn't mean it like that," he declared.

"Bullshit!"

"I *said* I was sorry. Are you going to let it lay or not?"

Hart felt the anger slowly begin to dissipate. "All right," he said reluctantly. He turned and began to walk away.

"Don't be in such a hurry," the rancher said, the words directed toward the back of Hart's neck.

Hart wheeled. "Now what?" He stood where he was, not bothering to return.

"Look, man. I don't have any riding job for you. But if it's work you want, well, I need a hey-boy for my cook. I'll pay twenty a month and keep. That's the best I can do."

Hart grunted. He bit off the words he wanted to fling down between them. It had been a long time since he had had steady work. He nodded. "You'll get your money's worth."

"I expect to," the rancher said. He had not expected any thanks. Both knew there was no charity being offered here. "The cook's name is Brown. You'll find his wagon at the loading dock over there. It has my brand painted on the side. V-Slash-4. Can you . . . ?"

"I can make it out."

"All right then." The man turned and went back inside the hotel saloon where Hart had found him minutes earlier.

Hart moved in the direction that had been indicated in a dimly seen wave of the hand. He found several dark, blurred, boxy shapes there and when he got close enough found the one with the appropriate, yellow painted brand on its side. Hart hopped nimbly onto the rough wood platform of the loading dock and entered the adjacent store.

Inside he was surrounded by smells. Oil and leather and, mostly, foods. The heavy odors of smoked meats and the sharper bite of brine, the faintly musty smell of dried produce and the sweeter, pervasive scents of dried fruits. Hart paused to sniff and to identify the odors and felt the rumble of hunger rolling over in his belly. If he could not ride, a job as cook's helper would be a welcome enough thing in its own way. He had had enough experience at in the past to know that.

Two white-shirted shapes moved at the far side of the store. Hart moved close enough to see that both were men. "I'm looking for a man named Brown," he said.

"That's me," one answered. At closer inspection he proved to be a burly, barrel-chested man in his late forties—or ten years younger with some exceptionally hard living behind him.

"Venable sent me to find you," Hart said. "I'm your new helper."

Brown took his time examining his new assistant before he answered. When he did it was with no apparent warmth. "That's what he says, maybe. If you lay off on me I'll kick your butt up around your ears. If I have to do it twice you're out, and I don't care what the old man says. Understood?"

Hart moved in until they were buckle to buckle. He searched the man's face, beard stubble to often-broken nose and all. "If you can get that job done the first time, I'll be damn well surprised," he said.

Brown nodded without a flicker of change in his expression, but the belligerence in his eyes seemed to soften. "We'll see," he said. "You got stuff to load onto the wagon now. Perce'll show you what to carry out while I go tend to some business." He started to turn away but paused. "What do they call you?"

"Hart. If you want the rest of it, most call me Gotch Hart."

"Like in Gotch-eye?"

"If you want, but you'd best be a bad news sonuvabitch to call me that to my face."

"Fair enough," Brown said. "I'll be back in an

hour or so. Take care of our order will you, Perce?"

"Sure."

It took a half hour or less to load the ranch wagon with the sacks of flour and cornmeal and salt, boxes of dried fruits and baking powder, tubs of lard, cases of evaporated milk, and a small keg of salt pork. When it was done Hart sat on a nail keg inside the door to wait for Brown's return. The storekeeper lingered nearby.

"Hungry?" Perce asked. Hart still did not know if this was the man's first name or his last.

"Broke," Hart answered.

"There's open kegs of raisins and crackers by the front door," Perce said.

"I told you I couldn't pay."

"I heard you the first time."

The offer seemed to take Hart by surprise. For a moment the customary cold, hard set of his expression softened. He started to speak but did not. The storekeeper nodded acceptance of the unspoken thanks.

Later, more than an hour later, Brown still had not returned. Perce helped a customer out the front door with her packages and came back to the nail keg where Hart was again waiting, the hunger no longer nibbling inside him.

"Brownie's likely been taken drunk again," he said. "You might want to dig him out before it gets too bad. Once he gets wound up past a certain point it can go on for days before he burns out."

"Well, I'm not much of a cook and don't 'specially want to get any better at it out of sheer practice. Maybe I better go find him."

"You might look in the Muleshoe," Perce suggested. "That's where he generally heads. Go up to the corner and turn right. It's two blocks on the right. Red painted false front place."

Hart had no trouble following the directions. He found the Muleshoe to be a rough and ready place given solely to beer and liquor for its attraction. No free lunch, no women, no gaming tables. There was not even a beaded curtain over the doorway to lend comfort by discouraging flies.

The interior was dark and smelled strongly of sweat and spilled beer and ancient tobacco. The floor was of rough wood, littered with trash and lacking even a sawdust coating that might have absorbed spills or tobacco juice. It was small enough to give an impression of being crowded by the dozen or so patrons there at the time.

Hart could not identify the V-Slash-4 cook among the customers. He made his way past a pair of rickety tables and some scattered chairs to the well attended bar. The bartender excused himself from a conversation with a ragged looking trio at his bar and moved to place himself in front of Hart.

"Beer, corn, or rye," he said. "Your choice."

He got a head-shake in return. "I'm here to collect Brown from the Venable outfit." If the bartender wanted to assume that Venable had sent him that was all right. Hart had not lied about it, and this way the cook might save face in his favorite bar. And after all, he thought, he and Brown would have to put up with each other for some time now.

The bartender's interest vanished. He hooked a thumb toward a back wall door. Hart nodded abruptly and turned toward the door.

The back room was even smaller than the front, but it was somewhat better lighted. Four cheap tin lamps were hung from the ceiling throwing light onto a pair of tables that were in better repair than those out front. Only one of the tables was occupied.

Brown and three other men sat around it with a deck of cards and several bottles before them. The table was littered with coins as well. The air of the room stirred when Hart opened the door, causing the lamp flames to flutter and dance. The moving light patterns reflected on the polished metal of the coins.

"Time to go?" Brown asked as Hart approached. There was no annoyance in his tone.

"Uh huh."

Brown began to collect the change in front of him, raking it into a pile and scooping the bright disks into a cupped palm. Hart thought he could see the glint of yellow metal among the coins. "'Scuse me, boys," Brown said, "though to be honest, the timing couldn't have been any better."

"Don't you think it's too early to quit?" another of the players protested.

"Not a bit," Brown answered cheerfully. He started to rise.

The man to his right grabbed quickly at Brown's wrist. "We deserve a chance to get some back."

For a moment Brown stared at the offending hand clamped on his wrist. "You had it when we started," he said coldly.

The other two men rose from their chairs and moved threateningly close. Brown grinned at them. Staring back at the two he held his left hand under his pinioned right and let his money fall into it.

Carefully he transferred the coins into his trousers pocket. He raised his empty left hand and turned it palm outward toward the two men. Still smiling he gave them a broad wink. And drove the toe of his left boot toward the nearer man's crotch.

The seated man flinched away and Brown, his right hand unexpectedly free, threw a punch at the second fellow's jaw. It connected solidly enough to jar both of them. The first man, hobbling from the pain of a kick on the muscle pad of his thigh, moved in beside Brown and began hooking short, chopping punches to the kidneys while his partner kept Brown tied up with a series of aimed blows.

The tactic probably would have succeeded—Brown certainly expected it to—except that the man who had been kicked found himself being yanked backward by his shirt collar. One moment he was concentrating on delivering maximum punishment to Brown's kidneys, the next he was being propelled in an arm-flailing rush across the room until his back was slammed violently into the wall. He hit with a crash, shook his head, and tried to draw a supply of air into his suddenly emptied lungs. His eyes focused in time for him to see a lip-twisting snarl of rage on Hart's face. Rage and something that looked close to a fierce kind of joy.

Hart was under the impression he was grinning at the man. He grinned all the broader and smashed a right fist low into the pit of the man's belly. The fellow doubled over nicely. Hart gave him time to finish gagging—he did not want to have to ride out to the V-Slash-4 with his pantlegs fouled by this man's previous meal—and lifted a knee into the man's face. In addition to the dull, meaty sound of impact there was a lighter, sharper crack as bone let go somewhere in there. Probably a cheek, Hart decided gleefully; certainly enough to put this one out of it. That left only one to go.

Hart turned and moved closer to the two figures that were still upright. He was disappointed to find that Brown already had the last man well under control. The cook was doggedly slamming one fist after the other into the man's paunch. He was no longer receiving even token opposition and when he quit the man let his knees buckle so he could slide down the wall to a sitting position.

Brown, dripping sweat but still cheerful, turned toward Hart. "I'd forgot all about you, boy." He looked happily around the room, ignoring the man who had remained seated, and said, "I don't think I'd want to do that again, 'specially if you was on the other side. What's your name again?"

Hart told him and with a smile Brown shoved a hand forward to be shaken. "Let's go home, Gotch. We got work to do."

II

Titus Venable's V-Slash-4 was a middle of the road outfit with enough size to make it respectable but not so much profit as to make it one of the grand spreads of the rolling grassland expanse that surrounded it. It was reasonably well watered by one year-round and several intermittent streams plus perhaps three dozen potholes and sinks where water could be found much of the year. Its grass was good, spotty, and sometimes early to brown but rich and full of food value wherever it grew, and a fair portion of the land was heavily grassed.

The history of the place was apparent from a look at the buildings. The oldest was a half-walled sod dugout now in disrepair and being used for casual storage. A handful of plank-sided soddies were used for bunkhouse, cookhouse, laundry, dry storage, smithy and tack shed. A low, clapboard house showing the remnants of scaling, faded paint and some old tendrils of pretty-up plants was now being used as the foreman's home. It would once have been the main house, the Venable family's own home.

The current main house was not pretentious but it definitely was a step upward from the past. It was an unadorned, boxy, two-story structure tightly built of milled lumber and painted a stark, sunglaring white. Shrubbery and young trees had been planted in an orderly outline around the foundations but had not yet had time to become established or to hide a sense of newness behind the softening patterns of leaves and branches. There was a covered stoop at the front but no broad porch or veranda such as had been placed along the front of the older house.

A maze of corrals and breaking pens extended across a baked clay flat beyond the buildings. A dry creek bed ran through the pens, and several hand-dug wells showed their low, circular walls in the yards between buildings.

"Can you make out what's what here?" Brown asked as they entered the headquarters yard.

"More or less," Hart said with a shrug. "Give me time and I'll have it all in place. Hell, I ain't blind, you know."

Brown grunted an affirmative but he wheeled the wagon in a serpentine route through the buildings so Hart could get a better look at them all.

"Who's the foreman?" Hart asked as they passed the old house.

"You couldn't properly say we got one," Brown answered. "Fella name of Early Wynn answers if you holler for the foreman, and he lives in the house. He's really more segundo than foreman, though. Ti mostly runs things himself. You won't have trouble from Wynn if that's what you're thinking. Whatever Ti says is the way it's gonna be."

Hart did not answer, but that was what he had been wondering. On some ranches a man hired without the foreman's say-so could be in for a rough shakedown and one that might last until one or the other of them quit. And the one to go would not normally be the foreman.

"How about the family?"

"Ti you already know. Good man, too. Easy to get along with. Works right along with the crew, whatever the job. Has one son and a pair of daughters," Brown said. "No missus. She died before I come here a couple years ago. Word has it that Ti's thinking of taking another woman, but you couldn't prove it by me. I figure he's entitled if he wants. Kinda lonely I'd say. But a good man sure enough." He pulled the team to a halt beside the cookhouse. "The boy's away to school for now," he went on, "and the younger girl too. The oldest of them's at home. You'll meet her soon enough. She runs the house, thinks she runs Ti an' every other damn thing too, and she'll try to run you along with all the rest."

"It sounds like she isn't your favorite person," Hart said.

"That'd be a fair way to put it," Brown said as he climbed down from the wagon. "You can make up your own mind about it, though. *I* ain't going to be the one to tell you anything there. Fetch this stuff inside now, and I'll show you where everything goes."

Hart lifted and lugged for the next half hour and spent nearly as much time again getting it all stowed away to Brown's satisfaction. The man was as picky-fussy as a barren old maid, with bins and drawers and shelves reserved for each particular item. His work area was as spotless as his storage was orderly. Hart had met a few such in the past and knew others who went to the opposite extreme of sloppy disorder. There seemed to be no middle ground, and of the two Hart was not sure which he preferred.

When he was done, Brown pointed to one of several doorways leading off the big kitchen. "That's yours," he said and disappeared through another of the openings, shutting the door firmly behind him.

Hart shook his head and crossed to the door Brown had indicated. Behind it he found a tiny bedroom holding a blanketed bunk and a small, bare table. There was a row of about a dozen wall pegs to serve as a wardrobe—not that he would need so many as to complain about a lack of storage—and a night jar under the bunk. Most of the wall space was taken up by sturdy shelving on which had been stacked piles of spare tinware, plates and bowls and cups and large rolls of canvas made lumpy by tableware rolled inside. A single, shuttered window had been set into the back wall. Hart went to it and shoved the shutters wide. The view gave him a hazy look at the corrals and at the moving blurs of dark color that would have been horses.

He sat on the bunk and for a moment stretched out there to capture the feel of being in his own bunk, in a room that was to be his alone. It was a luxury he had not expected.

After no more than seconds he jerked himself upright. There would be time enough later for lollygagging; now there were things to be done.

In the absence of instructions to the contrary he parked the ranch wagon next to the tack shed. He left the team in harness, though, while he first untied his saddle horse from the tailgate and tended to it.

Under a film of road dust the horse was a solidly built animal, well muscled and with an exceptionally broad rump. It was slightly taller than average, not far short of fifteen hands, and a deep blood bay in color. The head was well formed, with a small muzzle, widely flaring nostrils and small ears. Its only glaring fault was a high, curving crest that made the neck look perpetually arched. The crest with its unusual depth of neck gave the animal an unbalanced look that belied its ability to shift and turn in close cutting work.

Hart pulled his saddle and bridle and dumped them into the wagon bed, replacing the bridle with a short loop of rope that he draped over the neck and let fall to the ground in place of the more common hobbles or halter and tie rope. He took a piece of rough sacking and began giving the horse a thorough rubdown. The animal was spare of flesh, but the coat was bright with the sheen of healthy oils where he removed the dust of travel.

"Ugly son of a bitch, isn't he?"

For a moment Hart froze, startled by the unexpected voice behind him. He shook the dirt from his sacking, folded it and tucked it into a hip pocket before he turned to face the speaker. What he could see confirmed what he had heard. It was a woman's voice.

"Nope," he said softly. But he let his uncompromising stubbornness on that subject ring through in the tone of his voice.

"Then you're a poor judge of horses, whoever the hell you are."

Hart stepped closer to get a better look at this woman with the quick and roughened tongue. A man would have to be hard pressed or powerfully drunk to claim she was pretty. Her appearance was as severe and unadorned as her language. Plain gray dress that was normal and modest enough of itself but was short enough at the hem to reveal heavy, mannish boots. The sleeves of the dress were lapped up as well, and both her arms and her skin above the unbuttoned throat of the dress were deeply tanned. Her face was long and flat-planed, lips thin and tightly held in a firm, straight line. Her brows were dark and full, drawn primly straight over light brown eyes nearly the same shade as her tanned skin. Her hair was brown also, its length impossible to judge in the straight-parted, tightly clubbed bun she wore. She looked to be in her mid-twenties but much weathered. The only thing reasonably attractive about her was her eyes. They had a clarity and a snapping sparkle that spoke of quick intelligence under her rough manner.

"Who the hell are you, anyway?" she demanded.

"I'm a man that knows more than you about horses, for one thing. An' has better manners to boot."

She snorted. "I know more than any five hands about our own horseflesh," she asserted.

"Then prob'ly you've got awfully dumb hands working here. And anyway, this one isn't *your* horseflesh. It's mine, and I'm the only one as has to be pleased, which I am, for I know what I'm doing.

Which is more than I can say for you."

"That's quite a mouthful for a damned kitchen hey-boy."

"Which means you know good and well who I am an' knew it when you asked."

She ignored his logic and stepped close to the horse. She ran a practiced hand over the near flank and down the hip line. Rather than comment on the quality that could be found there, though, she faced forward and pointed a finger toward the neck. "If you don't call that ugly, you're even blinder than you look," she said bluntly. Again she snorted. "My guess is you thought you had you a world-beater in this old snide and didn't cut him until it was too late. Now you've got a cresty old stag that won't ever be worth anything, and you're too damn stubborn to admit it. If you think you can deny it, tell me so now and I'll eat my words, but you know I'm right and you might as well admit it."

Hart pursed his lips to hide the shadow of smile that was tickling the corners of his mouth. "Well now," he said, "first off, this is a pretty good blooded old horse. Goes back to Blackburn's Whip on four lines and grand-sired by Copperbottom on both sides." He waited for and got a grudging nod of approval and a hint of interest flashing in her eyes. The horse was indeed well bred, and there was no way she could deny that quality.

"As for the crest," he said, "that comes from being allowed to get hog fat in a cornfield as a yearling. Never lost the crest, that's all."

"Crap," she said distainfully. "He's an old stud you cut too late. You can't tell me otherwise."

"I'll wager I can," Hart said, working all the harder to avoid a smile.

She cocked an eye rudely toward his battered saddle and the tiny bundle of possessions tied in a roll behind the cantle. "You've got nothing to wager anyway, hey-boy, so it wouldn't be fair to be taking anything from you. But . . . ," she paused and pretended to consider the matter, but there was already a gleam of amusement and of sure success in those light brown eyes. "If this animal can't be proven other than what I say, then you damn well scrub my floors in the house. I *hate* to do floors."

"And if you do agree you're wrong, what then?"

She shrugged. The possibility of changing her mind seemed too remote to seriously consider. "Then I'll scrub *your* floors," she said, and flippantly added, "and kiss this ugly bastard on the nose as well."

"Done," Hart said solemnly. He extended his hand.

She looked at his hand and then into his face. She tilted her head back and laughed. "You really are a fool, but all right." She gripped his fingers and gave them a single downward tug to seal the wager. "Now you do your damnedest, hey-boy. Tell me one more time how wrong I am."

Hart allowed his grin to show itself now. He scratched behind his ear and felt of his beard stubble—not too far advanced at the moment—as he was in no hurry to end the fun. "Well-l-l-l," he said slowly, "maybe I won't have to work *too* awful hard at it. Tell you what, lady. Before you go up to the kissing end, why don't you go back and heist her tail so you can see for yourself."

"What?"

"What I said, lady who claims to know more about horses than me, is that this here's a mare horse."

"A . . . mare?"

"Uh huh. And an awful poor prospect for being called a stag."

She flounced with anger and wishful disbelief to the rump end of the mare and jerked the horse's tail up roughly. "Oh, my Gawd. It really is a damned mare," she wailed. She turned and ran for the house but not before Hart saw her cheeks begin to flush bright red.

Hart chuckled quietly to himself for a moment then took the sacking from his pocket and continued with the mare's rubdown. "By damn, Fancy old girl, I believe the lady forgot something," he murmured to the horse. "I believe she owes you a kiss on the nose." He hummed softly to himself as he finished the job.

III

"You'd have thought that damned woman would've come over here by now," Brown grumbled. "Usually she's underfoot anyway, trying to tell me how to run things. And with a new hey-boy to be looked over and chewed under, I'd sure have figured to see her by now. 'Specially since a box of this is stuff she wanted for over at the house."

"Do you want me to carry it over for you?"

Brown eyed him closely. "You didn't strike me earlier as being all that eager to take on extra work, so it stands to reason you got something else in mind. Like the boss' daughter maybe?" He snorted. "Maybe you don't know all you think you do then. Anyway, no. I'll carry it over myself. I need to see Ti about a few things, and I can do this at the same time. Being as you're so eager to work, though, you can get to splitting some stove lengths. The wood pile is around back."

Hart sighed. He should have known better than to open his mouth. Still, it would give him a chance to look around more. Brown took a wooden crate from his work counter and left, while Hart went out another door to the woodpile and its inevitable wedges and maul. He was still at work there when Brown returned.

"You surely made yourself quite an impression," Brown said with a chuckle.

Hart set the maul aside and wiped his face. "She told you about it, then?"

"Hell no. All she said was for me not to send that shifty-eyed sonuvabitch anywhere near her house or she'd take a whip to the both of us. What'd you do, anyhow?"

Hart told him.

Brown whistled appreciatively. "If I'd known that I would've asked when we could expect her over to do her scrubbing." He grinned. "Next time I see her I will."

"Oh, she'll get around to it," Hart said.

"Don't count on it."

"Care to make a little wager on that?"

Again Brown gave him a close look. He shook his head. "No. I don't think I will, though why I should pass up a sure bet I don't hardly know."

"Maybe it isn't all that sure."

"I don't know as I'm willing to go as far as to say that. Not yet. But then I ain't willing to strike your wager either, so we'll just drop it here for now."

"You know what you want to do," Hart said. "What's her name, anyway?"

"Twy, short for Twyla."

"Ti and Twy? That's a hell of a combination."

"Don't look at me. I didn't name either of them. Ti stands for Titus. Where him and his missus found a name like Twyla is beyond me. I never heard of it before or since." He grinned. "Wherever they got it, they must not've been too satisfied with odd names. The younger girl is Mary, and the boy's Richard."

"Is the young one as homely as her sister?"

"Wouldn't know about that," Brown said. "I've never seen her. She's been off being schooled since before I came here. I seen the boy, though, and he's all right. He'll come home for the summer each year and sometimes for Christmas. Not a bad kid though I think Ti doesn't know what he's got in that boy. The boy's sorta scrawny, and I think Ti is trying to push him into a city job. Don't know why he would. Ti Venable loves this land. An' knows livestock too. City ways ain't for him. Not that it's any of my never-mind, you understand. I wouldn't say a word about any of it."

"Of course not," Hart agreed seriously.

Brown had a talent for keeping his help busy, and by the time the evening meal and lengthy cleanup were finished Hart was more than ready for bed. But he was relieved to find that the cook had been accurate about the foreman's, or segundo's, influence around the place. After serving a meal to the full crew, Hart still was not sure which of the men was supposed to be the foreman, and he had been too busy to ask Brown at the time.

Breakfast was no more leisurely, but at least it was over and done with by dawn. The crew had long since chosen their day's mounts and ridden off about their business, each carrying with him a pair of paper-wrapped sandwiches so the work would not have to be interrupted for a noon meal.

"You have an easy life here compared to some places I've been," Hart observed when they were done in the kitchen.

"That's true enough," Brown agreed. "You have hey-boyed in the past then, huh? I kinda figured you had. The first time a fella is all thumbs and big feet. You ain't, exactly."

"Then you aren't going to crawl my frame today, old man? Or try to?"

Brown grinned. "I'll have to give it a try one of these days maybe, but I'll be needing a different excuse from that one."

"You don't need an excuse. Just say the word, and we'll have at it. Name your rules or go without, it don't make any difference to me."

"Hell, I think you mean that, too."

"I do."

"An' I just may take you up on it when I figure I'm having a good day. For now, though, the day's pretty much your own 'til after dinnertime. Then you might split some more wood, and we'll start getting ready to slop the hogs again."

"Would you mind showing me something then, if there's nothing else you need done right away?" Hart asked.

"If I can, sure."

Hart hesitated. "Well, you see, in town ... before I went looking for Venable ... some fella was telling me he owns a stud horse with Steeldust blood in him. I looked around for him some yesterday, but I sure hell don't think I found him yet."

Brown snorted. "Found you a stud out there in the pen and can't believe it's him, did you?"

"Uh huh. Near as I could make out without crawling in with that big sonuvabitch he's one of those rump-spotted horses, and I *know* that's not the one I want."

Brown threw back his head and laughed aloud. "Bad as your eyes are you can see a horse better than Early Wynn can. He trapped that wild bastard a month ago and wants to make a pet of him. He says that's a bunch of horse and he wants to put him to stud. But he hasn't been able to lay a hand on the bugger, hardly, since he brought him in."

"A whole bunch of horse, is he? Hell, I haven't seen one of those blanketed horses yet that was worth the price of a bullet to shoot it. No cow sense, no horse sense, nor any other kind of sense."

"Don't expect me to argue. Anyway, Ti does have him a good stud, but he's in a pen over behind the new house. Ti likes to be able to look at him whenever he's around home. C'mon. I'll introduce you to the gentleman."

Brown led the way around the Venable home. As they passed the house Hart found himself wondering if Twyla Venable were watching them pass, but if so he could not see well enough to spot either form or motion to catch her at it. He was half hoping to see her and half hoping he would not. He wanted to prod her again about the lost wager. But if Venable's stud lived up to the description he had been given, he would not want the horse to be compared with his mare.

The stud was in a solidly constructed run built five rails high and set onto posts not more than two paces apart. The far end of the run had been partially roofed to provide the stallion with shade during the summer months. Hart noticed that the inside of the corral was nearly as free of manure as was the ground around it.

"Somebody puts in a lot of time on this animal," he said.

"Ti and his eldest both do. Hand feed him twice a day. Hand water him too. All the time cleaning and brushing and fetching for him. Damn fool way to treat a horse if you ask me, but nobody ever does."

The stud had been at the far end of the pen. At the approach of people he snorted loudly, tested the air with an upraised muzzle, and trotted toward them, slowing as he neared them and reaching forward with his head to flare his nostrils and sniff.

"He's worth the babying," Hart thought to himself although he kept silent to avoid contradicting Brown's opinions on the subject.

The horse was a bright gray with black points although a good amount of gray lightened the mane and tail also. He was taller than Hart's mare, close to 15-2, and even more heavily muscled. He would have scaled well over a thousand pounds, probably around twelve hundred. Yet he had one of the finest heads Hart had ever seen on a live horse, as fine as an idealized head drawn by an artist. Hart whistled his admiration, and the stallion's ears pricked forward. Hart moved around the corner of the pen to look at him from another angle.

"Damnation," Hart said. "That's a horse."

"Ti sure thinks so."

"No wonder. There's more than cow pony and quarter running blood in this one, too. With those legs and that long body, there's got to be."

"Yeah. Ti told me what it was one time, but I disremember now. A Thoroubred, anyway. One of those distance running horses."

"Ayuh. I knew it had to be so. You can see it in the way he's built. Oh, that is a horse all right." Hart licked his lips. "D'you think Venable would mind if I was to crawl in there and feel of him?"

"Oh, he ain't a killer horse. I told you he's hand fed all the time. It's safe to get in with him."

Hart gave the older man a dirty look. "That is *not* what I meant. But a horse like this, well, a man has a right to expect some respect for it. What I want to know is would Venable care? I don't much mind what the horse thinks of it."

"Aw, I don't think he'd care. It's not like you're a passing stranger or something."

The words were no sooner out than Hart had swarmed over the rails and dropped inside. The gray did not react except to tilt his ears toward the man. The horse swung to face him and moved forward with short, stiff legged steps, inquiring ahead of him with his nose.

Hart muttered to him and rubbed his muzzle to let the animal take his scent. Hart moved around to the side and let his fingers slide across the shoulder and along the length of the deep barrel to the hard, bulky muscles of the hindquarters. He could feel the animal tense and quiver at the touch of an unfamiliar hand, but the horse refused to bolt.

"He's as solid as if he was carved to shape," Hart said over his shoulder.

"So they tell me," Brown said. "I don't like to mess with those stud horses myself. Cut 'em and use 'em, I say. At least you've got a manageable horse then."

"They're a nuisance if you aren't in the breeding business," Hart agreed politely. The truth was that he liked handling an animal with more strength and perhaps as much sass as he had himself.

Hart would have been quite content to let his fingers continue to learn the strengths of this horse, but a woman's voice interrupted from the other side of the rails. "What the hell are you doing in there, hey-boy?"

Hart straightened and turned with a deliberately insulting grin on his face. "Why, Miss Twyla. It sure is good we ran into you. I believe you owe my horse a kiss an' me some work."

"Be damned if that's so," she said angrily. She stepped onto the second rail so that her head and shoulders were visible over the fence. "Get away from that horse now before you make him nervous."

"He don't look too awful nervous." Hart had begun scratching the big horse on the poll, and the stud seemed to be enjoying the attention, lowering his head and shifting closer to give the man easier access to the favored spot. "What do you think, Brownie?"

"Don't put me in the middle," Brown said. He turned and headed back toward the safety of the kitchen, where he was the boss.

"Now if you would get the hell out of there... Or will I have to fire you to accomplish that?"

Hart let his grin dissolve into outright laughter. "Now if that ain't a helluva way to avoid paying a debt."

"You're not taking me very seriously, are you?" she asked. She sounded as much interested as angry.

"No real reason to as far as I can see," he said.

She flared, her eyes fairly crackling with anger.

"You damn well better take me serious."

Again he laughed, deliberately loud. The stallion's ears shifted back and it moved away. Hart, keeping one eye prudently on the hind end of the horse, drifted sideways and climbed to perch on the top rail of the pen. He returned his attention to Twyla Venable. "Just because you talk dirty don't make you any different kind of a woman," he said, the bantering tone gone from his voice now.

"Crap," she said emphatically. "You don't know what you're saying, not the first bit. You're just stringing words together, hey-boy. You're nothing but a stupid hey-boy anyway, and I don't have to listen to the likes of you." She stepped down from the rail on which she had been standing.

Hart shrugged. "Suit yourself," he said. "My name, by the way, is Hart. And I might not see so good, but that don't make me stupid."

"You're still nothing but a damned hey-boy." She had moved closer and was glaring up at him now.

"Uh huh," he said agreeably. "As I recall, that's the job that was offered. If you can't have what you want, you take what you can have."

"Just what is it you normally do, hey-boy?"

He laughed lightly. "Hell, lady, it ain't been regular enough to be called normal, but what I *prefer* to do is to handle horses. There's not too much I cain't do with one."

"Modest bastard too, aren't you?"

"Not so's you would hardly notice it, but if I don't toot my own horn, who will?"

"Why would you want it blown to me anyway?"

The grin came back. "Why, lady, I believe we

may find another way for you to square your debt with me." His hand shot up, palm outward. "And before you go denying that you've got a debt hung on you, you know damn good and well I'd've been scrubbing your floors before this if I hadn't won. I figure a wager works both ways, no matter who's the loser."

"You impudent son of a bitch," she said. But with less rancor than she had shown earlier. "Go do something to earn your keep, hey-boy, before I have you thrown off the place."

"Hart, ma'am. The name is Hart."

"Go to hell. Wear any name you damned please, but go to hell." She stalked away toward the house, leaving Hart chuckling atop the stud pen.

IV

"You're Hart, aren't you?" The lean man with streaks of gray tingeing his hair shoved a hand forward. "I'm Wynn, the foreman. More or less." He was smiling easily when he said it.

"Yes?" Hart could think of no reason for the man to be approaching him. Hart's job was certainly of no concern to Wynn, as foreman or segundo or simple ranch hand either.

"I've heard you could handle a horse," Wynn said. He shoved his thumbs into the waist of his low hanging jeans and began making patterns on the floor with the toe of his boot.

"Uh huh. It's a claim I make from time to time."

"Well, lookahere now, Hart. This is a busy time for me, and I have a rank stud horse that needs some manners. If you want to break and gentle him enough that he can be handled, I'll pay you ten dollars."

"That's twice the going rate," Hart said skeptically.

Wynn looked up at him. "Do it for five if you'd rather," he said. "I won't try to fool you. That horse is a real sonuvabitch. I figure it would be worth ten to get him broke. So tell me if you want to try him and for how much pay if you do."

"Hell yes, I'll break him for you." For some half-formed reason that he did not fully understand, Hart added, "For five dollars."

If a regular working hand with good vision got five dollars for breaking a horse, Gotch Hart was not going to take more for doing the same job. He regarded himself as being as good as the best, and any bronco rider was expected to take them as they came, wild or mild or anywhere between. Besides, someone had put Wynn up to this offer. Hart certainly had made no chow hall brags that could have reached the foreman's ears. If he were being tested in some way, Hart wanted to take it on as a rider and not as a highly suspect, half-blind heyboy.

"Has anybody ever accused you of being a damn fool?" Wynn asked.

"Uh huh. It happens pretty regular," Hart said without taking offense at the question.

"Well, I don't wonder. Five dollars. You're sure?"

"I said it."

Wynn shrugged. You got a deal then. I'll pay you the five the day I can walk to him, saddle and ride out without he tries to kill me." Wynn nodded and walked away.

Hart felt pleased as he watched the foreman's receding back. Breaking that bone-headed stud could mean more to him than five dollars. If he got a name here as a bronc peeler he might be able to get regular work at it, and at far more than the twenty per month and keep he was now earning. And a bronc rider commanded infinitely more respect than a kitchen hey-boy. Hart swung his arms to loosen his shoulder muscles and grinned to himself. He was looking forward to letting that big, spotted horse try him.

As soon as Brown released him after the breakfast cleanup, Hart slipped off toward the old soddy where the leather gear was kept. From the jumble of equipment hung on the walls, piled on shelves and thrown into tangled heaps on the earthen floor he selected a stout bosal and braided cotton mecate. There was a saddle on the floor that had to be the ranch's breaking saddle. The leather was cracked and ancient, its color almost lost under a thick layer of old and often applied mud and manure. The appearance did not matter, though. The seat was deep and formed of rough leather. The horn had long since disappeared—either smashed in a hard fall or deliberately removed. Either way there now was no danger of the saddle horn spearing an unfortunate rider if a rank horse should roll on him. A horn driven by the weight of a thrashing, frightened horse had crushed the chest or punctured the lungs of more than one bronc rider, and the injury was usually fatal.

Hart was pleased to see that the rigging was

nearly as new as the saddle was old and was cut from heavy leather, both sewn and riveted where it needed the strength. It was heavily oiled. If someone had taken that trouble to care for the rigging so well, he probably could trust the tree to be sound. But he checked it anyway. He took his own catch rope and lugged it all to the stallion's pen.

The horse was at the far end of his run, pacing the length of the short wall and peering into the rolling, sunlit distance beyond. As soon as the man approached the horse's ears swept back flat against its head and its teeth were bared.

"Hullo, you ugly sonuvabitch," Hart said, but despite the words he used, the tone of his voice was calm and gentle.

The horse did not respond gently. It squealed and charged the fence toward Hart, all of its fury focused on the man behind the rails. Yellow-white teeth gnashed together loudly but snapped only on each other as Hart withdrew his arm from the top rail.

Hart was safely protected behind the corral rails but even so he found himself recoiling and ducking away as the horse threw itself into the barrier. Hart could feel the force of that impact as much as he could hear it. The sharp odors of corral dust filled his nose as the horse angrily pawed the ground and struck at the lower rails with range-hard forefeet. Hart was angry with himself for flinching away but forced a sense of calmness through himself so there would be no anger in his voice as he cooed and murmured gently with wordless sounds to the infuriated stallion.

White-rimmed eyes flared and the horse's ears

stayed pressed flat against its large, Roman-nosed head. It shook its head and sent scraps of ratty mane and burr-clubbed forelock flaying. Again and again it tried to strike its way through the intervening rails to smash this man who was its enemy.

Hart grinned. "I don't think I wanta try an' choke you down nor bust you the hard old regular way, you old bastard," he said lightly.

He let the saddle and bosal drop to the ground by his feet and deftly shook a small loop into his catch rope.

With a flip of his wrist he brought the loop up and over the rails to settle around the neck of the furious horse. The horse squealed and darted to the side. Its anger was forgotten now as it tried to bolt away from the rope that threatened it as it had been held and threatened by such once before.

Instead of snubbing the free end of the rope around a post to hold and ultimately to choke into submission the stallion, Hart closed his fingers only briefly, enough to allow the horse's run to take up the slack and draw the loop snug around the throat. Immediately Hart let go. The free end of the rope was whipped over the top rail as the stallion thundered across the small, enclosed area, bellowing and shaking itself and flinging itself into the air until it could go no farther and crashed into another wall of rails.

The horse bounced back, became entangled in the length of free rope on the ground under its feet and began to strike with stiffened forelegs as if the rope were a snake. The efforts only further snared its legs and it fell panting in the dirt only to rebound to its feet and again offer fight. Within a few minutes the horse was sweat lathered from fear and exhaustion. Hart stood watching without expression.

"Huh. Lost your rope, didn't'cha, hey-boy?" someone said behind him.

Hart turned. The man came closer. Hart did not recognize his features but from the color of his checkered shirt and the peculiar, faded blue of his bandana, this was one of the hands.

"I said you went and lost your rope, didn't you?" he persisted. "Not that it's much loss. A hey-boy don't hardly need a man's tools, does he?" He was close enough that Hart could see he was grinning insolently.

A surge of joyous strength and reckless release swept through Hart. He grinned eagerly back at the man, measuring the look of the ropy muscles beneath the other man's shirt, the determination that might lie hidden under his beard-dusted jaw, the mocking disrespect that molded the set of his mouth.

"Think what you like, you dumb son of a bitch," Hart said happily. He knew he would not have to show any anger of his own to push this one into a fight. The one he could enjoy in his own way.

The cowboy clouded over with combined anger and disbelief when he heard the readiness in Hart's response. Still, Hart was nothing but a half-blind hey-boy, and the cowboy did not like him. "You cost me five dollars," he said. "I don't like that worth a damn. 'N then I see you're such an idiot you lose your own damn rope to the fool horse." He grunted. "I think maybe I'll take the rope an' the job of breaking that horse too, just to show you to keep your place around here."

"It'll cost you more than a lost five dollars, by God, if you don't turn tail and run, boy. Do it now or I'll spank your butt for you."

The cowboy stepped closer. He faked a looping right hand blow and drove the point of his right boot toward Hart's crotch.

Hart pivoted aside, whirling to his right and forward. He jabbed hard into the man's unprotected kidney and danced lightly backward. "You done set the rules, boy," he said. "Don't cry to me afterward."

He was behind the cowboy but only momentarily. The man swung to face him. A thin line of pain-sweat beaded his upper lip. It was too late to call back the kick.

The cowboy crouched and shuffled forward turtle-like under a protective armor of upraised forearms and elbows. Hart waited for him, standing loose and ready, his hands slightly lifted but not wasting the energy it takes to hold a fist closed and hard.

The man ducked and weaved a few times, but Hart was throwing no punches, only waiting with what seemed to be contemptuous amusement. The cowboy inched warily closer and began throwing overhand blows toward Hart's head. Somehow they never quite seemed to land. Hart barely moved his head but somehow there was always an unexpected forearm flickering into the way to deflect the punch and send it harmlessly aside. Worse, with each new attack Hart would grin at him and dance lightly away. Once he winked at the man.

With a groan of frustration the cowboy tried to

rush Hart. He tried to force his way inside Hart's shield so he could bury his fists into Hart's belly. Instead he found himself taking blow after blow in the hollow parts of his body, deep-driving, forceful punches so poundingly hard they could be only vaguely felt on the surface but drove in deep to sap his strength from within. His arms began to feel leaden, and there was a sick emptiness within him.

Hart bobbed backward, skipped lightly to the side and hooked a quick combination into the man's kidneys. When he turned Hart met him with a crossing left to the chin that sent him to his knees. Hart stepped back.

The cowboy looked up. His jaw was sagging from exhaustion, and a flow of bright blood was draining from the right side of his mouth. He nodded wearily and began to rise. He had had enough.

Hart's face tightened. He shook his head and stepped forward, and the cowboy felt an empty flood of fear in his belly. A boot toe exploded into his side and he fell doubled, retching but unable to find any relief in it. He was aware of no time passing, but of a sudden Hart's face was close to his and he could feel a tightly gripping hand at his throat, holding him up off the dirt.

"Don't play with me, boy," Hart hissed. "Don't you *never* do that."

The cowboy shook his head. "No," he whispered. Or tried to. He felt the grip loosen, and he thumped back onto the hard ground. A little later he rolled to his belly and pulled himself erect against the corral rails. Hart was no longer in sight.

The cowboy shook his head trying without success to throw off the nausea that rose up in his gorge. He stumbled weakly toward the bunkhouse.

V

The evening meal was piled in steaming bowls and platters across the long surface of the common table and they were ready for the hands to arrive when Early Wynn burst through the doorway and into the kitchen.

"Where's that damned hey-boy?" he demanded of the cook.

Brown nodded toward the storeroom where Hart was grinding coffee beans. Brown drifted quietly along in Wynn's wake as the foreman stormed across the room.

"Hart!"

"Uh huh?" Hart was a model of innocence as he stopped his work and looked up. "You appear to be riled, Wynn. Something I can help with?"

"*Help* with? Aye-God. This afternoon you could've helped. Now by damn, you're fired."

"All right," Hart agreed mildly. He set the sack of unground beans beside the big, red-wheeled mill and began to shoulder his way out of the small room.

"Don't you be going nowhere just yet," Brown said, blocking his path. To Wynn he added, "Just what in hell is this all about?"

"Him," Wynn declared, jabbing a finger toward Hart.

Brown looked at Hart. He got only a shrug in reply. "Well dammit, *one* of you is going to tell me something. And nobody eats around here until you do, hear?"

Wynn gave him a sour look, but there was no way he could counter that threat. The foreman resigned from the game and disgustedly said, "It's that damn hey-boy of yours." If he had to discuss it he could at least confine the discussion to a single direction—toward Brown. "This afternoon he let that stud of mine get away with his rope and to make matters worse, when Harry Grimes took a laugh off of it, your hey-boy beat hell out of Harry. The boy won't be fit to ride for a couple days. He's over in the bunkhouse passing blood and puking all over himself, or he was when I left."

"What's your side of this?" Brown asked Hart. "I suppose you got one."

"I got one."

"Then say it if you like, but don't expect me to beg for it. Say it if you want; leave if you'd rather."

Hart looked at Brown and reminded himself that the man had treated him fairly. And he did want to break that horse. "All right," he said. He turned to Wynn. "Your hand tried to kick my cods loose. I figure anything he got it's because he asked for it. As for your horse, that rope is right where I want it to be. If you want to take it off I expect you can, but you'll be getting someone else to break him for you."

"Why?" Wynn sounded skeptical but genuinely interested.

"You've choked that animal down before or he wouldn't be here now, right?"

Wynn gave him a grudging nod.

"I can't see that it done him a lot of good. Any more and you'll ruin him. Let him step on that trailing rope for a day or two, though, and he'll learn to give to it some without being scared of it all the time. It's as simple as that. If you want now, I'll take back my rope and leave. It's up to you."

The foreman rubbed unhappily at the back of his neck. "You coulda said something."

"You coulda asked."

"Those beans still need grinding," Brown injected.

Hart waited, looking pointedly at Wynn, the constant shift and dart of his eyes doing nothing to take away from the reminder that was in the stare.

"Go on and do your work," Wynn said. "Nobody's going to bother your rope."

Hart nodded and returned to his work. The foreman left.

Brown leaned against the doorframe. "Harry thinks he's pretty salty with his fists," he observed.

"Harry used to think so maybe," Hart said, cheerful now. "I don't think he'd want to talk about it at the moment, though."

"He thinks he's pretty good with a gun too," Brown said.

Hart snorted. "Let him have at it then. Don't own one myself, but if he wants to fetch one out with me around he'd best use it quick or I'll see how far I can plant it up his nose."

Brown started to make a retort, thought better

of it and said, "You don't own one yourself, huh?"

"Nope." Hart grinned. "I couldn't see good enough to know who I'd be shooting, so it never seemed like much of an idea to have a gun around. Wouldn't know how to use one even."

Aloud Brown merely grunted, but he made a mental note to make sure that Early Wynn—and through him Harry Grimes—knew that Hart did not go armed. He wanted that known before the evening meal was done.

Brown had his talk with Wynn while Hart finished grinding a sack of coffee. Grimes did not try to make the journey from bunkhouse to chow hall and so missed his meal. He was not sufficiently close to any of the other hands for anyone to volunteer to carry food to him, nor would Wynn have thought of having a meal sent to him under the circumstances. If he had, the only one he could have assigned the chore to would have been Gotch Hart as that would have been the hey-boy's job had Grimes been injured while he was working. Since the injuries were his own affair and not the business of the V-Slash-4, Wynn did not even consider the matter.

The next day the spotted stallion was still wearing most of Hart's rope. Hart checked on the horse as early as he could, postponing another bout of wood chopping in his impatience to make sure the animal had not injured itself. That danger he had not wanted to mention to Wynn.

The catch rope was considerably shorter than it had been the day before and was too frayed and worn for further use now. It would cost a dollar of his fee to replace the rope, but he counted it as money invested rather than lost.

"Not quite so wild with that thing now, are you?" Hart murmured softly as he slipped through the rails to place himself in the pen with the stud.

The business with the rope had done nothing to gentle the horse, nor had Hart expected it to. It merely gave the animal some respect for ropes. Not for men. As soon as Hart was inside the pen the stallion charged. It came at him in a scuttling, almost crablike run as it quartered to avoid stepping on the trailing rope end. Hart watched it come. With his right hand he unsnapped his heavy buckle and slipped his belt free of the loops.

The horse lunged, ears back and teeth bared. Before it could clamp its teeth onto the man the belt flashed in a quick, vicious arc, slicing across the horse's head and turning the charge.

As the stud shouldered by him Hart threw a boot toe into its belly and bent to grab the free end of the rope.

"Time to learn you some manners, you sweet ol' sonuvabitch," he crooned to it.

A jerk on the rope stopped it this time. The horse whirled to face him and charged again. Again the belt flailed, and again. Held by the rope and under attack from the whistling leather strap the horse became confused. The pull of the rope would not let it turn to run, and when it tried to race backward the man and the belt followed.

Hart charged the panicked stallion, the rope wrapped in his left hand and his right arm churning with the buckle-weighted belt. When the horse retreated he ran after it. Within a few strides the animal became overbalanced and fell, kicking up a cloud of powdery corral dust. Still Hart followed.

Dropping the belt now he flung himself onto the stud's head, twisting it and forcing it against the ground with all of Hart's weight pinning the head and upper neck into the dirt.

The stud squealed and kicked, but with its head pinned it was helpless, unable to rise.

Carefully Hart shifted until he was seated—more or less comfortably—on the stallion's neck. Dust was pasted to him in muddy runnels where it had landed on dripping fear-sweat. Had he not been fast enough or accurate enough with the belt, the horse could have won this fight. Now he was trembling slightly, more from aftershock than from fatigue after the brief but furious tussle.

Hart let out a long breath and reached into his shirt pocket for the makings of a cigarette that he rolled with every appearance of calm. He ignored the horse that lay beneath him until the smoke was made and lighted.

For long minutes then he sat on the animal, talking to it and stroking it wherever he could reach. The horse was heavily lathered with its own frightened sweat and gave no sign of response to the gentle voice or soothing touch, but gradually its muscles leapt slightly less when he touched it and the white-rimmed eyes seemed to roll less wildly with each new word or motion. It was enough for the first lesson, Hart decided.

Without alerting the horse by a change of position Hart rolled suddenly away and leaped to and over the corral rails. The horse was left lying bewildered on the ground, the rope still around its neck.

Hart went back to the corral that afternoon but did not try to enter the enclosure, standing instead behind the rails and talking to the horse in the same, soothing tone.

He talked endlessly and very nearly mindlessly, about any and every thing that came into his thoughts. He talked of past jobs and current hopes, of crib women he had known and of other horses he had handled. He spoke at length of his mare and smilingly told Wynn's unimpressive stallion that it would never service so fine a mare as his. He said nothing of his boyhood or really of anything that would have told an unseen listener much about himself.

The stallion's response to all was a wary nervousness. The horse stood in a corner of the pen, alternately shivering in frustration and stamping angrily. Its ears were flat against its head nearly the whole time Hart was close, although several times one ear would reluctantly, almost sneakily, slip forward to listen while the man spoke. After an hour Hart left the animal alone and returned to the cookhouse.

Brown looked up when he entered.

"I haven't forgotten your wood cutting," Hart told him.

"Well, I never said you did. Have a cup of coffee before you start on it."

Hart helped himself to the big pot, now containing the strong, bitter dregs of the morning's boiling, and sat lightly on a stool at Brown's big work table.

"You're spending an awful lot of time on that animal for a five-dollar breaking," Brown observed, directing his voice into his own mug more than toward Hart.

Hart shrugged. "The man wants the job done right, I figure. If it was up to me I'd cut the big bastard, give him a month or two to get the juices out of his system and then ride him down the same as any other horse. That ain't exactly what Wynn wants done with him."

"What you're doing is worth more than five dollars," Brown said. "More'n ten for that matter."

"We agreed on five," Hart said flatly.

"So you did." Brown took the hint and changed the subject to Hart's duties in preparing the evening meal.

VI

It took Hart four days more before he could approach the stallion without the certainty that it would attack. He handled the large, ugly animal several times each day, soothing and gentling it when it was peaceful, beating it as furiously as he knew how whenever it charged him. At the end of that time, though, he could enter the corral and walk to the horse. Only then did he remove what was left of his rope and replace it with a stoutly constructed halter.

From that point on the training process was simply a matter of patience, letting the horse become accustomed to one new thing at a time, being handled and rubbed, having its feet lifted, learning the feel of a saddle on its back and a hackamore on its head. And whenever the stud offered a fighting challenge it got a taste of Hart's belt and would end pinned helpless on the ground. When Hart finally did step into the battered old breaking saddle he sat on a nervous but docile animal. A few days more with rein and spur and Hart was satisfied. He talked to Wynn after breakfast the next morning.

"You can have your horse back whenever you want him," Hart said.

The foreman did no more than nod, but he looked pleased.

"Did you hear that, boys?" Harry Grimes spoke up from a few seats down the table. "The hey-boy claims to've broke that spotted stud. What do you say we watch Early get his butt dusted this morning?" He got an appreciative response from the other hands who had been noisily finishing their morning coffee. If Grimes was aware of the wildly erratic glare with which Hart was lacing his face he gave no indication of it.

"Watch if you like," Wynn said, "but I figure to use that horse today, boys."

"Two dollars says you don't get him outta the corral without him blowing up," Grimes said.

"I'll cover that," Hart injected quickly.

Grimes looked at Hart for the first time since the conversation started. The hey-boy's expression was coldly challenging. Grimes remembered only too well the punishment he had taken the last time he faced Hart, but he had opened his mouth and could not back down now without making himself the butt of countless bunkhouse jokes from then until he quit or the crew split up at the end of the working. He forced a grin onto his lips and said, "You're on. Two dollars he don't get out the gate." He was not at all pleased by the satisfaction he thought he could see in Hart's rapidly shifting eyes.

The other hands, seven of them at this time of year, began tugging their hats down onto their foreheads. Wynn tossed his coffee spoon onto his plate with a loud clatter to indicate that the meal was ended. The hands, including Grimes, scraped their chairs back and rose but this morning did not immediately begin to move toward the still night-dark doorway.

"Go ahead and get yourselves saddled," Wynn said. "I'll be out in a few minutes."

They left then, satisfied they would not miss out on any of the fun that might be yet to come. Hart noticed with disappointment that he heard no new wagers being made as they went out. He reminded himself bitterly that he should not have expected any of them to put their confidence in a cook's helper.

Wynn sat back and rolled himself a cigarette. "Do you want your pay now?"

Hart shook his head. "We agreed you don't owe it until you've used the horse."

The foreman shrugged. "Suit yourself. Me, I figure I'll owe it to you anyhow in a few more minutes."

A flush of gratitude spread through Hart's belly. He was barely able to keep it from reaching his face where it might have been seen. His only outward reaction was a cold-eyed nod.

Hart began clearing the table of the dirty plates and empty platters left from the meal, but he had no intention of finishing the job right then. As soon as Wynn was done with his cigarette and got to his feet, Hart muttered a quick explanation over his shoulder to Brown and followed the foreman to the stallion's corral.

The hands were already there in the growing pre-dawn light, slouched on the horses they had chosen for the day and waiting quietly. Hart noticed an extra horse and rider in the crowd. When he came nearer he could make out Titus Venable's fawn colored leather coat and narrow brimmed stockman's hat at the edge of the group.

"Your saddle's on the rail, Early," Venable called. He sounded as eager to watch the action as any of the other men.

"Yeah," another voice bantered, "we figured you might be needin' your strength so we fetched it over for you."

"Thankee kindly, boys," Wynn said. "I'll do something nice for you someday."

Wynn hesitated at the gate for a moment before he went in. The stud was at the far end of the pen pawing nervously at the ground. It had been some time since he had been close to so many other horses, and these were lowly geldings at that.

Hart walked through the group of standing horses and crawled up to sit on the top rail of the corral. Although he had not been able to see the man clearly enough before to tell who it was he found himself on a level with Grimes, whose patchy coated dun horse was standing droopy-eyed and patient nearest to the rails.

Wynn let himself in through the gate. "You been working him with a bit or a hackamore?" he asked.

"He'll take either one, but he's more used to the bosal still," Hart said.

Wynn nodded and draped his bridle over a post top, picking up instead the hackamore Hart had left there.

The foreman moved cautiously down the length of the pen. Hart wished he could see more clearly how the horse was reacting.

The stallion stood facing the man who approached him. One ear flicked back and forward, and he quit his pawing. The man and the saddle took his attention from the geldings outside the corral.

Whatever they had been expecting—and Hart was sure he knew what that had been—the hands got no entertainment laid on for their amusement this morning. After all the build-up there was simply nothing to see.

Wynn walked to the horse, slipped the hackamore onto him and saddled. He stepped back, shrugged once and moved forward to swing lightly into his saddle. The horse merely shifted its weight and waited for its rider's nudge of command.

Wynn took his hat off and resettled it more lightly on his head. It had been pulled tight until it rubbed his ears. "Well, I'll be a son of a bitch," he said loud enough to be heard by the hands. "Open the gate, boys. We got work to do."

The group stirred slowly into motion. Someone leaned over to slip the gate latch and pushed the gate wide. Wynn rode out to join them, the spotted horse obedient to his touch.

"I owe you some money," Wynn told Hart. He pulled a half eagle from his pocket and moved close enough to hand it across.

"So does Grimes," Hart said with a tight smile.

Grimes dug unhappily into his jeans. "That's all I got 'til payday," he grumbled.

"No, that's what you *had* 'til payday," Hart corrected him. "Now it's what *I've* got until then."

"Come on, gentlemen. Let's go do some work," Venable's voice cut through the morning but with a ring of good humor in it.

"You heard the man," Wynn said. "Let's go find us some bovines, boys."

They turned and jogged westward away from the ranch headquarters. As they went Hart could hear some voices being raised, tossing comments at a sullen and silent Harry Grimes. Hart grinned to himself and pocketed his seven dollars. He slipped down from the rails of the empty corral and walked lightly back toward the hey-boy work that was still waiting for him.

Hart leaned against the fence rails and admired the sleek gray stallion in Venable's stud pen. The horse had already come over twice to inspect its visitor, the second time stretching its muzzle forward to lip his hand and get slapped for the familiarity. Now it was posing at the far end of the pen, its head lifted and ears pointed toward the distant grass where the mares ran free. Its skin rippled tightly over hard muscles when it shivered a botfly off its belly.

Footsteps lightly crunching on gravel pulled Hart's attention from the horse. When she came close enough he could see it was Twyla Venable, plain and drab but clean scrubbed. A glow of health showing through from under the skin made her look almost presentable.

Hart reached up with the intention of sweeping his hat off in a mocking welcome but thought better of it at the last moment and merely touched his brim. He was in too good a mood this day to bait her. "Good afternoon," he said, making a point to be civil about it.

She gave him a quick, questioning look and then

seemed to accept the greeting as it had been meant. She climbed lightly to perch on the top rail and let out a low, trilling whistle that brought the gray's head around. The horse trotted to her to receive a thorough ear scratching. After a moment she shoved the gray's muzzle aside and it wandered away.

"Good looking bastard, isn't he?"

"It's a fact," Hart said.

"I didn't see Early's spotted stud in his pen this morning."

"Wynn's working off of him today." He paused and grinned. "I hope. Leastways they were doing all right the last I saw of them this morning."

"You finally got done with him then."

"Uh huh."

"Took your sweet time about it, too."

"Didn't have much to work with," Hart said. He pointed toward the gray. "Now a horse like that one there, him a man could do something with. I'll wager he was born knowing everything a cow might ever do. Has that knowin' clean down in his bones, I'd bet."

"Well, you'll damn sure never find out, hey-boy. That horse is here for one thing only, and that's to cover my mares." She bristled. "If you've got some thoughts about him you can just forget them. You hear that, hey-boy?"

He grinned, the rapid-fire shaft and dart of his eyes lending to the insolence that twisted the corners of his mouth. "The name is Hart, ma'am."

She cursed and ignored him for a time, giving her attention to the gray stallion again. Eventually, without looking at him, she asked, "What were you able to make of that bonehead of Wynn's, anyway?"

Hart shrugged. "He's a horse. He'll go from here to there. Put him to a mare and he'll throw you a colt just as bad as he is. All I could do was see to it that he could be handled and rode, but then that's all that was asked. I don't think he ever will have sense enough to do any real work. Wynn will have to control him all the time."

"You get paid yet?"

"I cain't see that t's any of your concern, but yes. I got my pay."

She laughed. "You can get yourself a new rope now."

"Uh huh."

She laughed again. "Aw hell, it was worth it."

"What was?"

"You'd hear about it sooner or later anyhow. I put Early up to giving you that stud to ride. Kinda thought you'd end up with a busted head or something like that. Tell you what, hey-boy. Save yourself the price of a rope, hear? There's a bale of manila in the shed. Cut yourself off whatever you want of it. All right?"

He gave her another lip-curled grin and said, "Sure. Why not? But if you think that makes us square, you're wrong as sin, Miss Twyla, ma'am. Wrong as sin."

She dropped to the ground beside him and glared up into his face. "The hell you say. I don't owe you a damn thing, hey-boy."

His grin broadened. "One floor scrubbing, ma'am. And a buss on the nose for my mare Fancy."

She stamped her foot in anger and whirled to leave with her chin lifted and shoulders straight.

"Thanks for the rope, ma'am," he called after her. "An' the name is Hart. Try to remember that." Her pace increased perceptibly.

Hart leaned back against the rails and chuckled for only himself and the gray horse to hear.

VII

The following day Brown stopped him as Hart was about to enter his room. The evening meal was over, the kitchen cleaned and ready for its next use.

"The man wants to see you over to the house, Gotch."

"Now?"

"He said as soon as we're done here. I expect that means now."

"Something in the wind?"

"He'll tell you about it." Brown acted like he knew what was coming, but Hart did not know when the cook could have found time to talk with Titus Venable. Venable had been out with the hands all day while Brown had been at the headquarters throughout the day, and Brown and Hart had been working together in the cookhouse since well before the men rode in for their night meal.

Hart lifted his shirt from a wall peg just inside his door and pulled the garment over his head. He tucked the shirttail inside his waistband and tugged his hat into place. "Ready for any damn thing," he told Brown on his way out.

Hart had never before been inside the Venable home. He mounted the three steps to the covered stoop, which was barely large enough to be worth the bother of building it, and rapped on the door frame. From inside he heard Venable's voice calling, "Come."

He stepped into a papered and wainscoted foyer that was undecorated except for a bench and a hat rack. To his left a double door opened into the parlor. There a floral patterned rug covered polished wood flooring. The wallpaper was in a smaller floral pattern. The furnishings were heavy, thickly stuffed and covered with a dark rose colored material. Several lamps were lighted although the room was not in use. Straight ahead was a steep, narrow set of stairs and, to the right of the staircase, a closed door. Hart guessed that would lead back to a large kitchen where the family, when it was assembled, would do most of their indoor living.

Another set of double doors, slightly ajar, was on the right. Hart heard movement from behind them and Titus Venable pushed the nearer door wide.

"In here," he said. He was in shirtsleeves. It was the first time Hart had seen the man without a coat. Normally, even when working, he was well dressed and carried himself with dignity without being standoffish about it. A gentleman in the best sense of the term.

The room was as large as the parlor but not so fully furnished. A massive rolltop desk dominated the room. A pair of large, leather covered chairs were arranged near a cast iron stove with a small table between them. The table top was inlaid with contrasting woods to form a checkerboard, but a number of pieces were ranked on opposite sides of the board, pieces that were oddly shaped and unfamiliar to Hart. There was a rack of rifles and shotguns on the wall. The foor was covered with buffalo hide rugs, shaggy and soft underfoot.

"Sit down, man," Venable said with a motion toward the leather chairs.

Hart slouched into the nearer of the two. He tipped his hat back and waited with an outward show of casual disinterest while Venable closed the roll front of his desk and seated himself in the chair across from Hart.

Venable pointed toward the board between them and politely asked, "Do you play?"

Hart leaned closer so he could distinguish the shapes of the pieces and then sat back in the chair. He grinned. "I don't think I do. Don't even know what they are."

Venable seemed disappointed. He stifled a sigh and said, "They're chess pieces, but never mind. That isn't what I called you over for." He paused as if waiting for a question, but Hart remained silent. Venable went on. "I saw the work you did with Wynn's horse."

Hart nodded. If Venable expected comment from him or questions, though, the man was disappointed again.

The ranch owner smiled. "I can't decide if you have good control of yourself or if you just lack curiosity, dammit."

Hart loosened up enough to let a half-smile tug at the corners of his mouth. He took his hat off and dropped it to the floor beside the chair. "All right, I'll bite. How'd the sorry bastard do?"

"Better than I expected, I'll tell you that. He goes where Wynn points him and doesn't blow up when he's roped off of. You did a good job with him."

Hart nodded his thanks. And was silent.

Venable shook his head. "You just don't keep a man jumping trying to answer all your questions, do you?"

"You'll get around to it," Hart answered mildly.

"All right, then. Here it is. My using string is long since broke out and working, but I have a crop of three-year-olds that need to be broke yet. You can have the job if you want it."

Hart felt a sudden swelling inside his chest. He was sure if he tried to draw a deep breath there would not be room in there for it. But he let nothing of what he felt creep onto his features for Venable to see. "What do you offer?" he asked, careful to keep his voice under control as well.

"I still need you to help Brown," Venable said, "and you're already drawing wages for that. Keep your wage and I'll pay four dollars a head for the horses you break."

Hart snorted. "You want me to work the stock in my free time, right?"

"Of course."

"And you'll want a full job done with Brown."

"That's right."

"And you want me to take less than is fair for what I do on my own time, right?"

Venable sat straighter in his chair. "Now I wouldn't put it quite that way, man. I surely wouldn't."

"I would," Hart said pointedly. "Five dollars a head is a fair price. I'll do it on my own time while I work with Brown or I'll move over to the bunkhouse and peel your horses full time. That's up to you. But you pay me five dollars a head."

"You're wanting to draw two full wages, damn it."

"I am not. I can't break horses near as fast while I'm doing your damned kitchen work, and you know it. So pick your deal. Or we can drop the whole idea." Hart felt his throat tighten at the prospect of the offer being withdrawn, but all he showed to the ranch owner was a calm patience.

Venable craned his neck and scratched under his chin, lost in thought. After a delay that brought Hart's nerve ends near a breaking point he said, "Five dollars. On your own time."

Hart, his face impassive, nodded curtly. "Have them brought in whenever you want them started," he said. He got to his feet. "Anything else?"

"No. The horses will be brought in tomorrow."

"Then I'll say good night to you."

Venable remained in his chair while Hart found his own way to the front door.

There were twenty-seven horses in the bunch driven into the stock pens the next evening. Hart was surprised. He would not have thought the V-Slash-4 would have had a mare band large enough to drop that many colts in a single crop, and each of these was a gelding. No fillies had been brought in among them.

The animals were coarse bodied and unpretty but they showed at least an average quality in the blood behind them, with little of the stringy, undersized build of the wild bands showing through. There was some of the mustang blood in them to be sure, enough to give them the toughness needed for day in and day out work but not so much as to take away from the bone and the muscle required of a working horse. Hart stood by the gate so he would be close enough to see them as they streamed past into one of the larger corrals, and he wondered if Titus Venable had the same weakness for horseflesh that Hart had himself. Hart looked at the crop of colts and thought of the gray stallion and wished he could get a look at Venable's herd of broodmares, wherever they were kept. He was willing to bet the sleek gray would improve on this lot greatly.

It took Hart more than a month to break the geldings to his own satisfaction, starting each of them by the tried and true method of riding them to a standstill but adding some refinements of his own to put a handle on them with rein and spur.

By the time he was done the spring cow work had been completed and the V-Slash-4 was nearly empty. Early Wynn and most of the hands had taken a herd of steers toward the nearest railhead. The few other hands had been paid off, and Hart was alone in the cookhouse. Brown was with the herd, handling those cooking chores by himself while Hart stayed with the horses.

The afternoon he moved the last gelding into the big, well grassed trap where the broken horses were being held, Hart decided he was ready for a trip to town. He sponged himself clean and put on his spare shirt before he presented himself at the Venables' front door. His knock was answered by Twyla.

"I was looking for your father," he told her.

She shook her head. "He rode off this morning."

"Ah hell," Hart blurted. "I sure wanted to get paid an' head for town tonight."

The girl frowned and her chin hiked itself a notch or two into the air. "I suppose you want to go get yourself all likkered up and find some saloon girl to paw at. Randy as a damn stallion in springtime and no more sense than one neither. Hell, you're all the same. Cowhands and hey-boys and horse stompers, you're none of you any good."

Hart took a half step backward as he recoiled in surprise. He felt his jaw drop open and clamped it firmly shut. He recovered quickly and said, "Lady, all I did was come asking to get paid. I just finished breaking the last of those horses, an' I figure your pa owes me a hundred thirty-five Yankee dollars for that *plus* two months wages that I ain't ever collected yet. Now if I done something wrong, you tell me about it, but don't go jumping down my throat for no reason, you hear?"

She let out a coarse oath that would have made a bullwhacker proud of himself and stood still for a moment. Her hands were twisted into the apron she was wearing over her plain, drab dress. Finally she let go of the apron and stepped to the side, swinging the door open wider.

"Look, I'm sorry, all right? I'm kind of upset about something else. Come on in if you like. I was just fixing a late lunch for myself. You can have some if you want." She took a deep breath. "And I'll see if I can find some money for you. I ought to be able to give you some of what Daddy owes you anyhow."

"Well . . ." Hart hesitated. "That'd be all right

then, I guess." He stepped inside.

She led him through the foyer and past the staircase into the large kitchen. Except for a walled off niche that he guessed was a pantry the kitchen took up the entire rear half of the downstairs floor.

A copper sink had been built beneath a pair of curtained windows on the back wall, and most of the wall space was taken up by cabinets and counters. The range was of the highest quality with a wide, deep woodbox and a hot water reservoir cast into the side, even a large warming oven built directly over the stove instead of being tacked onto the pipe like an afterthought. Several wooden rocking chairs were placed at the range end of the long room, and a large table occupied most of the other end. There was a single place setting of crockery tableware laid at the table.

"I've got biscuits in the oven and ham ready to fry," she said nervously. "Do you want some eggs to go with that?"

"Eggs? Whereat would you find eggs around here?" He had not seen—or been able to afford—an egg in more than a year.

"Daddy gets them in five-gallon crocks packed in waterglass. They keep for months that way, the ones that don't get broken hauling them in. I take it you want some?"

He nodded quickly. "That'd be a real treat."

A brief flicker of smile touched her lips and some of her nervousness seemed to dissipate. She smoothed away some of the wrinkles she had wrung into the cloth of her apron and said, "Sit down then. I'll be right back."

She disappeared into the pantry, and a moment later Hart could hear the distinctively chunky sound of a heavy crock lid being rattled. He found a wall peg by the back door to hang his hat on and sat in the straight backed wooden chair across the table from where her table setting had been laid.

When she came back she had a clutch of brown eggs held in a fold of her apron. She laid them out on the counter and began toweling them dry one at a time. "Fried be all right for you?"

"Fine."

The girl busied herself at the range, heating grease in an iron skillet, shifting golden topped biscuits from the oven to the warmer, fussily wielding a broad spatula. She laid a place for him at the table and poured a mug of coffee for him to occupy himself with while she finished their meal.

When the platters were on the table, filled heavily enough to satisfy the needs of three times as many people, she picked lightly at her food, her eyes staying mostly on her own plate. Hart stuffed himself with eggs and ham and sopped biscuit after biscuit in the thin red gravy she had prepared. When he could hold no more he shoved his plate aside and said, "You might not know much about horses, but you can sure as hell cook."

She looked up. Her expression was genuinely appreciative of the compliment but what she said was, "That's nothing but a damn hey-boy's opinion. What would you know about anything, horses or cooking either one?"

Hart grinned. "More than you about horses," he said. "Less about cooking. But I know I liked what I just had. If you don't know how to take some nice words about it, well, the hell with you then. I don't beg nobody to believe me, man nor woman either one."

He had meant it lightly enough and had spoken in a gentle tone. He was taken by surprise when she burst into tears and fled from the table. She bolted through the door to the front part of the house, and he could hear the rush of her feet clatter noisily up the stairs.

"Well, I'll be a son of a bitch," Hart muttered to himself.

VIII

Hart sat for several minutes wondering what he should, or could, do. Failing to find inspiration in a last cup of coffee he cleared the table, brought a bucket of fresh water in from the well and washed the dishes. He was toweling the last of them dry when Twyla Venable returned.

"I didn't know what to do with the leftover meat so I just laid it on a plate. It's under that towel there," he said, deciding to ignore her departure, at least for the moment.

"Oh, I . . . You didn't have to do any of this." She was wringing her hands in her apron again.

He grinned at her. "That's part of a hey-boy's job, remember?"

"Of course," she said, but her tone was serious, preoccupied. She took the plate of cold ham into the pantry, and he heard the snap of a tightly fitted door. There was a food safe in there, he guessed.

"Would you like some coffee?" he asked when she was back in sight. "Another two cups should just about finish this pot and I can wash it too then."

"No, I . . ." The gentle pressure he had applied sank in, as he had intended it to. "All right. Another cup won't hurt."

"Coming right up." He filled the two cups and emptied the coffee pot into the copper sink where Venable or some workman had fitted an open drain into a pipe that led not to a bucket—he had looked—but to somewhere under the house. He poured out at least a quart of hot coffee when he dumped the pot. "There you are." He put one of the mugs before her and dropped into the chair across from her.

"Thank you," she said in a small voice.

"Sure." Hart's attention was on his mug as he stirred sugar and evaporated milk in until it was of a syrupy color and sweetness. "You can tell me about it if you want to," he said, still without looking at her.

"No," she said quickly. She sipped nervously at her coffee and made a loud slurping noise, and sudden embarrassment sent a tinge of color into her cheeks. Hart said nothing. After a moment she said, "There wouldn't be anything you could do about it anyway. You probably wouldn't even know what I was talking about."

"You're more than likely right," Hart agreed, still speaking to his coffee cup. "Telling somebody else about troubles practically never makes them any better." He paused. "Funny how it makes a body feel better about things, ain't it? Doesn't seem like it ought to."

"No, but it . . . Why, you did that on purpose, didn't you?"

He looked up at her. "Did what, ma'am?"

"Led me right into agreeing that . . . Never mind," she finished firmly.

Hart looked back down toward his mug, consciously trying to hide from her the involuntary shift and dart of his eyes. "You know," he said quietly, "there probably isn't a safer person around here you could talk to. I don't have anyone to carry tales to. And anyway I keep my mouth shut pretty good." He could not stop himself from grinning at her and adding, "Besides, since I wouldn't understand any of it, I wouldn't know what to repeat even if I wanted to."

"I think maybe . . ." She shook her head.

"You do what you think best," he said, sipping at his coffee.

The girl got up from the table and crossed to the cast iron range. She pulled the firebox door open and stooped to peer inside. "I really ought to clean this soon," she said.

"Too hot now."

"I suppose." She clanged the door shut and returned to the table. She fidgeted with her spoon and vigorously stirred her black, unsweetened coffee. "Have you ever had troubles, hey-boy?"

Hart barked out a short, ugly noise that might have been intended as a laugh. It did not sound like one. He fixed his eyes on hers and said, "Ask me that again."

"I'm sorry," she said. She sounded like she meant it. "It's just . . ."

"I know. You don't have to explain anything to me. Remember?" But he sounded bitter now.

"Look, I *said* I was sorry. I'm just . . . not thinking very well today. You know what I mean?"

"I will when you tell me about it."

She sighed. "It probably isn't anything, really. I just worry too damn much. Daddy tells me I do, anyhow. He's probably right."

"What is it you're fretting about, girl? You got man troubles?"

This time it was her turn to snort. She tossed her head and said, "At least that's one problem I'll never have."

"What then?"

Her expression softened, turned inward and more pensive. "Oh, it's just . . . I'm worried about Daddy." She paused and looked at Hart but he did not interrupt, just waited for her to continue. She went on. "He isn't like himself lately. He's never sent Early Wynn off alone with the market herd before. He goes out a lot at night now. He never used to do that. No so much, anyway. And when he is at home he doesn't . . . laugh and make stupid little jokes or . . . sing when he's shaving in the morning. As long as I can remember that's the way I could tell it was time to get up. When I heard Daddy stropping his razor and singing to himself. He's a good man, hey-boy. This place, the family, have always been everything to him. Now he . . . frowns a lot. He's always been, well, he hasn't many friends outside the family and the ranch. Now somehow he seems all alone and kind of sad." Again she snorted, but more softly. "Doesn't sound like much, does it?"

"I'm not in any position to judge that. But I guess you are. If you're worried maybe you've got reason to be. Where does he go when he's out like that? Why'd he send Wynn off alone this year?"

She shook her head. "I don't know where he

goes. I don't know where he is right now. He just tells me he's going for a ride, says he wants some air. He's always told me *every*thing before about where he'd be and what he'd be doing. Now he doesn't even tell me about the ranch work. And for sending Wynn off he made up some excuse about the foreman handling more of the responsibilities. Said if anything should happen to him Wynn would have to run the place for us kids." Again she snorted. "Hell's bells, hey-boy. I know more about this place and how to run it than Wynn ever will, and Daddy knows it. And Richard knows nearly as much as I do even if Daddy has kept him away at school so much. Mary, she doesn't care anyway. She'd rather Daddy sold the place and bought a house in Boston or some such damned place. I don't know how she ever got to be part of the family in the first place." She giggled and for a moment amusement softened her plain features. The sparkle returned to her eyes, and she looked almost pretty. "I tried hard enough to keep her out of it. When we were little I bumped her into the well one time and then tried to bean her with the bucket, but I missed and she hung onto the damn thing. Everybody thought I'd thrown it in to save her. They treated me like some fairy-tale princess that day, I'll tell you." There was an appealing wistfulness in her voice when she spoke the last words from that memory.

Abruptly she stopped talking and a look of astonishment widened her eyes, the whites of her eyes standing out clear and almost bluishly white between the tan of her skin and the tan of her eyes. "Why . . . I never told that to a soul before today. Not even to Richard. You won't . . ."

"Of course I won't be telling that to anybody. What the hell do you take me for, girl?"

She looked at him blankly. "I don't know," she mumbled. She seemed shaken and the mood that had generated her chatter was gone. She jumped up from the table. "You needed some money, didn't you? I'll see what I can find."

She swept out through the door to the front of the house. He heard no steps on the stairway and assumed she was in her father's office. In a few minutes she was back, wearing an apologetic look. She handed him a ten-dollar eagle and said, "This is all we can . . . this is all I could find. Will that be enough? I mean, I have some savings up in my room. I could get you some from that if you need it."

Hart shook his head. "No, this is fine. A couple beers, and I'll be all set 'til the next time. Your pa can give me the rest later. But I do thank you for the offer. I mean that."

She nodded. "Sure. Well . . . I have work to do. I'll see you tomorrow maybe. Maybe you could, if you want to that is, maybe you could work the gray horse some for me. He's getting a little soft, you know."

Hart nodded. The horse was as solid as sun baked clay, he knew. She was trying to offer him something special but whether in apology or in gratitude he was not sure. "I'll stop by tomorrow some time," he said.

She turned toward the sink, and he let himself out the back door.

A trip to town with seventeen dollars in his pocket was going to be far different from the excursion he had promised himself while he was absorbing punishment on top of those V-Slash-4 geldings, but it would have to do for the moment. Besides, his mood was not quite as loose and expansive as it had been.

He saddled his own mare for the trip and felt her shift and quiver between his knees in her eagerness to be let out into a run after so much confinement. The feeling of controlled power that flowed out of her pleased him, and he was smiling even as he snatched back on her mouth to keep her from bolting when he leaned from the saddle to swing the gate open. "Mind your manners, Fancy old girl." He let her take a fast lope and held her in it for most of the three-hour ride to town. She was well lathered but far from being spent when her hooves hit the rutted clay streets of the town. "You're soft, ol' girl," he told her as he stepped down. Enough of the sass had been ridden out of her that she would be content to stand tied for a while, he knew.

The only bar he was familiar with here was the Muleshoe, and it had not exactly met his tastes. He certainly had no desire to go out of his way to find it again. It was easy enough to find another. At this hour, with darkness just fallen, most businesses presented dark faces or at the most low-trimmed glows from counter lamps left burning overnight. Most of the few lighted windows in the business district could guide him to a beer.

He tied the mare in front of one of these that had the added attraction of piano music coming through the open doorway.

The place was brightly lighted inside and not very crowded. It must be a week night, Hart decided. He had no idea what day of the week it was, nor did he particularly care. He took a place at the end of the bar and ordered a brew, then turned to hook one elbow on the unpolished but solidly built bar surface while he listened to the piano.

Whoever was at the keys was doing a good job of it, the notes clean and the tunes gay. Eight or ten others stood along the bar, and three of the eight tables were occupied. Card games were in progress at two of those tables, while the third was ringed by bareheaded, city dressed men in quiet conversation.

Hart was pleased to see that his beer was served in a glass mug. This would not be a brawler's hangout. For some reason he did not much feel like getting into a scrap this night.

He finished his beer, found the backhouse and ordered a refill. When it was gone he asked the bartender, "Where could a man find some company around here?"

The man took the empty mug and sloshed it in an undercounter bucket of cold, soapy water, rinsed it in another and set it back on the shelf. "What kinda place are you looking for?" he asked.

"Decent place. Nothing fancy, mind. Just a nice, clean kind of place."

"Up to the corner then and turn left. Last house on your left."

"All right, and I thank you." Hart laid a quarter on the counter and went out. He untied the mare and swung onto her, nudging her into a slow walk along the dark street.

He turned at the corner and went up a slight grade, passing the red painted front of the Muleshoe. There was a railroader's red lantern hanging over a doorway in the alley beside the Muleshoe. He was glad he had asked directions from that bartender.

For some reason he was concerned now about the diseases a man could pick up in places like that one was sure to be. He never used to give a thought to such things. Getting old and cautious, he told himself without believing it. But he did not know what else it might be.

He found the place he wanted and slipped the mare's bridle free, tying her by a halter instead of the reins. He expected to be a while, and even a well trained horse can become impatient. And he had no desire to walk the thirty-odd miles back to the V-Slash-4. Not only would that be uncomfortable, it would be downright embarrassing. Twyla Venable especially would get too big a kick out of it to take a chance on it happening. He gave the mare a pat and went inside.

IX

"Your pa's not here today?" he asked.

"No." She did not seem inclined to pursue the matter, so he let it drop.

The girl slipped inside the gate, Hart behind her, and whistled for the stallion. The gray horse had its attention far across the grass but it turned and came sulkily toward them.

Twyla Venable was as plain as ever and dressed as drably, but today she was at least clean scrubbed and perhaps more neat about it than usual. Hart could catch a lingering soap-smell in the air around her, and her dress was lightly starched and newly pressed. Her hair, too, looked to be clean and soft although as always it was pulled severely back into a primly tight and homely bun. Hart wondered briefly what her hair would smell like. And wondered next where such an odd thought might have come from. Stray thoughts left over from the night before, he decided and pushed it out of his mind. *That* did not belong here. Still . . . he could not deny a growing interest.

The horse walked to her and shoved its muzzle against her stomach impatiently as it looked for a tidbit to make the trip across the pen worthwhile. She slapped it hard on the jaw and was rocked backward when the finely molded head was tossed and the big eyes widened. Hart noticed that the horse's muzzle left a wet, dirty smear on the front of her crisply washed dress. "You know better than that, buster," she warned with a raised fist. The horse backed away nervously.

She glanced at Hart. "Pet or not," she said, "if you don't keep your eye on the big bastard he might take it in mind to kill you."

"They're notional," Hart agreed. "What's the horse's name, anyway?"

"Daddy named him Gray Lad. I mostly call him Horse. Or just cuss at him. He doesn't know the difference anyhow."

Hart tugged free the rope halter that had been shoved into his waistband. He stepped forward and slipped the halter onto the fine, gray head. He shoved the black hank of forelock aside and shook his head admiringly. "Look at them knowledge bumps, will you? Like a pair of fists planted up there. This horse has to have more cow in him than any I ever seen. Except my mare, maybe. What's your fee for breeding to him, Miss Twyla? I hate to ask you straight out like that, but I got to do it."

"I told you before, hey-boy. This stud won't cover any mares but our own. Not until he's built a name for himself, he won't. Ask me again in five or six years."

"Nobody's mares but yours? Hell! He isn't even doing that, and it's 'most past the breeding season already. If your pa waits much longer you'll be carrying a crop of suckling foals into the winter. Lose half of them and ruin your mares too, I don't doubt."

He saw a kind of pain film her eyes, and she turned away.

"Uh-oh. I put my foot down smack on another of your troubles, huh?"

He could see her shoulders rise and fall in a small shrug. "Part of . . . the same ones. It doesn't matter."

"It does matter," he insisted. "What is it?" The gray horse wandered away from Hart's fingertips on its halter. He let it go. "What is it?" he asked again.

"Daddy said he's thinking of selling Gray Lad. And he was talking about selling our mares too. He said there may not be any point in breeding them. Besides, he's too *busy*." She bore down bitterly on the word. "Too damn busy to have the mares brought in."

"It takes an awful busy man to let a horse like this stand idle."

"Doesn't it, though." She turned. "Listen, I don't feel much like fooling with him today, all right?"

He thought for a minute and nodded his head. "Yeah, I agree. There's more important things can be done." He took her by the elbow and led her out of the enclosure. She was quietly crying.

"Listen," he said, "you tell me you know your mares. Do you think you could find them this time of year? Point them out to me?"

"What do you mean?" she asked as he latched the gate behind them.

"Listen, Miss Twyla, there's no way I could go out and hunt up your mares. At any distance I couldn't even spot them for horses much less for being the mares you want. But if you could find them for me, I could bring them in. Put those geldings back in one of the pens and turn the mares—just the best of them, mind—into that trap. The grass is still good in there, and they'd have water, and the free running studs couldn't get to them. Then turn your gray horse in with them. They won't all be bred yet. You'd have *something* on the ground from him next year anyhow."

"You'd do that?" Her eyes were large. And hopeful.

"I'd ask payment." He could see her drawing back, disgust beginning to curl the corners of her mouth.

"I might have known . . ." she began.

He cut her off. "The first mare he covers," Hart said quickly. "I want to put my mare to him. I'll pay you a fair fee. Whatever you think it's worth. You can take it out of what your pa owes me. That's what I'd ask. If you don't want to pay the price, well, we'll go get your mares anyhow. But that's what I'd want."

Her look softened. Interest returned to her eyes. "It's too late to start after them today," she said speculatively.

"First light tomorrow," he said quickly.

"The two of us could bring them in easily enough," she said. "We'd lose some of them, but we could drive most of the good ones in. Is your mare in season now?"

"No. It will be . . ." He stopped to figure.

". . . another week or so."

"You could put her in the trap with the others," the girl said.

"That'd be fair," he agreed. Hand breeding would be more sure, but the stallion probably had never been handled before for breeding. "All right."

"First light then, hey-boy. And bring one of those geldings for me to use. I'll see how good a job you've done with them." She started toward the house, her step light and eager.

"Miss Twyla?"

She stopped. "Yes?"

"The name is Hart, ma'am. Try to remember that, will you?"

"Sure, hey-boy." But he thought he heard a small chime of laughter float over her shoulder as she walked away.

"Where are you going?"

Hart had not seen him in the half light of early morning. Venable was under the roof overhang of the shed where they hung saddles. Around the corner Hart could hear a horse stamping and pawing impatiently.

"Out," Hart said, bristling. He thought he could detect implied accusation in the question, as if he did not know his job, as if someone had to keep an eye on his work. "Anything wrong with that?" he demanded.

"No, of course not," Venable said quickly. "I'm just going out myself." The older man hefted his saddle down from a wall hung brace and carried it out of sight. His tone was friendly enough, and

Hart wondered if he might have been too quick to take offense.

Hart could hear the slap of leather as Venable's horse was saddled and the latigos yanked snug. A faint creak of aged and oiled leather told him the man was mounting. Venable walked the animal to the front of the shed and started past.

The light was not good but the bald, white smear around the horse's muzzle was unmistakable. "That's one of the three-year-olds I just broke for you," Hart said. Venable tightened his hand, and the horse stopped.

"It is," Venable agreed. "Twy said they were all done. I thought I would try one today."

"Uh huh." Hart waited but the ranch owner merely nodded and squeezed the horse into a walk. He was at a lope before he was out of the V-Slash-4 yard. It irked Hart that Venable had not mentioned the pay that was due him for the breaking.

Hart took only his own gear from the shed, saddled his mare and used her to go into the trap and rope a horse for the girl to use. It irked him, too, that Venable had chosen the baldfaced chestnut to ride. It was the horse he had wanted to put the girl on. Somehow he resented Venable being able to pick out the smoothest and the quickest of the young geldings.

On the mare he prowled through the fenced pasture until he found a short coupled blue roan that he liked, drifted close and dropped a loop over the surprised animal's head. He led it back to the shed and strapped on a lightweight saddle that he assumed belonged to the girl. There were no sidesaddles in evidence anywhere on the place or he would have noticed them long since, and somehow she did not look like the kind of female who would demand such—to his mind—foolish equipment.

He led both horses to the back door of the house and knocked.

"Come in."

"All three of us?"

"What?" Her voice was faintly heard through the closed door. She opened the door and leaned out. "What? Oh. No, just you. *They* can stay outside. Will the colt stand tied?"

"He'd better."

"All right. Come on in, then. I'll be ready in a minute." She was gone again.

There were no large trees around the still new house and no hitching rail. The only fence nearby was the stud pen, which would have been asking for trouble. He tied the horses on opposite sides of the family's backhouse and left them there with a silent hope that they would not pull it over.

The girl was washing dishes when he entered the kitchen. "Sit," she told him. He took the chair he had used before and did as he was told.

She poured him a cup of coffee and stirred in canned milk and sweetening before setting it before him. She dropped the sugar-sticky spoon into the dishwater and went on with her chore. "I won't be long," she said.

"Whenever." He wondered about the roan, though. He had not spent much time giving the geldings their manners.

Twyla Venable finished the dishes and left them on a rack to dry. "Be right back," she said. A moment later he could hear her feet on the stairs.

Hart sat back, relaxed in the warmth of the big

kitchen, and nursed his coffee. He was surprised to find that it was fixed exactly to his taste. He had not thought she would have paid any attention to such details the other time he was here. But then, he reasoned, most cowhands took their coffee the same way. She probably had plenty of experience with them, helping with things when there was no cook on the payroll or when the cook was sick or taken drunk. Brown was about due for a binge, Hart mused. So was he, he thought. Past due.

The girl came back, the clatter of hard heeled boots on the stairs preceding her. She had changed clothing. It was the first time he had seen her in anything except a drab, severe housedress.

Not that there was much of an improvement, he thought, but then she hadn't much to work with. And in truth, he decided, there really was some improvement there. She was wearing a long, split riding skirt of some dark blue material and a lighter weight shirtwaist that almost but did not quite match the color of the skirt. The sleeves of her brown blouse were lapped up on her forearms, and the blouse was open at the throat. She was wearing a battered, wide-brimmed Stetson that must have been a hand-me-down from her father judging by the amount of use it had seen in the past. It was dust- and sweat-stained and had long since lost its original blocking until now it was virtually shapeless although still as serviceable as a spanking new one would have been.

"All set," she said. She looked and sounded quite eager. She was smiling, her teeth white and even, standing out against the tan of her skin. Smiling and with her bun hidden beneath the crown of the old hat she did not look quite so completely plain. Hart realized this was also the first time he had seen Twyla Venable smile with anything like a degree of joy touching her eyes. He had seen amusement there before. And solemnity and anger and pain. But never joy. He found it rather nice to see now.

He drank off the last of his coffee, rose and set the empty cup into the now dry dishpan. "Let's go do some work then."

They hazed the geldings out of the trap and into one of the larger corrals without losing any of them. The girl rode well enough to help with the herding, he was pleased to see, and the blue gelding responded well to her control. Once the geldings were settled they left the wide, double gate of the trap standing open, and he followed her lead across the rolling grass to the northwest.

X

The land they crossed was, to Hart, an undulating blur of dusty green. The grass was thick, with the red soil showing through but rarely, and was hock deep. The few watercourses were marked by darker color shadings that would be low thickets dense enough to provide windbreaks during the winter's harder times. Even with as little as he could see of it Hart knew this was prime livestock country, bountiful for horses or for cattle.

They rode for little more than an hour before they began to encounter bands of free running horses. When they did, Twyla Venable reined her blue roan to a stop.

"Did you see some you want?" Hart asked,

"What?" She seemed preoccupied. She stood in her stirrups and turned to look closely at the countryside around them, beginning here to rise and to become more choppy, the grass somewhat less thick. "No." She did not explain further but booted the gelding ahead and to the top of a sharply rising slope. There she stopped again to look around her.

"What is it?" he asked. "Those are horses down below us, aren't they?" To Hart they were a shifting brown blur dimly seen against the reddish green background of grass and soil.

"They're horses all right," she said. Her voice was grim. "The question is whose horses they are. I've never seen a one of those animals before."

"Are you sure?" He sounded uncertain. A cowhand, now, he would trust to know if he had ever before seen a particular horse, and most could recognize individual cattle even in a large herd. But this girl would not have their day in and day out experience. She could well be mistaken. "Maybe we should take a closer look," he suggested.

"I damn sure am sure," she said, "but you can just bet we'll take a closer look, hey-boy. I want to see what brand they're wearing. Some son of a bitch is about to have himself some trouble." She kicked the blue horse and sent him into a rump-sliding descent down the steeper far side of the hill they had just climbed.

There were easier routes she could have taken and Hart thought her choice particularly foolish on a just-broken green horse, but apparently she was too upset to have thought about that. Or simply did not care. He sent his bay mare in motion at her heels.

They bottomed out into flatter ground, and the girl quirted and spurred the gelding into a hard run toward the front of the horse band. They were close enough now that Hart could distinguish individual animals in the bunch. He broke off to the right at a slower pace so he could turn the band when they reacted to the girl's charge.

As he had expected, the strange horses bolted away from her circling run. They wheeled and tried to thunder free only to be met by Hart's mare. Since the girl wanted a brand to inspect Hart shook a loop into his rope and dropped it onto the neck of the first horse to pass him.

To his surprise the animal acted like a wild one when the rope pulled tight. It squealed and reared, striking with its forefeet and trying to wrench itself free at the same time. The animal, a scrubby dun, bared its teeth and charged Hart's mare.

The mare had been backing away to keep the rope taut but now as the dun neared she lunged forward, battering the strange horse off its feet with a blow from her chest and taking the time to rake its crest with her teeth before she again backed away to tighten the rope. Hart rode out the brief storm, staying in the saddle by unconscious shift of balance while he concentrated on trying to keep his rope from tangling in the mare's legs. It was sheer luck, he knew, that the mare's feet had not been enmeshed.

They backed away and the mare hit the end of the rope hard and continued to back under Hart's urging. The dun was flat on the ground. Each time it tried to rise Hart ran the mare backward.

Twyla Venable raced to them and slithered to a jittering, ragged stop on her gelding. The horse needed to learn about stopping on its haunches, Hart noted out of habit.

"Hold that bastard where it is, hey-boy," she cried. She dropped out of the saddle and ground-tied her roan. Or tried to. Hart had given the young geldings no training in that.

"Don't . . ."

Barely in time she realized what she had done. She managed to grab the trailing end of one rein before the now unsettled three-year-old could escape from all this strange activity. "Jee-zus!" she yelped. She had her hands full of frightened horse for several uncertain moments but managed to bring its front end back down on the ground and get it under control. "Hold this bugger for me, hey-boy," she said, leading the horse to him and jamming her reins into his left hand.

Hart shook his head. She wanted him to handle all three animals at once. But he was shaking his head in wonder, not refusal. She was no longer there, having turned to run toward the fallen dun as soon as he had his hand on her reins. "There's no rush now, you know," he called to her. She did not seem to have heard.

He dropped his own reins, grateful the mare would respond to knee pressure and weight shift, and gave his attention to Twyla Venable's nervous gelding and to the half-wild animal at the end of his rope.

The dun horse tried to rise as the girl neared it but whether to fight or to run Hart could not know. He stabbed his mare's shoulders with his toes and sent her backward again, dragging the dun in the dirt and drawing from it a loud squeal of frustration. The girl had been running down the rope and for a moment was in the path of the dun horse's churning forelegs as it was dragged toward her. She leaped aside with a loud curse. She stood out of reach of the strange horse's hooves and planted her fists on her hips.

"I'll be billy blue damned," she said. "Come here a minute, will you?"

Hart gave her an odd look that she was too preoccupied to notice. He got more of her attention when he laughed out loud. "You've got to be kidding," he said past the laughter. Her blue roan reacted to the sound by trying to pull away again, nearly taking Hart out of the saddle with it until he regained a small measure of control. The mare continued to back on the rope.

"I guess you are kind of busy," the girl admitted. She looked around. The band of horses they had chased was gone, even the dust of their flight now settling. "I'll take him now," she said, walking back to the roan gelding. "You can turn loose of that dink."

"What is it?" he asked with a nod toward the dun as she reclaimed her reins and mounted.

"It's a gelding. Six, maybe seven years old, I'd say. It's hard to tell."

"No, I mean . . ."

"Oh. Whose is it? I told you to start with it wasn't any of ours. Never saw this brand before, and it's kind of smeared at that. Looks like a Box 11. It wouldn't be worth the trouble of shaving it to find out for sure."

Hart grinned. "Probably no need to. That sounds like a good brand. You could burn it real pretty with a straight iron or just a cinch ring held between some sticks. Good brand for a fella traveling light." He kneed the mare forward and whipped the slack in his rope until the loop opened. The dun threw the loop and came angrily to its feet. It shook itself like an overlarge dog and snorted its defiance before it wheeled and plunged after the remainder of its band. "Skittish bugger, isn't he?"

They watched the horse gallop out of sight, its head and tail held erect.

"What I want to know," she said, "is where that animal came from. And what it's doing on our mare range. Nobody but us has ever run horses here. And where the hell *are* our mares, anyway?" She shook her head in bewilderment.

"We can go look for them, I guess."

She sighed. "Yeah, I suppose we'd best do that, hey-boy. But I sure don't know what to think. Box 11. Damn!" Again she shook her head.

They spent the rest of the day covering the higher ridges of the broken country where the Venables held their horses, and everywhere there were horses to be seen. Far too many animals for the grass to carry through fall much less through a hard winter with cold winds sweeping down off the open plains to melt fat off the best fed horses. But everywhere the horses in sight were the same. Rough, indifferently bred animals in only fair condition, unfamiliar horses wearing poorly drawn Box 11 brands.

The girl saw only two bands that she recognized as V-Slash-4 animals. Both of those were groups of yearlings separated too early from the mares and without the protection of older, more experienced horses among them.

She insisted on riding down into the first such group she spotted. The young horses eyed them with more eagerness than anxiety at their approach.

"They keep hoping to find their mamas with us," Hart said as they eased quietly near the yearlings.

"Yeah," the girl said absently. "Dammit, they've been worked or they wouldn't be away from the mares now, would they?"

"Nope. They wouldn't for a fact. Be another year anyway before they'd go off on their own or be run away by the mares."

"There's not a one of them been branded. They're ours all right, though. See that liver colored colt with the white star? I remember seeing him last fall. I remember his dam real well. Kind of a showy looking thing with a good build. One of our best mares, I always thought. And that buckskin. I'm sure I've seen him before. We don't get many that color, and I was wondering about wild studs getting their blood into our herd. I remember thinking that at the time. But there's not a brand been put on any of these, and the colts are still whole, not a one of them cut like they should have been if they were being worked anyway. You don't see any geldings there, do you?"

Hart chuckled. "Girl, it's all I can do t' see those little horses. Don't you go asking me for more than that now, hear?"

She looked at him with no sign of embarrassment. "Yeah, I guess I forgot that. Never mind then." After a pause she said, "Dammit, hey-boy, those mares have *got* to be somewhere out here."

"If you say so."

She gave him a closer look. "What do you mean by that?"

"Nothing. Let's get back up to higher ground." He turned his mare away from the yearlings.

The other band of yearlings was only a few miles away. They did not bother to ride close to them. By mid-afternoon they had passed several hundred Box 11 geldings without a sign of the Venable mares.

"It's time we started back," he told her.

"Not yet. These breaks run north a good ways yet." There was a tiredness in her voice that he was sure she would not admit even to herself if he called her on it. "There's a lot of country we haven't covered yet."

"Uh huh," he agreed mildly, "and it's too late to be trying today. It will be coming dark by the time we get back as it is. If you're gone past dark your pa will be worried."

She let out a long, shuddering sigh. "I suppose you're right. But even so . . ."

He turned the mare back the way they had come.

"Maybe tomorrow . . . ," she said. Her voice tailed away into another sigh. Fatigue pulled at the wrinkles sun and wind had created around her eyes and at the corners of her mouth. Wisps of limp hair that had strayed out of her bun were escaping now from under the much abused sweatband of her old hat. Her cheeks looked more hollow than usual, and she looked pale beneath the false front of her tan. "All right," she said. "Let's go home."

XI

The crew that had been with the market herd got back that night, or what was left of them. Early Wynn returned, driving the cook wagon, and two of the hands, Harry Grimes and a man known as Spud because of his fondness for potatoes. Grimes and Spud were both unusually quiet, apparently still suffering the aftereffects of their payday.

Hart helped Wynn unload the few foodstuffs remaining in the chuck boxes. When they were done he asked, "What happened to Brown?"

Wynn grinned. "Same as the rest of them. Taken drunk, and too pleased with it to want to work again for a while." He shrugged. "Can't see as we need much of a crew until the fall work anyways. And, say, that stud horse you broke for me?" Wynn's grin widened into a broad, satisfied smile.

"Uh huh."

"Some fella gave me a hundred dollars for him. Hell, I grabbed it. That fool thing didn't have enough sense to know which end of a cow he should chase, but the man paid for him anyway.

Said he was gonna cut him and put him in harness. Liked those damned spots on him real well." The foreman chuckled at his good fortune. The only money he had had in the horse was the five dollars he paid Hart to break him. And even Wynn was admitting now that it had been a twenty-dollar horse at best.

"You made out all right then," Hart said.

"Like a bandit," Wynn said happily.

Hart fingered his chin and mused, "A man might make out all right with some mustanging, I wouldn't wonder."

"Not me," Wynn said as he clattered a still dirty coffeepot and box of tin mugs onto the kitchen work table. "It's a bad time to think of that. I heard at the railroad that the damned Army has quit buying remounts for a year or so. Fella at the shipping yard said it's cut 'way back on their traffic in horses already. No market at all for saddlers all of a sudden, and everybody an' his brother trying to unload what they've got. I wouldn't count on being so lucky a second time."

"Oh well," Hart said without interest. "I was just airing my teeth anyhow. I can break them, but there's no way I could go out and find them." He grinned. "With my eyes I'd manage to pen some fella's branded stock and get myself hung."

"It'd serve you right, too," Wynn said agreeably. He patted his pockets, located a pint bottle in one of them and offered it to Hart for a long pull before he drank himself. "Gotta go find my bed," Wynn said. "I know I left it around here somewhere. Are you gonna wake me up with coffee in the morning?"

"The hell," Hart said with a smile.

"Yeah, well, it's a tough old life, ain't it? See you tomorrow if I wake up before dark."

The foreman walked a slightly unsteady line through the door, and Hart realized that Wynn was more drunk than he had thought. Not that Hart blamed him. The drink Wynn had given him burned comfortably in his belly. A heavier load of that would have been pleasant.

Hart looked at the boxes and bags piled in the kitchen, said the hell with it and blew out the lamp. It could wait until morning.

He went into the room he had been given and undressed by the moonlight streaming coldly through the window. He lay on his bunk and felt at peace, aware of his surroundings although there was too little light to see them. He liked this room. It was the first he had ever had all to himself, and it gave him a good feeling to be able to shut the door and find privacy while under a roof, with no wind or threat of rain to disturb his rest. He liked that too.

Since there was no one else to do it, Hart fixed a breakfast of sorts in the morning and called the three-man crew to it. They were still in too much of a stupor to complain about the cooking, and when they were done they dawdled over coffee well into full daylight. Hart ate in the kitchen as custom required but joined them with a cup of coffee afterward. They were listening to Spud tell about a run of luck at a faro table when Venable came in.

The owner spoke a hello to Wynn and nodded to the two hands, but he ignored Hart and chose a seat at the far end of the table from him. He had always before been reasonably friendly, ready to joke with the hands, relaxed and easy-going. "Did you have a good trip, Early?"

"Fair," Wynn said. "We lost eleven head crossing the Arkansas and paid another beef to some louse-running batch of Indians." He smiled. "They didn't look like much, but they seemed to have a good bit of ammunition with them and they kept pointing their guns at our bovines."

Venable nodded, accepting Wynn's judgment in the matter. It was something nearly all drovers faced at one time or another.

"Anyway," Wynn went on, "we made it in good enough shape, and they hadn't dropped too much weight."

Hart kept his thoughts to himself, but his opinion of Wynn fell a little. Hart had twice been on drives working for a man named Peters, one as a hey-boy and the second time as nightherder for the remuda. Peters carried his beeves along slow and steady, and at the end of the drive he would have added an average of fifty pounds to each animal in the herd. Walking the tallow off an animal only meant the job was not being done right. Venable said nothing, however, nor did his face betray any change.

"We only had to wait a couple days for our cars," Wynn said. He paused. "But we, uh, didn't quite meet the price we'd hoped."

Hart wished he could more clearly see Venable's face, that the man had not chosen to sit quite so far away.

"How bad?" Venable asked. His voice sounded casual enough.

"A dollar thirty per head under what you'd figured," Wynn told him.

"That was twenty cents better than the Fishhook outfit got," Spud put in, "and they got there the day after we did."

Venable grunted.

"It was a good price, everything considered," Wynn assured him. "So I took it and paid off the boys and did your banking, just the way you said to." He fumbled under his shirt and dipped his fingers into a money belt buckled there. He pulled out a folded scrap of paper and handed it to Venable. "There's your receipt," he said. He sounded uncertain when he said it. Few cattlemen trusted paper. Most dealt only in currency, and some clung to the old habit of using only hard money, coin, in their transactions no matter how large.

"You did right then, Early. Nobody can get more than the buyers will pay." He sighed. "You boys go on out without me today; I have some things to do. You can check the water, doctor for screwworms if you see any. Whatever needs doing. You know the work as well as I do."

"Whatever you say," Wynn told him, puzzlement creeping into his voice. Venable had always been a man to work beside his crew, not to order them out while the boss relaxed elsewhere.

Still ignoring Hart, Venable left. Wynn and the hands drifted out a few minutes behind him. Hart began the chore of cleaning up from breakfast and the mess Wynn had brought in the previous evening. Before he was done he heard four horses ride out, one of them heading away from the open grass.

When he was finished Hart dumped his buckets of wash water outside the back door, dried his hands on an almost clean towel and rolled his shirt sleeves back down. He walked out into the clear, bright, already heating light of the morning and stood for a moment letting the breeze ruffle his hair before he tugged his hat on. He would soon have to find the barbershop in town, he reminded himself.

For a time he wandered idly among the pens and the sheds that made up the working area of the V-Slash-4. They felt empty now, deserted. While he walked he wondered why Venable had been so pointedly uncivil that morning. The man had always been straight with him before, had never seemed to look down on him the way some did. That was one of the reasons Hart had been coming to like this job so well. He had even been given some proper work to do here. Surely he had done it well enough.

Briefly Hart wondered if the owner might have had trouble with the horse he had used the day before. That might account for it, he decided, although there should have been no problems with that one. It had been by far the best of the string of three-year-olds. Hart's steps lengthened and became more purposeful. He went to the pen where the young geldings were corralled, let himself in and walked among them so he would be close enough to identify each. The baldfaced chestnut was not there, which meant that Venable was probably using it again. If it had given him trouble he probably would not have taken it out again so soon, Hart reasoned. And the man probably would have mentioned that it needed touching up. The other horses arched their necks and shied timidly away when he passed, but they did it as a matter of form, without any show of real nervousness. He was satisfied that he had done his job well with all of them.

He let himself out of the corral and found himself drifting toward the stud pen where the big, gray horse was kept. He hooked a boot onto a low rail and leaned against the pen. The horse came over to investigate, extending its nostrils and snuffling loudly into his shirt sleeve. It tried to lip his wrist and he backhanded it in the muzzle, then murmured softly to bring the small, delicately set ears back forward. "What do you think, old boy?" he asked the horse. Talking to horses was a habit of long standing. He probably had more practice at it than in talking with people. Horses were always reasonable, listened patiently and never argued.

Venable could have been upset that Hart had ridden with his daughter out to the mare range, he thought. That would seem more likely than the man having trouble with the chestnut. He might have decided the girl was not safe in the company of a half-blind hey-boy.

Of course she seemed competent enough to go anywhere she liked, alone if need be. But then he did not know how a father might view such things. Hart wondered if the man was going to give him his time. He hoped not. With the season's work at its end and even the poorest trail jobs long since taken, this would be a bad time to be looking for a bunk. It could have been worse, of course. He had a good bit of pay coming, more than he had ever held in his hand before. If he was careful he could stretch that out through winter if necessary.

But he had really been hoping to get that Fancy mare bred. He looked at the gray horse standing quietly near him and thought about the kind of foal he should get if he could mate a horse like that one with his mare. You never knew, of course, but one like that one, a cross of two fine blood strains, might be the kind of foal a man dreams about, the kind of horse a man is lucky to find even once in his lifetime. The kind that cannot be bought but can only truly belong to a man if he is the one to mix blood with blood, planning and hoping a year ahead of time. Then the satisfaction would be all the greater, a satisfaction the wealthiest of men could not purchase. It had to be earned through the long, slow, hopeful gamble of the mixing of blood.

Hart could envision the foal clearly. He would hope for a colt and would leave it whole. A colt like that could support a man, no matter where he traveled. South Texas, now. There was a place where they appreciated quick-footed animals. Especially if they had the muscle and the wind to run quarter-mile sprints on a Sunday afternoon. A man could make a good living with a stallion like that along the coastline.

Hart sighed. First he had to get the service of the gray, and his mare would not be in season for several days yet. There was nothing he could do to change that, no way to hurry it. And he had never bred the mare before. She might not settle the first time. He might need a full month to be sure of her. He hoped he would have it. That month, that colt, could be his whole future, the difference between being a hey-boy for the rest of his life. Or the owner of maybe the best sprinting stud on the Gulf coast of Texas. He had never really allowed himself a dream before. Now he held one in his thoughts.

And he was afraid it was going to shrivel and be blown away before he hardly had the chance to reach out for it. The fear was new to him also. He shivered despite the sunshine that lay hot on his shoulders.

XII

The gray horse became tired of standing close and being ignored. He wandered away in the awkward looking hip-fall motion of his kind to stand at the far end of the corral gazing endlessly toward the broad, free grass. Hart watched without really seeing him.

Hart felt alone this morning, a feeling that was foreign to him yet which lay emptily in his belly. He wanted to talk with someone, anyone, on any subject. The only other person at the headquarters, though, was Twyla Venable. And if her father was angry about him riding with her in search of the mares it would be best not to look for an excuse to approach her. He looked at the gray horse and grinned to himself. On the other hand, he reasoned, if she should want to talk to him there was not much he could do about it. And she *had* asked him to work the horse.

He turned away and walked purposefully toward the tack shed. He collected a braided rawhide bosal and a thick cotton rope to use as a mecate. Those should be enough, he decided. He carried them back toward the pen behind the Venable house.

The stallion came to his outstretched hand and sloppily lipped a fistful of barley from his palm. Hart slipped the bosal onto its head and took up the buckles of the drop strap—the animal's head was more delicately made than he had realized—until the hard braid of rawhide fell just over the most sensitive part of the nose, above the wide nostrils. Any lower and it would restrict the horse's breathing when the crushing pressure was applied. Higher and it would lie on the flat, hard facial bones that formed the front of the skull. Where he placed it the innocent looking braid could inflict harsh and sudden pain without causing injury. As such it was much better for what he wanted than the cutting steel of a bridle and bit.

He hummed softly to the horse and the gray, incurious, stood patiently while Hart looped and wrapped the cotton rope to form reins and built the excess into a weight-balancing knot on the bosal beneath the horse's jaw. When he was satisfied with the construction of the knot and with the reins that would not burn his hands no matter how violently they might be taken away from him, Hart stepped back a pace to admire the big horse.

The gray was calm and accepting. It eyed him with interest but without wariness. Hart stroked the thick, powerful neck and ran his hands across the hard, sculptured muscles of shoulders and flanks. The horse accepted the attention without trying to sidle away. Hart smoothed his hands down the length of the broad, gray back, the spine no bony ridge here but a shallow valley surrounded by muscle and by healthy fat.

"Big old lazy thing like you," Hart scolded in a soothing tone of voice whispered only loud enough to reach the horse's ears. "Stand around hog fat and handsome as a new-dropped calf and never done a lick of work yet," he said. "You an' me will talk more about that," he cooed.

With his hands lightly steadying at the gray's withers, the reins firmly held in both fists, Hart seemed to bend forward more than he leaped upward but he was suddenly astride the blockily built animal, his legs clamped firmly around the broad barrel of its body, his own torso loosely upright and leaning slightly back. "Oho, old boy," he whispered. "Something new for you."

The gray's first reaction was one of confusion. It had known the touch of men's hands for as long as it could remember, and it knew that was no threat. But it had never borne weight from such touching before. It had never had anything placed on its back. And it had never, certainly, had anything clamp around its body like the man's legs now tried to hold it. It stood and began to tremble.

The gray and black head raised, and the wide nostrils flared in search of danger scents. The small ears were suddenly laid flat in anger.

"Atta boy," Hart whispered. "Go ahead an' blow right up."

The trembling stopped and through his legs Hart could feel loose muscle harden into solid slabs. A sense of enormous, tightly pent power flowed to him from the horse, more than he had ever felt, more than he would ever have thought to find in one animal. He smiled and waited for the head to drop in readiness for the first bucking explosion of that raw power.

The gray half turned its head so it could more clearly see the man on its back. It seemed still more confused and angry—perhaps *annoyed*—than frightened. Hart set himself for the explosion and leaned further back so his weight would be balanced and firmly in place when the head dropped and the hindquarters rose in that first thrashing kick meant to unseat the thing on its back.

The head did not drop. The gray humped its back and crouched. It shivered heavily as if to shoo a massive and unwelcome fly.

Unprepared, his weight already shifted backward, Hart felt himself not violently flung from the unbroken horse but ignominiously—almost gently —almost *casually*—dumped onto the ground, the cotton reins still in his grip.

The horse quickly, nervously now, pivoted on its front legs to face him with one ear cocked forward in curiosity but the other still pinned in uncertain alarm.

Hart bounced to his feet and the horse backed away, muzzle low and the head weaving from side to side. An angry man it understood, and it was now more fearful than it had been when the man was on its back.

"Well, I will be a total son of a bitch," Hart breathed, more to himself than to the horse. The gray reached the limits of the reins and waited nervously. "You sly old bastard, you," Hart said. But he said it more in amazement and admiration than with resentment. "I hain't been spilled like that since I was a pup. Maybe not then neither," he said more loudly. The horse responded to the voice. Its tension began to ease.

From a few feet away Hart heard the tinkle of

bright laughter. He turned and the girl was there, her head barely visible over the top rail. Hart ducked his head. His face was beginning to redden.

"Lordy, but I'm glad I got to see that," Twyla Venable said.

"You'd best go inside," he said. "What I'm thinking right now ain't fit for you to hear."

She laughed again and crawled up to sit on the rail. She was bareheaded, back in her usual drab housedress. She was plain and unpretty with her hair in the stern, uncompromising bun. But when she laughed her teeth showed white and even and her light brown eyes were lovely, and she was less homely than usual. "I swear I wouldn't have missed that for the world."

Hart reluctantly allowed his wavering eyes to meet hers. The corners of her eyes were crinkled with amusement. A slow grin began to spread across his face. "Damnedest horse I ever crawled onto," he muttered.

"I believe it," she said amid more laughter. "You should've seen the look on your face when your butt hit that dirt." She tried unsuccessfully to stifle her laughter behind the long, slim fingers of a sun-browned hand.

Hart took the gray's reins loosely into one hand —the horse was quite calm now—and removed his hat. He mopped sweat from his forehead onto his shirt sleeve and used the brim of his hat to slap dust and powdered, dry manure from his jeans. He replaced his hat and led the horse to the rails. The gray moved with him willingly. The girl leaned forward to scratch the horse on the poll.

"Gentle soul, isn't he?" she asked with mock innocence.

Hart's grin returned. "He is for a fact. Not a mean bone in his body. You know," he mused, "I'd swear he wasn't mad about a thing there. He just didn't know what was expected of him an' figured he ought to get rid of that nuisance on his back. Clever bastard, too. He did it without getting all het up about it. Just went an' did it. There's not many can unload me no matter how they try it, and I *never* saw one that could do it so damned, awful easy. But I'll know better the next time."

She sat upright on the rail and looked down at him. "I suppose you figure to get back on him."

"Got to now that I've started. You know that. Unless you want this boy to get bad habits set in his head."

"I know that, damn you. I just don't want to miss anything." She giggled and made a show of squirming in anticipation of what was to come.

Hart resettled his hat and tugged it down firmly against his ears. "If you'll excuse me then. . ."

"And pick up the pieces later? Go ahead, but you can expect to have an audience."

He thought he heard another muffled giggle as he turned away. He shook his head. Such girlish sounds seemed most uncharacteristic coming from Twyla Venable, but he could not have been mistaken.

He led the gray to the center of the corral and again gathered his reins while he soothed and gentled the horse. This time when he sprang onto its back the animal was better prepared for what was to come. And more inclined toward anger than confusion. The thick neck swelled and heavy pads of muscle pulled tight. Hart grinned happily in anticipation of the fight.

The big gray bogged its head, and Hart let it take as much of the rein as it wanted. When the powerful hindquarters exploded into rising motion—but this time not a moment before—Hart swayed back to meet the movement.

The horse leaped and twisted. It flung itself as violently as if a catamount were riding it. Sharp hooves pounded the earth and sent corral dust billowing into the air. The broad, gray back lifted and twisted at seemingly impossible angles but through it all the rider stayed upright, his legs locked around the gray's body, his toes locked into the sockets behind the horse's forelegs. If anything, that made the gray more angry.

The bone jarring explosion lasted less than a minute. As soon as Hart felt the gray change from bucking into a run as a means of escape, he took a shorter rein in his right hand. When he felt all four of the horse's feet on the ground he doubled the gray, hauling back with all his strength. The braid of the bosal gouged cruelly into the tender nose flesh of the gray and its head was forced unwilling toward Hart's knee.

Denied by pain the control of its head and its balance destroyed, the horse fell heavily onto its left side. A wave of dust flew dry and sharp-scented into Hart's nose as he landed on his feet but still astraddle the kicking gray horse. Immediately Hart threw rein to the animal, giving it back its head. This one he did not want to humiliate by forcing it to lie helpless in the dirt.

Still game, the gray surged to its feet again, picking up the unwelcome rider as it rose. Hart began to talk to it, his voice as calm and as soothing as if he were feeding it barley mash. The words he used were meaningless sounds. Had anyone asked he could not have told them what he was saying. He was not listening to them himself.

The horse bucked again, but only briefly. That tactic had not worked before, and the animal put little effort into the second attempt.

Again it tried to bolt out from under Hart. The rider gave it time for two powerful, reaching strides before he again snatched back on the bosal to double it. They were close to the corral rails, and the horse lurched sideways as it tried to maintain its balance, to keep its feet so it could continue to fight.

Horse and rider slammed against the wood rails. The impact was enough to send a rush of hot breath out of the gray's extended nostrils. Hart could feel the sudden heat through the fabric of his jeans. He could more acutely feel the sheet of pain that swept through his other leg as more than a thousand pounds of unbalanced bone and muscle crashed into the rails with his left leg between horse and wood.

The horse leaned there for a moment. The eye that Hart could see was rolling wildly, and saliva spilled from the opened jaws of the black-muzzled head.

Hart was white-faced with pain, and he willed himself to not stiffen against the bone-deep hurt. He had to keep his muscles loose now at all cost. Rigidity would send him tumbling into the dirt, and only a fool would want to be flat on his back with an angry stallion standing over him. Hart unclenched his jaw and, his voice calm still and soft, spoke more of the meaningless words to the horse.

He gave the gray a foot of rein, and the liquid

brown eye rolled less wildly. The horse shivered and its feet scrambled to regain balance. Hart's leg was scraped against rough wood and he could feel splinters drive into the meat of his thigh, but the horse had its feet properly under it again.

Hart drew the fine head back toward him, released it, pulled it slowly back again. The horse made no immediate effort to bolt. It gave readily to the bosal, avoiding pain by giving to the braid before it could dig into the sensitive flat of its nose.

"You're a learner, you are," Hart whispered to it. "And I think you and me have learned enough for this day."

He gave the horse more rein until the head was almost straight. He let the animal move a few uncertain, slowly taken steps off the rail and again doubled it to the right but more slowly, giving the horse time to yield itself willingly to the bosal. When it did, Hart was pleased. He cooed and murmured again to the sweat-drenched animal and without warning dropped to the ground between the horse and the rails. He did not want to have to run if the gray should blow up now. His left leg had no more feeling in it now than a two-by-four propped under his hip.

Hart yielded with the right rein and pulled carefully on the left until the horse's head had been pulled around near him. The gray gave Hart its head but anxiously sidestepped away so that the man would no longer be in a position to mount.

"Are you all right?"

"Huh?"

"I asked if you are all right. You look kind of pasty." There was concern in Twyla Venable's voice. For a time he had forgotten she was anywhere near. Now she was standing just opposite him outside the corral rails.

"Yeah. Fine." He carefully shifted both reins to his left hand and reached slowly out with his right to stroke the sweaty poll of the horse and to scratch soothingly in the deep pocket under the jaw. The horse's breathing was still labored but its ears were no longer pinned so angrily against its head. One ear twitched tentatively forward. It was beginning to calm. The danger of it attacking was less.

"Listen," Hart said, "do you think you could hold this brute a minute while I crawl outta here? I'd just as soon be on that side of the fence when I pull the bosal."

"Sure." She stepped onto the bottom rail and hooked an elbow over the top to steady herself. She reached out to accept the reins, and Hart hobbled carefully backward, paying out rein length as he moved. He did not want to ask the horse to follow yet.

"I have it," she said. "Get over here."

Hart tried to step onto the rails, winced as new pain flooded through his leg and changed his mind. Beads of cold sweat popped out on his forehead.

"You should get a look at yourself," she said quietly. "Like a damn ghost."

"Don't watch me, for cryin' out loud, woman. Keep your eyes on *him*." Hart dropped to his belly and rolled beneath the bottom rail. He lay on his back for a moment, relief moving through him like slow waves coming across a Gulf of Mexico sandbar. He was conscious of the sun heat on his chest and of her booted feet near his head. He forced himself to breathe more slowly and climbed hand over hand up the rails until he was on his feet, propped with his weight on his right leg and gaining support from the fence. "I can take him now," he said.

She offered no protest but returned the thick cotton reins to him. Hart clucked to the horse and tugged it toward him. The gray's ears twitched skeptically but after a moment it took a step forward and then another. It thrust its head over the rails and allowed itself to be scratched. Hart slipped the retaining straps past its ears and allowed the bosal to drop into his hand.

The horse stood still for a moment, apparently uncertain whether it was free. The animal backed away a foot or so, shook itself and threw its head into the air. It snorted loudly, then ducked its head and wheeled. It thundered tail-high the length of the corral and slithered to a dust-raising stop. It threw itself once into the air, landed on all fours and raised its muzzle to bugle a war cry over the open grass beyond the far fence.

"By God, that's a horse," Hart said.

XIII

Hart tried to walk away from the pen. The leg buckled and he saved himself from falling only by a desperate clutch at the rails.

"Come over to the house," Twyla said. "I'll help you."

He shook his head. "Cookhouse. Just need t' rest it a bit."

She ducked impatiently under his left arm and draped it over her shoulders. "Listen you silly sonuvabitch," she snapped, "I have to carry you wherever you're going, and my kitchen is a damn sight closer than yours. You go where I put you or you crawl, hey-boy."

"I can do that too if I have to," he said.

"Not you, b'God. I won't believe that. Now put some weight onto me and do what you're told."

With her help he was able to move slowly and painfully toward the back of the house. Half way there they paused to rest.

"That's enough lollygagging," she said after only a moment. "Let's get on with it."

Hart grinned into her serious, straight-lipped face so close beside his that he could see her clearly, really clearly, for the first time. "Have you ever considered enlisting in the Army, Miss Twyla? You'd make one hell of a top sergeant."

"You're just full of flattery aren't you, hey-boy?" While they limped forward on three legs she asked, "Have you ever been in the Army, hey-boy?"

The good humor died on his face. His expression became stony. "I guess I earned that dig, didn't I?"

"What do you mean? I was serious. If you don't want to tell me, just say so." She seemed genuinely puzzled.

"Sure," he said. The single word had been drawn from a deep well filled brim-full with bitterness. It was bile in audible form.

She stopped without warning, and he almost fell. "What the hell's gotten into you all of a sudden?"

"Have you ever been in the Army, hey-boy?" he parroted at her in an unkind falsetto imitation of her question. "Shit! Make fun of a man and the next breath butter wouldn't melt in your damned mouth." He jerked away from her and tried to limp toward the cookhouse. His left leg still would not support his weight and he fell, catching himself on his knee but paying for it with a jet of pain in his good leg when his kneecap landed on gravel. "Jeez!"

She was beside him almost before he hit, trying to help him back up.

"Leave me *alone*, dammit."

"I *won't*." She hauled him upright with more strength than either of them thought she had. When he was standing she positioned herself defiantly before him and glared up into his face. "Now what is this all about? What is wrong with me asking you a simple question like that?"

Hart's lips curled back into a sneer. "You just gotta prod at it, don't you? You just gotta make fun of me. Well, I'm as good a man as any other, miss high an' mighty, and if I cain't change what my eyes are like I can at least know better than to go around asking questions just to poke fun at people that never hurt me."

First hurt and then comprehension came into her eyes. She grabbed roughly at his shirt sleeves when he tried to turn away again. "Listen, you oversensitive baboon, I wasn't mocking you nor a damn thing about you. How am I supposed to know how long you've been like that? Hell, I thought maybe you got wounded or something. So maybe it happened when you were little. All right. I apologize. I didn't go to hurt you. I'm sorry if I did. But don't you go jumping down my damn throat for something I never did." She looked and sounded at least as belligerent as he was by the time she was through.

Slowly his expression softened. He looked away from her eyes, and his hands flopped emptily in his embarrassment. He started to speak but clamped his mouth shut. She maneuvered herself in front of him, but he would not look at her.

Twyla positioned herself under his arm again. She met no resistance. "Come on, dammit," she ordered.

They made it the rest of the way to the back door steps and—more from her effort than from his—inside. She helped him to the long table and shoved him forcefully into the nearest chair. "I'll get you some coffee," she said.

She fed wood into the firebox first and then filled two cups from the big pot on the back of the stove surface. She laced his heavily with sugar and tinned milk before she carried the cups to the table. "Here," she said. "Stretch your leg out. Better yet, pull that next chair out and prop it up. Do you want me to check and see if it might be broken?"

"No, it isn't busted. I'd've heard it pop if it was. It was just bashed some."

She nodded and sat near him. An awkward silence lay in the space between them. It stretched uncomfortably until half their coffee was gone.

"Look," Hart said, breaking the discomfort finally, "you said you were sorry. I guess I can do the same. You didn't mean anything like what I thought you did."

"All right," she said quietly. After a moment she added, "Do you want to tell me about it?"

He shrugged. "There's no accident to tell about. I was born this way." He was not looking at her. "My ma knew I would be. If I was a boy, that is. If she'd had a girl it would've been all right." He could not suppress a shudder that he hoped she did not see. "My pa left her not long after he saw what I was gonna turn out to be." Had he looked at her he would have seen the sympathy in her eyes, but he did not.

"The way it works," he continued, "it carries in the blood somehow. But not every time. Her pa was this same way, but she's all right. She had three brothers, and they're all right. They got a mess of kids. Every one of *them* is all right." There was a distinct but distant, hopeless envy in his voice. "I asked a doctor about it one time. He didn't know much more than me about it, but he said the seed, whatever it is, is carried in the woman but only comes out in the man. If I was to have kids they'd be just as normal as any kids. If they was boys, the seed would die right there, see? If they was girls, and they had kids, their girls would be okay too. But any boys they might have, well, they'd have eyes just like mine. No way to stop it. No way at all." He finished his coffee and sat for a time staring toward the wall.

She took his cup, refilled it and took a long time adding the milk and sugar. When she came back to the table she remained standing beside him. Her fingertips hovered near his shoulder for a moment, but she withdrew them without him seeing they had been there. She returned to her chair. "None of it is your fault, you know," she said softly.

His head snapped around so she could again see the erratic, uncontrolled motion of his eyes. The bitterness was back in his voice when he said, "I carry it in my blood. Say whatever you like, but that's the damned truth. I carry the seed of it in my blood, the same as my ma did, the same as her pa did. The seed is there and no way to kill it."

"So what?" she asked.

"So *what!*" He tried to rise but was driven white-faced and sweating back into his chair when he tried to put pressure on his leg. "So I won't ever be like other people, that's what. So if I was to ever have kids I'd put the same seed into their blood, that's what. So I . . . ah, never mind. It don't concern you anyhow."

"No, but it sure God builds a fire in your belly.

Look, it isn't your fault. If you ever find a woman you want just tell her what the story is. She can make up her own mind what to do about it. You said yourself if you had sons they'd be all right. If you had girls it would be up to *them* to worry about it." She took a deep breath. "Anyway I don't think that's what galls you so much. I think you're trying to take all the guilt for your father leaving your mother. Don't you see that that is *his* problem? And hers if she never told him about the seed in her blood. But it *sure* isn't your fault. You told me you're as much man as any other, hey-boy. Well maybe I'm more willing to believe that than you are." She got up from the table. "What do you want for lunch? I have some corned beef. Maybe some eggs to go with that? And fresh biscuits with milk gravy. How would that be?"

"Yeah," he said absently. "That would be fine." He could not have repeated back to her what she had just said. Not the last part, anyway. He sat deep in thought while she prepared the meal.

When she brought the food to the table neither of them wanted to continue the subject. It was still only mid-morning, far too early for lunch. He realized she had wanted the cooking as an excuse to occupy herself for a while. They ate and when they were done he said, "Damn good. If I could make biscuits like that I'd be a cook and make more money." He patted his stomach to emphasize the compliment. He got a smile in return.

Twyla refilled the coffee cups. "You'd give up working with horses in return for a kitchen stove? Hell, I was just about to start believing you're half as good as you say you are. Maybe I was right to start with."

"I don't seem to have made much money with them." She began to look embarrassed and he quickly added, "Hey, I didn't mean . . . I wasn't talking about right now. I meant the whole time since my ma died. I didn't mean here."

She nodded.

To cover the renewed discomfort he had caused he quickly asked, "Say, did you get a chance to ask your pa about those Box 11 geldings out on your grass? I've been wondering about them."

She made a sour face. "I sure did," she said disgustedly. "Those dinky bastards belong to us."

"Lord Almighty," he blurted. "Whatever for?"

"Daddy's always been horse crazy anyhow, horse poor really, and somehow he got it into his head to buy that bunch of worthless scrubs and resell them. He got a hell of a deal on them if you listen to the way he tells it. Six hundred of them at seven dollars a head. Big deal!" She sounded upset.

Hart shook his head. Of course they had not seen all of the animals, he told himself. In that many of anything there should be some that would be decent. Venable probably figured on selling those at twenty dollars a head. Call it fifteen dollars for the run of the bunch. Even the worst of them would be worth four dollars for hide, hair, and bone. So maybe it wasn't all that bad a deal. Still, there was something. . . He could not remember but there was something, maybe something he had heard in town, about the Army.

The thought of the Army turned the key in his mind, and the conversation came tumbling back to him. It was not in town, it was just the night before when Wynn told him the Army remount was full and the horse market had gone to pieces without warning. Too few buyers and too many horses right now.

Hart thought about that further and decided that was probably what Venable had in mind all along. That was probably why he had been able to buy the herd at seven dollars a head. Buy them cheap, carry them on free grass until the Remount Service pumped life and money back into the horse market—say until next year or at worst the year after—and sell them for a nice profit. Venable should double his money at the very least. Damn good business, Hart decided. He nodded to himself. A man could do worse than to pay attention to Titus Venable, maybe.

"Don't worry about it," Hart told the girl. "Your pa just might have himself a good idea there. Let him run it out, girl. I think he knows what he's doing."

"Do you really?" she asked skeptically. "Those miserable things?"

"Yeah, I do. Really. Don't you go fretting about it now. I'm betting your pa knows just what he's doing. It won't hurt you to trust him about this."

"Well, it hurt my damn feelings, I'll tell you, that he went and swapped our mare herd on those dinks. We had some awfully nice mares in that bunch."

"Ah, you can replace them. You know that." He snorted. "Practically nobody pays any attention to mares any more. Foolish if you want my opinion. Far as I can tell the mare puts in half of your blood, but if you ask any of these old boys they'll tell you it's all the stud. Tell you the mare's just a carrier." He grinned. "I got that good Fancy mare of mine for seventeen dollars, and the fella wasn't even broke at the time. He figured that was all she was worth. And that's a hundred dollar horse if ever I sat one."

She looked a little less troubled. "If you say so." She left the table and put a fresh pot of water on the stove to boil more coffee.

Hart watched her. It occurred to him that for a change she seemed willing to take his opinion about something without an argument. From a feisty bit of a thing like her that seemed quite a compliment, and he savored it within the privacy of his thoughts until she returned. He decided he was liking it here more and more. And he was really in no hurry now to limp back to the cookhouse. Another hour or two of rest would do his bruised leg no harm at all.

XIV

There was no need for him to stay around the V-Slash-4, not enough of a crew to need their cooking done, Venable not at home except perhaps a few hours at night for sleeping purposes. Hart certainly was not going to crawl back onto that gray horse until more of the bone-deep ache went out of his leg. He decided to give himself a few days in town. He got another ten dollars from Twyla—her father was not there, and he suspected the handful of bills came from her own savings—and saddled the cresty bay mare.

He took his time covering the miles, but the mare had an armchair road jog that gave him no pain. He stabled the mare when he got into town and gave the hostler a dollar in advance to cover two nights' food and care. Just in case he managed to be taken broke before he was ready to go back. Not that he was in much of a mood for it this time, but like most others he knew he had lost more than one horse when he came off a drunk too flat in the pocket to buy his animal out of its feed bill. It seemed a cheap and unfair way for a livery to acquire horseflesh as far as he was concerned, but it was the law and there you had it. A poor man could not argue with the law.

He paid up front for a hotel room as well and spent the remainder of the afternoon sipping slowly at mugs of nearly cool beer in the easygoing saloon with the bright and lively piano player. Come evening he got a hunk of cheese and a double handful of crackers from the man called Perce. It would do for his supper. He chatted with Perce until the man closed his store and then drifted back onto the street, munching comfortably on crackers pulled from his coat pocket.

The town was closing down, businessmen and last-minute shoppers hurrying past him on the board walkway. They would be going home to loaded supper tables and lighted windows. The thought did not bother him. At times in the past he had been envious of such people. Or falsely contemptuous. Now he merely nodded to them and stepped out of their way. He was in no hurry himself.

He came to the street corner and leaned for a while against the sturdy, weathering brick of the town's bank. The bank building was a squat and undersized structure but the brick construction gave it an air of substance and dependability among the wooden false fronts of the other businesses.

Hart stood and watched until the flow of traffic along the streets was ended and the pattern of lamplight had shifted from the business district to the houses surrounding the town center. A faint piano tinkle carried to him on the soft air of the evening. He pulled the last cracker from his pocket, ate it and ambled without urgency up the cross street toward the house he had visited before. The ladies there had been both pleasant company and very clean. He could only afford one trip upstairs and maybe he would go this night and maybe the next. He could decide that later. In the meantime he could sit with them to talk and have a few drinks from their liquor cabinet.

He passed Second Street and went unhurriedly on. The slight incline pulled at the remaining ache in his leg like a tongue-tip on a sore tooth, but it was not bad. He passed a few darkened shop windows and stepped down off the sidewalk to cross the alley that separated the rank of shop fronts from the Muleshoe saloon. As he was about to remount the boards two men pushed noisily through the open doorway of the Muleshoe. They seemed to be arguing about something. He stepped aside to let them pass.

"Well, look-a here, Sonny," one of the men said. "It's that same gotch-eyed bastard that busted your face a while back." The two men squared their shoulders and began sidling toward the street edge of the sidewalk to block any sudden retreat. The second man laughed.

Hart had been in a good mood before. Now his spirits fairly soared. He felt light and free and ready. He rolled his shoulders to loosen the muscles there and grinned happily at the two men. To the one nearer the saloon wall he said, "Sonny, huh? I'll just bet I know the rest of it. It's Sonny-bitch, isn't it?" The two men launched themselves at him.

Hart stepped quickly back around the protection

of the building corner, cutting the first man off from being any immediate danger. As Sonny came past Hart drove a hard left low into his belly. "Just like the first time, Sonny," he said.

Sonny doubled over and Hart delivered a short right that landed with all the authority of an ax handle beneath the man's left ear. Sonny went to his knees.

The other man had turned the corner, but Hart had his back to the lapped board wall of the Muleshoe and Sonny was between them. The man tried to close. He threw a flurry of punches across Sonny's back. Sonny rolled sideways into Hart's legs, pinning him against the wall. "Take him, John," Sonny yelled hoarsely.

Hart did not have the freedom or the balance to weave away from John's blows, and they were coming too fast in the darkness of the alley mouth for him to block them all. A wildly looping right burned across his cheek and sent the back of his head slamming into hard wood behind him. A wave of dizziness slowed him, and John landed two good shots to the body.

Sonny was getting his breath back. He scrambled forward on all fours and rose to join the attack.

Hart was grinning again. His feet free, he dodged to the right and blocked a punch. He threw a quick, straight right, lightly so he would not break his own hand, to the bridge of John's nose. It would bring a rush of tears to the man's eyes, he knew, and would fog his vision for several seconds. Makes us even, Hart thought happily.

John pawed at his eyes. While his attention was diverted Hart crunched a knee into his groin. John collapsed with a shriek of pain.

Hart had lifted his right knee without thinking about it. The shift of weight onto his left leg was more than it could take. The leg buckled and he lurched against the wall.

Sonny threw himself across his partner and head-butted Hart in the stomach. Both men went down, rolling into the mouth of the alley.

They grappled in the dirt with Sonny on top, his face jammed against Hart's chest, clubbed fists pounding into Hart's ribs.

Hart reached around Sonny's shoulders and grabbed him by the neck. By main force he hauled Sonny higher against his chest. Hart bent his head down and clamped his teeth onto Sonny's right ear. He ground his teeth together and a sweat-sour taste in his mouth was quickly replaced by the copper sweet flavor of blood. Sonny screamed.

Hart felt a boot toe thud into his ribs. John seemed to be back in the fight. Hart flung Sonny off him and rolled the man into John's legs. Free at least for the moment Hart rolled to his left and shoved himself upright.

He stood half crouched and fists ready. He was winded and panting but so were they. He shuffled sideways until he had the security of a wall at his back again. He did not trust his leg enough now to press them in the open.

Sonny came to his feet and mopped a torn coatsleeve over the wetness on his ear and neck. "You like to . . . bit my ear off, you son of a bitch," he panted.

Hart grinned at him. "I might have . . . better luck . . . next chance I get."

Sonny moved forward. His partner plucked at

his sleeve. John was still white faced and haggard with pain that spread sickeningly from deep in his belly. "Wait a minute," he pleaded. It was clear that he had had enough.

"What the hell's the matter with you?" Sonny snapped. "He's near finished." Sonny wiped at his ear again and moved ahead. John came reluctantly at his side.

Hart had his wind back. The joy of the fight sang sweetly in the pounding behind his ears. He chuckled as he stretched to his full height and loosened his shoulder muscles in glad anticipation. "Come ahead, boys," he crooned happily.

John faltered—he wanted no more of it—but Sonny pressed forward.

Sonny crouched low, his fists weaving back and forth like a pair of snakes waiting to strike. John was still holding back.

Sonny stepped close to Hart and aimed a hard right at his jaw. Hart's forearm flicked the punch away, and he drove his own right hand into the cheek that he had broken the first time they fought. Cold sweat formed on Sonny's face and mingled with the blood still flowing from his torn ear.

The pain drew Sonny's guard up, and Hart ripped a three punch combination over Sonny's heart followed by a slugging underhand right to the gut. Sonny went as white faced as his partner still was.

Hart sidestepped to the right, closer to John. He looked the man in the eye. "You next?"

John shook his head mutely. He crept backward, placing his feet carefully, his eyes locked onto Hart's disturbingly joy-filled face. "Not me, mister," he said. He turned his back and moved away, tottering bent over and slow like a man fifty years his senior. He did not look toward his partner again.

"You're all alone, Sonny," Hart said cheerfully.

Sonny was sucking in air in fishmouthed gulps. He raised his eyes and glared at Hart. He staggered backward and bent lower. He fumbled with the cloth of his trousers leg and from a boot top drew out a slender knife. A glint of red light from the cathouse lantern deeper in the alley outlined the blade.

"You're kinda making this serious, Sonny. Are you sure you want to do that?" Hart's voice was calm. If he felt a surge of fear he did not show it. He shifted his hips and tested his weight on his left leg to see if he could count on it. It hurt but seemed strong enough if he would remember to place it carefully. He moved out away from the wall. With only one man facing him he wanted the greater freedom of the open alley now. The wall was too restricting.

Sonny inched toward him, crouched even lower now. He held the knife low and forward, the blade slanting up and the cutting edge uppermost, ready to slash toward the thin and relatively soft pad of muscle across Hart's belly. It was obvious he was no stranger to the use of sharpened steel.

Neither was Hart.

They circled each other warily, neither anxious to close until he could see a clear advantage. The first move would probably also be the last. There is virtually no such thing as a lengthy knife fight.

Hart concentrated on keeping his weight evenly balanced on the balls of his feet. He hoped Sonny had not earlier noticed his favoring that leg.

They circled, and the cold sweat continued to dot Sonny's forehead. He was reluctant to make his move against this man, and it struck a throat-clenching clutch of fear into him when he realized that this was so. The man he faced held no weapon; his hands were empty. Sonny had the keen-honed blade that had been filed to perfect balance. He had used it before, had slived bright blood onto the skin of several men in the past. One had died after a deep thrust from that knife. He should have felt confident and eager. He did not.

Hart found a position he liked. The pale edges of sidewalk lamplight beyond the alley were poor at best. Here Sonny was in silhouette against what little light there was. He stopped, shifting carefully back and forth.

Puzzled, Sonny stopped also. He vaguely understood that he was allowing Hart to position him, but he did not know what to do about it. It could have been some sort of ruse. He was not sure.

Sonny feinted with a snake-quick jab that he immediately withdrew. For all the reaction he got, Hart might not have seen the knife move. Perhaps he did not, Sonny decided. The man's eyes were bad. The light was bad. He might have seen nothing of the blade held with Sonny's body between it and the faint light at his back. Sonny began to relax. He was breathing easier now. He edged forward, all of his attention on Hart's hands.

Almost as if by mutual consent the two men closed until Hart was well within the arc of Sonny's reach. Sonny began to smile. His blade flicked out and then up, a long feint toward the belly and a ripping, upward slice toward the face. Lay a man's face open and he would never be the same again.

Sonny was feeling good about it.

A moment later he was not. He realized with an empty feeling in his stomach that he had not felt the whispery drag of sharp metal through flesh transmitted from the blade into his sweaty palm. The stroke had not connected. Hart had bobbed sideways even quicker than the knife had slashed upward.

Sonny's arm reached the top of its arc, the momentum of his stroke carrying it high before he could regain control. He felt a sharp flutter of fear in his belly. Anticipation, felt more than reasoned, turned quickly to reality.

Hart stepped in under the upflung arm. He grabbed Sonny's wrist in his left hand and curled his right arm behind to lock Sonny's elbow against his forearm. Hart turned his head and hissed into Sonny's ear, "You lose, fella." There was a wild, fierce joy in his voice.

"OhGodno," Sonny whimpered.

Hart pushed slowly forward on his extended left arm, putting his weight behind the insistent press that bent Sonny's arm to and beyond the limits of tendons and bone.

The knife dropped loosely from Sonny's grasp as growing pain drove all strength from his hand and his fingers splayed open in involuntary response to the agony that already seared his arm like open fire from shoulder to fingertips.

Hart grinned and shoved again. Both men heard the ugly, distinctive snap as the elbow socket moved past the limits brittle bone could endure. Only Hart heard the groan escape from Sonny's lips. Sonny had fainted.

Hart let go and allowed Sonny to fall unprotected to the dirt with a sound like chilled beef being dropped onto a stone floor. Hart found the fallen knife, stepped on the shining blade and tugged sharply on the slim handle. The knife broke at the haft. Hart bent and carefully tucked a broken section of the knife into each of Sonny's trouser pockets. He lifted Sonny's limp left arm, placed it across his knee for leverage and broke it at the elbow too. From somewhere in the unknowing depths of his faint Sonny found enough awareness to feel the new pain. He groaned and writhed, drawing his knees into his chest.

Hart rose. He felt light on his feet, his leg no longer bothering him. He resumed his walk up the dark street, now at a quicker, surer pace.

XV

Wynn and Spud seemed glad enough to see him back at the headquarters. Harry Grimes ignored him, and so did Titus Venable. If anything Venable was more hostile now than before. Hart still did not understand why.

He got back early in the afternoon, feeling loose and relaxed. His leg was no longer so sore although it would be several weeks probably before the last of the blue and yellow bruises faded. Another day or two and he could give the gray horse another lesson. Twyla had not told him to stop the project. Her father had not told him anything—period— although the man had been leaving the ranch yard when Hart rode in. It almost seemed odd now to see Titus Venable in broad daylight.

Hart was in fact every bit as poor a cook as he fancied himself to be, but he went ahead and prepared a meal for himself and the few remaining crew members. If they did not like it they could shift for themselves.

The crew came into the cookhouse before full

dark. They were stepping easily, with none of the dragging fatigue that characterized the cowhand during the spring and fall working seasons. Then they pressed themselves harshly from first light to last. Now they were still fresh at the end of the day.

Wynn looked at the three plates laid on a table long enough to accommodate them and a dozen more. He shrugged and told Hart, "You might as well fetch your plate out here too. It ain't like we're crowded these days."

Hart brought the food out and took a chair opposite Grimes. "Bitch if you want to, boys, but it won't get any better for letting it get colder." He helped himself to a chunk of boiled beef, dug a fork into it and wondered briefly what he had ever done to deserve being stuck with his own cooking.

When they were done Wynn looked at Hart, his expression serious. In a dry voice he said, "Now that was really . . . *interesting,* Gotch. Sure was." Spud looked amused. Grimes kept his attention on his plate.

"Why, I thought so myself, ramrod," Hart said just as seriously. "It was kinda like an experiment to see if we could save some money."

Wynn leaned forward propped on his elbows and urged, "Good idea. Go on."

"The way it was, you see . . . Say, do you remember . . . no, of course not. You boys were still on the road then. Anyway, a couple weeks ago, just after you boys left, an old fella came through here ahorseback with a couple burros on a string to carry his possibles. One of the canaries had took sick on him, so we swapped him a green horse for the burro and a fry pan and ten dollars hard money." The others, even Grimes, nodded.

"Poor little bastard never did seem to get any better, and that constant braying was getting on everybody's nerves in short order. It upset the horses something awful, and the burro just kept getting poorlier and poorlier until finally we decided the only kind and proper thing to do was to put it out of its misery. The only thing was, it was cute as a new pup and twice as friendly. If you didn't watch out it'd totter up behind you on them weak little legs and try to crawl in your pocket looking for the candies that old boy used to feed it.

"And, boys, there was just no way anyone could look into them soft, brown eyes and go to do the little thing any hurt. Still, it was driving us purely crazy with its hollering day and night, and that handsome gray stud horse Mr. Venable fancies so much was starting to shed tallow like a hot stove sheds snow. I mean the weight was just melting off that poor horse. Looking real gaunted, he was. And to make matters worse, that little burro took a special liking to that stallion. Kept trying to sneak into the pen with the horse, and when it couldn't do that it'd stand outside the rails and bray. And bray. And bray some more.

"Well, you know how much store Mr. Venable sets by that stud horse. He kept watching that horse go down and down, getting weaker and gaunter its own self the weaker and the poorer that little burro got, and he just couldn't stand it any more. He decided the burro just had to go, one way or another. He got himself a long knife and went to stick it, but that sad little burro looked at him with those big, brown eyes and tried to get into his pocket for a candy. He just couldn't stick the little thing and it watching him. So he got himself a gun and went out to shoot it. Found it standing beside the stud pen as usual, braying and hollering and making a fuss over that gray horse as usual. So Venable ups with his gun and draws back the hammer, but that little burro seen him and let out a bray of real joy and came pitty-pat over to him on those poor little hooves like it had just found its long lost mammy. It shoved its nose into his pocket, and what could he do? He gave it a candy and went inside.

"He couldn't shut out the noise it was making, though, and the little critter just had to go, there wasn't any two ways about it. Well, boys, Mr. Venable got to thinking that he couldn't shoot the thing 'cause he kept seeing those big, trusting eyes every time he went to put the burro down. But he figured the way I am, I wouldn't have that problem. If you know what I mean. So he went and got a big old shotgun that his daddy used to use to shoot ponded ducks. Big old long-barreled thing you could put a saucer down the muzzle of it pretty near. He loaded that sucker with some bolts and all the bent horseshoe nails he could find and put it all over a heavy charge of coarse powder. He wasn't taking any chances. He carried the gun out two-handed it was so heavy and gave it to me and said, 'Gotch, we gotta do this to save my horse, but I don't want the poor li'l thing to suffer. I just couldn't stand for it to linger and be hurting. So what you gotta do is take real careful aim and blow its head off with the first shot. This old gun will do the job, and that little burro won't feel a thing. It's the only decent and humane thing to do.'

"Well, boys, I took the gun from him, and it was a heavy old pig, 'specially after he got done pouring all that trash down the barrel. He must've put two pound of scrap metal in there just to make sure it would do the job. Anyway, I followed my ears out to the stud pen and there was that pitiful little burro, just a-braying and carrying on something terrible. I don't mind saying I felt kinda bad about what I had to do, but there it was. Had to be done. I hefted that old scattergun and rassled with the hammer until I got her back to the last notch. Damn thing had a hammer on it like a cow's hock, it was that big. But I got her done and managed to get the gun up to my shoulder, which wasn't any mean trick in itself, I'll tell you. Still, I got it up there, and I took real careful aim. I didn't want to mess this up any more than he did. So I drawed down a close bead the best I could, though I don't see good enough to find the sights and had to go by where the barrel was pointing. Irregardless, I drawed her down close and sort of apologized to that little burro, and I touched her off.

"*Wham*, that old gun hit me like a runaway beer wagon and, *wham*, all that stuff hit that poor little burro, and sure enough the charge he'd put into that gun was enough to blow its head clean off with the first shot." Hart sighed heavily and shook his head. He looked miserably sad.

"The only thing is, boys, I don't see so good, you understand, and I'd been aiming at the wrong end of that burro. Musta scared him awful bad, 'cause the last we seen of him he looked as spry and lively as ever a burro could and was in a hard gallop toward California." Again he sighed and almost as an afterthought added, "Oh, yeah! What you boys just had for supper is the meat I blowed off his butt." He grinned. "Cut it off neat as a butcher knife could've." He sat back in his chair and took a sip of coffee.

The others nodded their heads solemnly. None showed any hint of amusement.

"Uh huh," Wynn said finally. "Kinda tasted like it too."

"Good, though. Damn good, Gotch," Spud said quickly. He despised having to cook for himself and was afraid it might come to that if Hart decided to refuse the chore.

Grimes looked up and gave Hart a tentative half smile. "Yeah, Gotch. Not too bad. Considering."

Hart nodded to him and raised his cup a few inches off the table in a small salute. Grimes allowed his smile to spread a little wider.

The gray horse was nervous when Hart approached him in the pen, but he allowed himself to be caught after only a token show of refusal. Hart haltered the animal and tied him to a sturdy post. He used a quick release knot that he could jerk free if the horse got into a storm. It would not do to allow this one to panic and perhaps break its own neck in a struggle to get away from what was coming next.

The horse stood patiently and allowed itself to be soothed by Hart's hands and voice. When it was calm Hart slipped outside the corral long enough to retrieve a blanket and the much abused breaking saddle. Twyla Venable joined him at the rail.

"A body would think you spend all your time standing at a window admiring this horse. Or guarding it," Hart said. "Seems like I can't be here five minutes without you showing up to criticize what I'm doing."

"Huh. You need more protection from him than he needs from you, the way I see it. And I haven't hardly fussed at you once about this horse, now have I?"

"Maybe not," he said grudgingly.

"Do you think you ought to be on him again so soon, though?" She giggled, and again the sound seemed to him highly incongruous coming from her. "He got you pretty good the last time you tried him. You looked awfully funny when he dumped you, too."

Hart shrugged. "If I don't go back to him soon he'll have forgotten what he learned the last time. Besides, I'm all right now."

"If you say so, but I still think you're being foolish. And I can't see that you taught him all that much so far."

"He was standing still when I got off him, wasn't he?" He crawled back through the rails, dragging the saddle and blanket behind him.

Hart let the blanket fall and held the saddle in front of him with both hands. The horse eyed him warily and sidled away as far as the tie rope would allow. Moving slowly Hart stepped closer along the fence. He hung the saddle on the top rail beside the post where the horse was tied and moved back to where Twyla was standing.

"What was that all about?" she asked.

"Let him smell it a while. Damn thing might bite and scratch for all he knows."

They stood leaning on opposite sides of the rails and watched. Almost as soon as Hart was back beside Twyla the gray stretched its muzzle searchingly toward the strange article that cluttered its fence. Its nostrils were flared and its ears pricked forward. Its eyes were wide. It stretched close, snorted, and scared itself with its own noise. It recoiled to the end of the tie rope and rolled its eyes. When the saddle did not respond it moved forward again. Within a minute it had carefully smelled every part of the saddle. Satisfied that the thing presented no danger, the horse snorted again and butted the saddle with its nose. It turned its head and ignored the now familiar object.

Hart picked up the blanket and draped it over the saddle to let the horse repeat the process in its own time.

"Are you sure you know what you're doing?" Twyla asked.

"Reasonably," Hart said. She acted as if she expected him to continue, but he did not.

"Everybody I've ever seen before just puts a saddle on and rides them down," she said. It came out as more of a question than an observation.

"Uh huh," he said agreeably.

"You can be a close-mouthed bastard, can't you?"

"Uh huh," he repeated. "Ladies shouldn't ought to talk like that."

She tossed her head. He thought the gesture seemed more defensive than defiant. "Nobody ever mistook me for a lady."

"Uh huh." He smiled.

"He's done admiring that blanket. What do you do now?"

Hart walked back toward the horse. He took the blanket down and carried it a few paces away. The horse was watching him closely.

He unfolded the blanket and flapped it vigorously in the air. Matted horse hair and old flesh scale and dried sweat flew from the cloth. The horse rolled its eyes and backed away the length of the tie rope. The commotion was taking place just far enough away that it was not quite a direct threat. The horse was disturbed but not enough to panic. When Hart quit shaking the blanket it calmed.

Hart carried the blanket to the gray's head and let it smell the article again. When the horse had reassured itself Hart stepped beside the animal. He draped the blanket loosely over the broad back. The horse flinched.

He talked to it and soothed it. While he did so he draped the blanket again and again over the horse, dragged the heavy cloth off, dragged it back over the wide rump. He murmured and rubbed and petted, all the while pulling the blanket over the horse's hide, eventually running the cloth over its legs and under its belly. Within twenty minutes there probably was not a ten-square-inch patch of gray hair that the blanket had not touched. The horse by then stood unconcerned while it accepted his attention.

Hart turned his back and walked away, the blanket trailing in the dust behind him. He tossed the blanket over the fence, dumped the saddle behind it and untied the horse.

"Now what?" Twyla asked.

"Now nothing, that's what."

"Do you mean you aren't even going to try to get on him? You aren't going to ride him? Do you mean I've stood here all this time waiting to see you raise a dust with your ... backside, and you aren't even going to *try* to ride him?" She seemed quite indignant about it.

"*Ride* him? Why, girl, I got a sore leg. He'd dump me quick as a cat has kittens. Hell no I ain't going to ride him today." He let the horse go and crawled out of the pen. He grinned at her cheerfully.

Twyla muttered something under her breath and stalked away toward the house. Hart picked up the saddle and blanket and walked away whistling.

XVI

Twyla burst through the doorway just as Hart was putting the last of the breakfast dishes into a tub of warm, soapy water. He was surprised but recovered quickly enough.

"I wanted to see you today anyhow," he said. "My mare's coming in season."

She ignored him. She poked her head into the entry to the deserted chow hall and turned back into the kitchen with an expression of disgust. "Damn!" she said. She glared at him as if the whole thing—whatever thing it was—was his fault. "Where are all the hands?" she demanded.

"The hands," Hart said, "all three of them, are where they're supposed to be in full daylight, which is out working somewhere. Your pa I ain't seen today. And me, I'm right where I am supposed to be, which is right here." He wiped his hands dry and threw the towel onto the work counter. "I think that takes care of everybody."

She cursed, and again he had cause to admire the breadth of her vocabulary. He started to speak but she raised a hand palm outward. "I know. Ladies aren't supposed to do that. You tell me that. I tell you I'm no lady. You agree." The words ran together in a rush. "We been through all that. But *damn* it all anyhow." She planted her hands on her hips and eyed him. "You'll just have to do it, that's all. Come on."

"Do what? Go where? Girl, you'd better slow down." But he got his shirt from the peg, pulled it on and turned his back to tuck it into his waistband. He got his hat. "Now tell me just where we are going."

"To town. In the wagon. To get Richard, of course."

He shook his head. "You lost me."

"Do you *have* to be so dumb? Good Lord, heyboy. The Marlow boy just brought a note out from town. Richard got in on the night stage last night. He's waiting in town with boxes and boxes of things to be carried out here, he said, and he's anxious to get home. So will you *please* get the wagon hitched and get us on the way? I'll be dressed by the time you get the team in harness. All right?"

He shrugged. "It's okay with me." He deliberately slowed his pace to tease her. "By the way, who's Richard?"

"My *brother,* stupid," she responded.

Hart nodded his head and drawled, "All-l-l-l right. He's your brother Stupid. Can I call him that too, or is it a family name?" He had forgotten about the hearsay brother and sister she was supposed to have.

She stopped and glared at him again, then caught herself and laughed out loud. "Okay, heyboy. Maybe I was getting a little excited, but Richard is my very most favorite brother, and I *do* want to see him. You will hitch the team, won't you?"

"I will. And drive. And load. And all that stuff. And I won't call Richard Stupid. Not 'til I decide for myself, anyway. And I *will* be ready before you if you don't go get dressed now. Scoot!" He barely recognized his unthinking impulse in time to avoid slapping her bottom to send her on her way. He wondered where *that* might have come from.

She gave him a brief smile of gratitude and hurried back toward the house.

Hart pondered what she had said about those boxes and boxes of things Richard wanted brought out from town, but there was little choice in the matter. The V-Slash-4 had only two horses that had ever been in harness although there was an ample selection of both heavy and light harness cluttering the tack shed walls. He laid everything in readiness, led out the horses and had the wagon ready to go well before she appeared.

When Twyla climbed to the wagon box beside him close enough that he could clearly see her he was surprised anew. She almost looked like a real girl, he decided. She was wearing a fluttery, full-skirted city kind of dress made of some soft material about the color of a robin's egg. Her bun was hidden beneath a frilly white bonnet. More surprising, suntan and all, she carried a pale blue parasol. And most surprising, she smelled of some lilac-scented toilet water. He found that to be as much disturbing as it was surprising. She even smelled like a girl.

"Well, you don't have to *stare* at me, damn you."

"Oops. Sorry." He settled his hat and picked the

team up into the bits and slackened his reins just enough to signal them. Old partners, the unmatched pinto and seal brown horses smoothly rolled the unloaded wagon into a brisk road gait. "Town it is, Miss Venable, ma'am," he said with just the smallest touch of sarcasm in his voice. She smiled behind a gloved hand although she need not have bothered. Hart was looking only at the team and the wheel tracks ahead of them.

"You handle a team pretty well," she observed after they had traveled a mile in silence.

"It's another of the things I've done before," he answered mechanically. In her kitchen he probably would have told her about the job he had had driving an ore wagon in Butte or his two-day-long stint as a hansom driver in St. Louis—until repeated passenger complaints brought it to his boss' attention that he could not find his way around the unfamiliar city. For some reason the passengers had objected to his frequent stops to ask directions. But that would have been in the relaxation of her kitchen. And her plain, almost tatty clothes. Now he was not in a mood for conversation. Now he faced straight ahead and gave his attention to what he could feel being telegraphed to his fingers through the driving ribbons.

That had been a good job in Butte, though, he mused. He still regretted that syndicate buying out the mine and refusing to keep him on. He had enjoyed working with those big horses. Power flowed out of those huge bodies like there was no end to it.

"What are you thinking about?"

"Huh?" He snapped back to the here and now of the light ranch wagon and the lightweight, unmatched pair of ranch horses.

"I asked what you were thinking about. You were sitting there smiling about something."

"Oh." He shook his head. "Nothing. Nothing at all."

She looked disappointed. She turned her head away and stared silently out across the dusty green grass that flowed slowly past their wheels.

They reached town before noon, a trip made in near total quiet save for the sound of the animals and the sliding crunch of the iron tires. "You can park in front of the hotel," she instructed, breaking the silence of more than an hour. She had calmed down during the drive but now was beginning to become excited again.

The vehicle was scarcely at a standstill before she jumped out in a swirl of petticoats and was racing across the sidewalk to the hotel entrance. Her parasol was forgotten on the wagon bed behind the padded seat. Hart shook his head. He collapsed the parasol on his third fumbling attempt and stowed the article beneath the seat. He dropped to the ground, took a pair of hitching weights from the driving box and clipped their leads to the bits of the patient horses. Finally he headed for the hotel.

The hotel was narrow and dark, a cluttered maze of wicker bottom armchairs, smoking stands and unlighted lamps. A pair of poorly mounted buffalo heads hung over the clerk's desk. The clerk himself was not exactly Hart's idea of a town clerk. He was tall and burly, with forearms thick as stovepipes. He looked like he would have been capable of taking the buffalo trophies alone and barehanded, maybe both of them at the same time. Hart found a path through the chairs to reach him.

"I'm looking for the Venables, Twyla and, uh, Richard."

The clerk used a boulder-sized chin to point to his left.

Hart looked puzzled. "Isn't that the saloon?"

The clerk shook his head. "Not that door. The one further back. Got a restaurant in there. Good one, too."

Hart nodded his thanks and moved in the direction indicated.

The restaurant was nearly as small as the lobby, and six square tables left it nearly as crowded. All the tables had white cloths draped over them, though, and the place was well lighted. The floor was clean, and lamplight gleamed on its polished surface. Two balding gentlemen sat at one of the tables. Twyla and a young man were in the far corner.

"Over here, hey-boy," Twyla called too loudly across the small room. She was still excited by seeing her brother.

Hart joined them and sat gingerly in the chair Richard indicated. He felt uncomfortable here, out of his element. When he realized the source of his awkwardness it amused him and he began to relax.

Twyla performed sketchy introductions, insisting still on referring to Hart as Hey-boy. Hart corrected her and shook hands with her brother.

Seen together there could be no question that they were brother and sister. Both with the same trim frames, the same long, even planes of facial features, the same thin lips and full brows, identical brown eyes and hair. Yet the features that made Twyla plain and unremarkable were, in a masculine setting, finely molded and youthfully handsome on Richard. He was a good-looking boy. Or man, Hart amended. At his age Hart had been fending for himself for half a dozen years and had counted himself a man grown for most of those years.

Richard's expression was open and friendly, his eyes alight with the enthusiasm of his homecoming.

"You can't know how I have been looking forward to this, Mr. Hart. It is good to be back," he said.

"I'll just bet it is, fella. But say, your eastern manners are showing. Nobody ever named me Mister." Hart looked at Twyla. "Not that I'm complaining, mind. In fact, your sister could stand to take some lessons from you."

"Long habit, Mi . . . Gotch," he said with a laugh. "As for Twy, I am afraid the abrasiveness of her nature has become ingrained. I have no hope for her." Twyla dug an elbow into his ribs happily and was rewarded with a yelp of pretended pain.

Hart decided he liked Richard. And he liked the light, free mood Richard generated in the girl. She did not seem so unnatural in her town dress now beside Richard's neatly vested suit and correctly fashioned bow tie.

"You're in school back east?" Hart asked politely when the disturbance subsided.

Richard smiled and sighed. "I am afraid so. Under protest, I assure you. Latin, Greek, the classic readings. I cannot see how they apply to the real world, but that is what I am required to learn." The smile widened and warmed. "So I study those as being necessary and study the Chicago stockyard reports as a more useful occupation. I am afraid my heart lies more with the production of beefsteak than sonnets."

"I wouldn't doubt that you can do both just fine," Hart said. And was surprised to discover that he meant it.

Richard accepted the compliment easily, with a smiling nod of his head. He turned to his sister. "Tell me how things are going at home, Twy. Dad never wrote me a word about the spring work or the market herd, not even about those damnable mares you and he are always fussing over. And Gray Lad. I haven't heard a word since you wrote to say you bought the damn horse." It took Hart a moment to make the connection. Richard must have been talking about the stallion. Hart did not remember hearing its name before.

Twyla's excited good humor faded, and Richard was quick to catch the change. "What is going on, Twy?" he asked. "Something is wrong, isn't it?"

She glanced nervously at Hart and shrugged. "I don't really know what to tell you, Richard. Daddy doesn't tell me much of anything either these days. He's hardly ever home for me to ask him anyway."

Hart coughed and cleared his throat. He stood. "Look, you two have some family talking to do here. I'll go find a bite of lunch and then load the wagon if you'll tell me where your things are, Richard." Twyla looked grateful.

"Fine, Gotch," Richard said. He rose to shake hands again with the ease of practiced formality. "My boxes are on the platform at the express office. Or they were the last I saw them." He grinned. "Everything is marked with the V-Slash-4. Reminders of home in a distant land and all that. Shall we meet you out front in an hour then?"

"Sure," Hart said. He glanced at Twyla. She looked uncomfortable, and he wondered briefly if she might feel embarrassed about excluding him from discussion of the ranch's troubles, whatever they involved. He rejected the thought quickly. No, he decided. She was worried about those troubles themselves. Maybe she had a right to that worry. He had no way of knowing. Hart turned and went to find an eatery that catered to working hands. He fingered his pockets and wondered if he had enough money to buy himself lunch when he did find a restaurant. He shrugged. If not, he was not going to keel over in a faint before supper. Behind him Twyla and Richard bent their heads close together in low-voiced conversation.

XVII

Spud did not come in for supper the night following Richard's return. Hart had the meal on the table waiting for them when Wynn and Harry Grimes came into the chow hall. They hung their hats on wall pegs and looked around the room.

"Where's Spud?" Wynn asked.

"Hell, I haven't seen him today," Hart said. "Wasn't he with you?"

Wynn shook his head. "We split up today to ride the water holes looking for bog-downs. But Spud had the shortest circle of the three. I figured he was already over here cooling coffee when we didn't see him at the bunkhouse."

"Come to think of it," Grimes said, "his saddle wasn't on the wall. I never paid it any mind. Figured he'd slung it onto a rail or something."

"He hasn't been here," Hart said. "And I told him this morning I'd fry potatoes for supper tonight. He wouldn't want to miss out on that."

Wynn began to look worried. He glanced at

Grimes. "You didn't see a smoke off in his direction today, did you?"

Grimes did not bother to answer. He did not need to. They both knew that Wynn was buying himself time for thought while he talked to keep the worry in abeyance. If Grimes had seen a smoke he would have ridden to it. Wynn would have done the same.

Wynn pursed his lips and reluctantly laid it out into the open air. "He could be down," Wynn said.

It was something that could happen to any of them, at any time, in any one of countless ways. Rough horses, broken country, wild cattle with sharp, curving horns. Any of those could exact a painful toll without warning. No rider could work day in and day out on any string of using horses without losing his saddle from time to time, and they never knew when their luck might be bad in a fall. No rider could scramble across rough country, perhaps in pursuit of a wormy cow, without exposing himself and his horse to the danger of hidden holes or sudden dropoffs into rocky washes.

They had been searching for mud-bogged cattle that day. At times it was possible to drop a rope over the angry cow's horns and pull it free of the sullen, stubborn power of down-sucking mud. Often it was necessary to slog into the mud with the bovine and dig it free before it could be pulled to firm ground. At times a man had to trust his horse to hold an ungrateful cow and dismount to tail it back onto its feet once it was free. An unattentive horse and a horn-slashing sweep of the aggravated cow's head could sink a thick spear into a man's belly as easily as into a horse's. That danger was one of the things they lived with each day. It came with the job.

Wynn looked outside. It was already nearly full dark. "We'll give him a half hour."

Hart carried the food back into the kitchen and shoved the bowls into the tacked-on warming oven over the stove. He carried the big coffeepot out and set it on the table. No one would be hungry just now.

They waited in silence, ears tuned to the world outside the open door. They strained to catch the sound of approaching hoofbeats. Cups of coffee sat untouched and cold before them. After twenty minutes Wynn could stand it no more. He stood.

"Gotch, how 'bout going over and rousting out the old man and Richard. They'll want to come, and we might need them. We'll saddle horses for them too."

"Saddle five," Hart said. "My eyes are as good as yours after dark."

Wynn nodded. "We'll saddle five."

Venable was cold and hostile when Hart appeared at his door, but the expression quickly shifted to concern. Richard was behind him and had heard. They both headed immediately for the saddle shed, Richard not taking time to change out of the town clothing he wore.

The five men mounted, Hart on a short coupled brown that he remembered as being unusually touchy about the use of the spur. He did not have to worry about that now. He had not taken time to get spurs from his room.

"You place us, Early," Venable said. "You know where he was working today."

Wynn bobbed his head nervously. "We went out

together to that forked tree pothole. Harry rode wide to the south and back on a big circle. I dipped south and back. Spud came back. . ." He hesitated and corrected himself. "Spud started back just to the north. He was to ride that snaky creek—it's starting to dry now—and push back anything that looked like it was moving up onto the horse range. He could be anywhere along a twenty-mile stretch there. I figure we should ride in a wide line abreast of each other and holler for him. If there was a fire to see, we'd have seen it earlier. If anyone sees anything, he can sing out for the rest to come in. If that don't work, build a fire. Anybody sees a flame, ride to it." He paused. "I'll take the middle. Gotch, you ride off my flank. You don't know this country so stay on me, all right?"

"Yeah." Wynn was right. The others undoubtedly knew the exact route Spud's circle should have taken from whatever place they called the forked tree pothole. To Hart the directions were just so many words. Still, his presence would extend the search line by at least a short distance. If it was only by a few yards it might help.

They rode tightly bunched for only the first half mile and then by mutual consent began drifting out to the sides. Their pace slowed to a walk, and they formed into a line. Hart could hear their voices yipping shrilly into the darkness and calling Spud's name. His own voice joined them.

It did not help that there would be no moon. In starlight the ground was lost to Hart. He guided the horse with knee pressure and trusted it to choose its footing in the general direction he wanted. He took that direction from the sound of Wynn's calls to his left as Grimes would be guiding on Hart further out to the right. Hart could not see any of the other riders. He could occasionally catch the faint sounds of Richard on the far right, less often those of Titus Venable beyond Wynn on the left. Hart wished he could see better, but he knew that the others were little better off than he now. They all rode blindly and with little hope of success. If Spud had not been able to light a signal before, it might be days before he would be found. And there might be little left to find. Still, none of them would give less effort than they would hope for if they themselves were down somewhere.

The night dragged on. Their voices grew hoarse. The calls were less shrill and less frequent. The sounds would not be carrying so far.

After three hours or so Wynn called them together where they picked up the muddy run of one of the several streams that watered the V-Slash-4. Wynn stepped off his horse and loosened his cinches.

"We'll give the horses a breather here," he said. "Rest your pipes, boys. We got a ways to go yet."

They dismounted and slipped their cinches and hunkered in a small circle nearby. No one was in a mood to talk.

Night sounds closed in on them, the whir and chirp of countless insects and the overloud leaf rustle caused by unseen small creatures. Normally those sounds would have been more comforting than soft music. Now they seemed alien and threatening. The men rested for only a matter of minutes before the buzzing irritation of the nocturnal noises drove them back onto their feet. Richard was the first to rise; the others quickly followed. The insects and frogs were stilled by the sharper sounds of slapping latigos and stirrup leathers.

"Same line as before, boys," Wynn said to the dark shadows around him. "I'll ride the south edge of the creek, Gotch on the north. The rest of you spread on the way you were."

They scattered slowly and walked the horses on. The other noises were lost in the call of their voices and the steady, insistent swish of hard hooves through unseen grass.

Hart kept just outside a line of low, scattered brush that marked the creek flow. The scrub was more felt than seen, black on black ghost-shapes on his left. He watched his horse's ears rather than trying to rely on his own senses. A dead horse would certainly catch the animal's attention. A dead man might also.

More than an hour later Hart heard Grimes cry out to his right. Slightly ahead and well off to that side on a slight rise he saw a flicker of light. That would be Richard calling them to him. Hart turned in his saddle and yelled the word to Wynn before he hauled his horse around and booted it, hoping as he did so that it had good night vision.

Richard and Grimes were huddled over a figure on the ground. Spud's shape was defined on the edge of firelight that made a flickering circle of moving shadows around them. Hart swung down. Wynn had already come up, and Venable was not far behind.

Richard was kneeling in the dirt, ignoring the condition of his tidy, fine-fabric clothing. "He's still alive, by damn," Richard said triumphantly. "I heard him groan. That's what brought me to him. My horse damn near stepped on him it was so dark." Richard's face was pale in the firelight but excited and pleased. The others bent close.

Spud was out cold, mercifully unconscious. His head and face were a raw and purpled mass of dried blood and torn flesh. His right ear had been nearly torn away. It dangled by a strip of skin and gristle less than an inch wide. His hands were bluish and swollen until the skin swelled near to bursting. His fingers looked like so many acutely painful sausages. The men winced when they saw him. They could not avoid imagining themselves in such condition. Even the thought was painful.

"He musta been drug," Grimes said in a hushed voice. "Hung up in the stirrup. It's a wonder he come out of it at all, I reckon."

"If he does," Wynn said.

No one was touching Spud. They seemed awed by his injuries, not yet certain of what they could do to help.

Hart coughed softly into the silence that had again come over them. "He wasn't drug," Hart said. He sounded very positive. The others turned to stare at him. The looks they gave him were almost accusing except for Richard. Richard's expression was one of curiosity.

"I said he wasn't drug," Hart repeated more firmly. "Look at his face. There's no dirt or gravel bedded in the meat. Look at his shirt. It ain't torn the least bit, and there's hardly any dirt on it either. No more than he'd get from wallowing on the ground there. I say he ain't been drug." They looked back at Spud. Hart was right.

"What then?" Wynn demanded. He sounded angry. "Kicked, maybe?"

"Hell, I couldn't say," Hart retorted. But it seemed almost as unlikely. They could see that when they looked. There was too much injury, spread too far. No single hoof-strike could have done that damage.

"That doesn't matter right now anyway," Richard said. "Did anyone think to bring any water?" No one had.

"I'll go down to the creek and wet a cloth or something," Hart said. He turned toward his horse.

"Bring in some wood, Harry," Wynn said behind him. "We'll want to build this fire up." Wynn sighed heavily. "Might need to keep it going quite a while too."

Hart made his way back down to the creek run and walked the horse in the bed until he found clear water by listening to the suck and finally to the splash of the gelding's hooves. He carried no cloths with him and wore no bandana, so he stripped off his shirt and leaned far down from the saddle to sop it in the water. He carried the dripping garment back, the night air chill and unnatural on his ribs.

Richard accepted the wet shirt from him. Richard seemed to have taken charge of Spud's care. He sat spraddle-legged on the ground with Spud's head in his lap. He squeezed a trickle of water over Spud's battered face and used a wet shirtsleeve to wipe gently at the wounds. The raw places began to seep fresh blood. Some of it ran slowly onto Richard's leg.

"I don't know what to do about that ear," Richard said.

"If we had the stuff to do it with we might could sew it back on," Wynn said.

"It might work," Venable said.

"Do you think so?" None of them knew.

Grimes came back from the direction of the creek with an awkward load of dry drift balanced across his pommel. He remained mounted and dropped the wood beside the fire. He turned away without a word and went to find more. Venable got stiffly to his feet. His knee joints popped. He began feeding fresh wood onto the fire.

Hart thought for a moment. Wynn would not want to leave. Spud was his hand, his responsibility, now more than ever before since he was being asked to act as ramrod instead of just carrying the name. Venable looked old and tired now. The night had taken a hard toll from him. Grimes was busy finding wood. They would need a good bit of it.

"Richard, how about coming with me?" Hart asked.

"Where?"

"Back to the headquarters. You can borrow a needle and thread from your sister while I get the team in harness. We'll bring the wagon out. We'll need it to carry him back."

"You couldn't do that alone?"

Hart shook his head. "Sorry. I couldn't *find* it alone. Not 'til daylight. I'd hate to wait that long. 'Specially if we wanta do something with that ear. It'll mortify for sure if we let it go too long."

Richard considered what Hart had said. He nodded. With great care he supported the back of Spud's head, withdrew his leg and placed his own hat on the ground to act as a pillow. "Let's go," he said.

Wynn nodded to them. The old man—Hart had not thought of Venable as being old before; now he did—seemed unaware of what they were doing. Venable was paying attention only to the fire.

They mounted and wheeled their horses. "Can you ride, fella?" Richard asked.

"Anywhere you put that horse, I'll be beside you."

"Good. We'll see how much these horses have to give." Richard let out a short screech and sent his horse thundering down the slope and across the creek bottom.

XVIII

It was still dark when the heavily lathered horses fogged into the ranch yard, but the eastern sky was beginning to pale. Hart had been glad it had been Richard who set their pace. At least they had been his horses to kill if he wished, and he had come close to doing it. It would be some time before either of them could be used again.

Richard led the way into one of the smaller pens, stepped off his horse and turned it loose. "Just let them be," he said. "I'll tell Twy to pull the saddles and tend to them later."

"All right." Hart was already speaking to Richard's back.

Hart headed first for the cookhouse. He grabbed a sack and dumped in some towels and dried beef, added canned tomatoes, a small coffeepot and a double handful of ground coffee that he wrapped in a twist of cloth. He also took time to get his one spare shirt from his room before he went to the wagon. Richard was already back outside.

"I'll get the harness ready," Richard said. "I

don't remember which animals are our driving team these days."

They were hitched and rolling within minutes. A door slammed as they were about to wheel out of the yard, and Twyla ran out to them. She thrust a sack into Richard's hands. "There's some food in there," she said. "The little bottle is laudanum. It will ease the pain if you can get him to take a swallow." She stepped back and waved them away.

The drive back was slower. The sun was well off the horizon before they found a place to take the wagon across the creek bed and up to where the others waited. An extra horse was standing in the hobbled and unsaddled group of animals the other men had ridden on their search.

"How is he?" Richard asked as soon as they were close.

"About the same," Wynn said. "Stirring now and then."

Hart stopped the wagon and Grimes set out the hitching weights while Hart carried his sack and Twyla's to the fire. They had let the fire die down in the daylight, and he had to build it up again. There was a wide ring of white ash around the remaining coals. Hart looked over toward Richard. The youngster was studiously poking thread at the eye of a needle. He seemed to have that business well in hand, and any of them could have done a job of sewing. It could not be too much different from repairing a torn saddle skirt or stitching an open wound on a horse. Hart concentrated on the foodstuffs.

Twyla had sent cold meat and tinned peaches, more coffee and a can of evaporated milk. That Hart set aside. If Spud came around he could warm the thick milk for him. It would be nourishing if not tasty. He put coffee on the fire to boil.

He heard Spud groan. Richard was bent over him with the needle and thread. When he was done they all came silently to the fire. Richard's hands were bloody, but they seemed satisfied that they had done what they could. They chewed the cold meat and hacked open the canned goods while they waited for the coffee. Hart had forgotten to bring cups so they would have to use the empty peach and tomato cans.

"Is that Spud's horse over there?" Hart asked.

"Yeah." Wynn looked uncomfortable. "He damn sure wasn't dragged or kicked by it, either. Harry found it tied to a bush down in the creek bottom."

Grimes nodded. "About a quarter mile away. Wasn't tangled neither. Somebody's tied it there deliberate as hell."

"It wouldn't run back to the ranch that way, and Spud sure couldn't reach it in the shape he's in. Who in hell would do a thing like that?" Hart mused. No one answered him. But each would have liked an answer.

They finished eating in silence and drank coffee through an oily scum of floating peach or tomato juices. They had to drink it black. Hart did not offer to open the canned milk.

Spud groaned and rolled his head. They gathered around him.

"He's starting to come around," Richard said. "Do you have that laudanum, Gotch?"

"Yeah. Just a minute." He went back to the fire and cut open the can of milk. He spilled some of it onto the ground to create space in the can and poured a quarter of the small bottle of laudanum into the syrup-thick milk. The quantity was guesswork and hope. He had no idea how much Spud should be given nor how much of the milk they could get him to drink. When the mixture was warm he carried it to Richard.

Grimes supported Spud's head while Richard dribbled warm milk into his mouth. He had to pull Spud's lips apart with his fingers to get any in. Most of it ran back out and had to be wiped away with what was left of Hart's shirt. The shirt had been torn into rags. Wynn carried fresh water from the creek, using the coffeepot as a vessel, and Hart got the clean towels from his sack. They were able to do a better job of cleaning Spud.

"He didn't get much of that laudanum," Richard said. "Is there any more of it?"

Hart gave him the bottle. Spud seemed to swallow some of the medicine by reflex when it was put into his mouth but they could not be sure.

"I think we should move him now," Wynn said. "If he got any of that stuff in him it'll be a help." He looked at Venable but got no response. Venable had not spoken in a long time. He only watched.

Hart got the wagon and parked it beside Spud. The others bent over him, Richard and Wynn at his legs and hips. Grimes reached for his forearms to lever his shoulders up.

Spud screamed. The sound was shrill and piercing. Startled, Grimes let go.

"Oh my God," Grimes moaned. "I could feel bone shift in there."

They cut Spud's sleeves open.

"Some son of a bitch has broke both his arms," Grimes said.

Hart felt himself go white with anger. It was too much to be a coincidence. He hunkered down and wiped Spud's face with a wet towel and began to talk.

They put Spud in the big house where Twyla could tend him when the others were away. That night Richard joined them in the chow hall while Hart and Wynn and Grimes were at supper.

"Spud woke up a while this afternoon," Richard said. He looked worried. "He was quite groggy. Too much so to get a clear story from him. He did say there were three of them, apparently no one he knew, and he kept saying something about horses. We couldn't tell what he meant. He may have been trying to say something about their horses, perhaps their brand. He took more laudanum, anyway, and that seems to be giving him some rest."

Wynn shook his head. "I damn sure can't figure it. Harry?"

"Makes no sense to me."

"Me neither," Hart said. "If somebody has a beef with me over that fight the other night, I can't see them taking it out on Spud. I don't see a connection there, but that business with the busted arms sure makes it look like there is one. I wish I knew."

"None of us does," Richard said, "but I suggest for the time being, Early, that all ranch work be done in pairs at the very least and that we ride armed."

Wynn nodded.

"I don't own a gun," Grimes said. "Sold it to Charley Burwell when we got paid off."

"I can loan you one," Richard said. "Dad keeps a number of them at the house."

"If you say so," Grimes said. "Seems kinda unnecessary to carry all that weight around all day long, but I'll go along with it if you say to."

"Hart?"

"I wouldn't know what to do with one, Richard. Anyway, I stay around here most of the time. I won't likely need one."

"Suit yourself, but if you do need one there are some in my father's office. Including several shotguns. I'll set out a box of shells with buckshot just in case."

"All right. I sure hope Spud comes to his senses soon, though."

"If that will do us any good," Wynn said. "If he didn't know those fellas... well, hell. We might not know any more after he does talk to us."

"Don't even suggest such a thing, Early," Richard said. "He just has to be able to tell us something."

"Listen, boy," the foreman said, "maybe I'm out of line to be asking it, but how's your pa taking this now? He seemed awful shook up this morning. Not like himself at all. I'd have been expecting him to be ranting an' raving and burning the air, but he drawed into a shell today like a damn turtle. If he's not blowing a mad this must be bothering him down deep where it hits the hardest."

Richard's face clouded. "I think you are right, Early, but he hasn't spoken to me about it either. Right now he's sitting in the room with Spud, just sitting there very, very quietly. I don't mind telling you, that worries me too." Richard left and shortly afterward Wynn and Grimes left too. None of them had gotten any sleep the night before.

Richard came back the next morning. The foreman and single remaining hand had long since left, with revolvers strapped at their sides.

"Could you come over to the house, Gotch? Spud is awake now. Maybe you can make something of what he is saying. We can't."

"Sure."

Richard took him through the entry and up the steep, narrow staircase. As they passed the door to Venable's office Hart caught a glimpse of the old man seated at his desk with a ledger book before him. Venable seemed to be staring straight ahead, though. There was nothing before him but the cluttered pigeonholes inside the tall rolltop.

The second floor of the house was divided into four small bedrooms. Richard led the way around the landing to the right. Spud was lying on a four-posted bed with a frilly canopy suspended over it. There were miniatures on the walls and curtains at the front and side facing windows. A bureau held a clutter of jars and boxes, and Hart guessed that if he opened the massive wardrobe he would find ladies' clothing if it held anything at all. The room was probably that of the absent daughter. He could not remember her name.

Spud's head was wrapped in bandages. The exposed surfaces of his face were shiny where they had smeared some sort of ointment. Both arms were outside the covers. They were bandage-wrapped firmly to wood splints. Hart thought the Venables must have had a time getting the arms set. He thought with a moment of regret that he should have offered to help them, but he had been busy with the team and saddle horses when the others brought Spud upstairs.

Twyla was seated on a cane-bottom chair beside the bed. Two other chairs had been brought in as well. A soup bowl sat on a bedside table, but from the skin that had formed across the top of its contents the soup had been cold for some time. Twyla nodded a hello as they entered. She looked exhausted, and Hart guessed that she must have spent the night on that chair so her father and brother could get some sleep.

"He's dozing again," she whispered.

Spud's eyelids fluttered and crept open. He did not try to move. " 'Lo, Hart," he said drunkenly. His voice was weak and he was deep under the influence of the laudanum they had spooned into him.

" 'Lo, Spud." Hart took the chair next to Twyla's. "You look awful, Spud, but a lot better than the last time I saw you."

"Sonsabitches, Hart," he slurred. "Sonsabitches. Said they wished was the gotch-eyed bassard 'stead me. Mussa been you, huh?" The words came out slowly and indistinctly. He did not seem to be in much pain now, though.

"What'd they look like, Spud? Anyone you know?"

The man tried to shake his head and winced as pain cut through the fog of the drug. He held his head stiff. "Three of 'em. Movin' on horses. Horses." It seemed meaningless. No one was likely to be out that far afoot, and there was no wagon road near.

"That's the same thing he told us already,"

Richard said. "He keeps mumbling that they were on horses."

"No, dam't," Spud corrected. He tried again to shake his head and moaned when the wave of pain hit. He closed his eyes and lay still for a moment, rigid against the pain as if he thought he could hold it off that way. "*Our* horses. Rid'n down on *our* horses."

"They were riding V-Slash-4 horses?" Richard asked skeptically.

Spud breathed a few cuss words, and Hart was glad he knew they were already familiar ones to Twyla. Another female might have been quite thoroughly shocked.

"Do you mean they weren't *on* V-Slash-4 horses but were *after* them?" Hart asked. "Like chasing them? Rounding up a bunch of them maybe?"

Spud's lips parted in what might have been a smile, although the resemblance was scant. "Thas it," he said. "Horses." He closed his eyes again.

"That explains it then," Richard said. "Horse thieves. He had the bad luck to ride into them while they were making a gather." He breathed a sigh of relief. "It appears that the boys needn't worry about riding armed after all. They will have made their raid and be long gone by now. I dare say I'm as pleased as is possible under the circumstances. I would rather we lose horses than men, and I know Dad feels the same way."

Twyla nodded her agreement. She stood and said, "If you two are going to be with him a few more minutes I'll go get some hot broth. Maybe he can take some more now."

Spud was getting good care, Hart thought. Not that he would trade places with the man just now, but it would be nice to be fussed over like that some time. Twyla left the room and Richard sat back in his chair looking much less worried. Somehow Hart was not so sure they had reason to feel relieved, but he was not sure why.

XIX

Hart worked the gray horse that afternoon, more because he wanted to keep busy than from any desire to handle the animal. He had discovered long before that when he felt troubled he could put his mind and his muscles to other tasks, and sometimes the worries would resolve themselves, if only in his thinking. He did not really expect that to happen this time.

He flopped the blanket over the big horse, saddled him and slowly drew the cinches snug. He let the horse wear the saddle for half an hour before he hung the bosal on it and mounted. The horse pitched, but without real fear. He rode it just long enough to work out the first kinks, to show it he would come off at his command and not the animal's, then he hauled it through a few tight circles to left and right and dismounted.

He gave the gray a thorough rubdown with comb and brushes, thought for a moment and grinned to himself. He went to get his mare and turned her in with the stud.

The two horses approached each other on stiff legs, sniffed and squealed loudly.

"Fancy girl, you sound like a damn pig. Bad as your boyfriend there," he said cheerfully.

The mare turned and flirted her tail, and Hart nodded his satisfaction. The stallion trumpeted again and mounted. A few minutes later Hart picked up a pitchfork in case he would have to fend the stallion away from the mare and led the bay out. He had no trouble with the stud. "At least he's a gentleman," he told the mare.

He was returning the pitchfork to its place when he saw Twyla Venable approaching. He opened his mouth to speak, with only the most polite intentions, when she cut him off.

"Damn you, hey-boy, you are an evil, no account, sneaking son of a bitch, you are."

Hart grinned happily and said, "You sure have me pegged, don't you? But you needn't be so shy. Next time feel free to speak right out. No need to beat around the bush."

Her step did not falter but the hard set of her jaw did. She came and stood defiantly under his chin and tried to maintain her anger. She failed. In another moment she laughed. "You're as brassy as hell, aren't you?"

"I have my moments," he confessed.

"Did you honestly think you could breed that mare without me knowing about it?"

"Of course not." He managed to look insulted and indignant about it. "Loud mouthed thing like that was sure to go bragging to the whole world. Not that I blame him. That's the finest mare *he'll* ever cover."

She shook her head but laughed again. "I swear,

hey-boy, you've got solid brass b . . ." She snapped her mouth shut, and a deep red blush began to show under her tan. Hart pretended not to notice.

"Anyway, it's the truth," he said. "And you *did* say I could use the horse."

"Not exactly. Not the way I remember it, but . . ." She shrugged. "The damage is done now anyhow."

"Ain't it, though?" He did not sound at all displeased. "And that being the case, I'll just carry her back to him for the next three days or so to make sure she catches."

"All right, dammit," she said with a sigh.

Hart grinned and said, "I sure am glad you finally made it official." In an innocent tone of voice he added, "A man could get into a bunch of trouble using somebody else's property without permission. It's a good thing I know better'n that."

"The hell. You've had your mind on nothing else since the day you came here. I think you'd have done it in the dark of night and then gone to jail if you had to. Well, you got what you came for." She stopped and cocked her head to the side, eyeing him closely. "Come to think of it, I wouldn't be surprised if that was the only thing that brought you here. Was it?"

"Just about. But I did need a job. If I hadn't found work here I guess I'd've come back with cash for a breeding when I could."

"You really think your mare's that good, don't you." It was not a question. "It really is important to you, isn't it?"

He became serious. "Miss Twyla, if my mare throws a colt next year it could be my whole future, right there on four wobbly legs."

She nodded gravely. She seemed to understand all that he had said in those few words. "And if she throws a filly?"

Hart smiled weakly. "Then I guess I try to find some cash and come back. And hope the horse is still here." The smile became teasing. "Unless, of course, that gray horse of yours throws dinks. You can't ever tell when you know the stud's not as good as the mare."

She doubled her fist and punched him in the stomach. Hart gave no sign that he had noticed it but the fact was that she surprised him. Her fist was small, but she had a sting like a hornet. When he did not respond she punched him again.

He laughed and asked, "Was there something you wanted, little one?"

She was satisfied. She had scrapped with her brother enough to know that he would be rubbing the sore spot on his belly if she were not watching.

Hart set the pitchfork aside and by unspoken consent they wandered toward the pen where he had put the mare. Neither felt any particular desire to look at the horse. They leaned on the corral rails and Hart asked, "What about you? What is it you want out of life in the time down the road?"

She was silent for a long time, long enough for him to think she would not respond at all. "I guess . . . this place. Take care of Daddy as long as he needs me. After . . . run it myself or take care of Richard." Her shoulders lifted a fraction of an inch, then dropped. "That's all, I suppose." She forced a smile that did not quite ring true. "I can't see much else in store for me."

"You don't ask for much if you want no more than you've got," Hart said. He pursed his lips and exhaled loudly. "By God, I'll tell you the truth," he declared. "I'll tell you just what I think. I think you told me what you expect. I don't think you said the first word about what you *want*."

She looked startled. And troubled. "What if I tell you you're wrong?"

"Convince yourself of that first. Then tell me."

"There are times when you see just too damned well, you gotch-eyed son of a bitch." Her voice was unsteady. She turned and ran toward the house.

Hart watched the pale blur that he could see as she receded. He was feeling a deep, quiet sadness that he did not fully understand. And did not want to.

Wynn and Grimes came in reporting no incidents out of the ordinary during the day. Harry Grimes was already complaining about the uncomfortable drag of a loaded revolver at his belt, the more so when Richard told them what Spud had said about the men being horse thieves. Richard had joined them again after the evening meal.

"How is Spud, anyhow?" Wynn wanted to know.

"He's sleeping an awful lot. Every time he wakes, Twy pours him full of soup and puts more laudanum in him. We don't know if that is the right thing to do, but it seems to be working so far. At least he is comfortable now."

"Good. I never seen a man beat any worse than him and still be alive. A bad horse couldn't have done him any worse than that." Wynn seemed ready to dismiss the subject then. Spud was all right, and they still had a ranch to run. "Is there anything your pa wants done now? Anything in particular?"

Richard sat back in his chair and swirled coffee in the bottom of his mug. "Well . . . he left no instructions. But I really think it would be a good idea for you to check that horse herd tomorrow. I would like to know how many we lost. I assume you can get a count."

"Do we have to wear those damn guns?" Grimes asked.

"Oh, maybe a little longer." Richard smiled sympathetically. "A few more days shouldn't hurt. After that, I guess we can call it over and done with."

"It'll take us that long to comb the horse range anyway," Wynn said, "if you want a decent count. We'll carry food with us and plan on staying out a night, maybe two."

"All right."

"You said your pa didn't leave any instructions," Wynn said. "He's gone for a while?"

"Yes. When he left this afternoon he said he might be away as long as a week. He didn't say where he would be." Richard sounded slightly miffed about that oversight. Hart thought Richard probably did not know how much his father had been away during the early summer or how little he had been letting his hands know about the ranch business. Hart guessed that that probably rankled Wynn also, although the foreman had never said anything to indicate that it did.

For the next two days Hart busied himself with the gray horse, working the stallion in the mornings and returning the mare to him in the afternoons. The second afternoon she refused him, nearly connecting with a pair of hard flung hooves when he tried to mount. It was a good indication that she was safely in foal.

Richard was very much in evidence around the headquarters, but Hart did not see Twyla outdoors. She even was ignoring the young garden she had so carefully planted.

Although they had taken food for three days, Wynn and Grimes returned the second night. Their news was not good.

"There's more than a hundred head missing," Wynn reported, "and that ain't the worst of it. They're still being taken."

"You're sure?" Richard asked.

"Hell yes, I'm sure. We went out to where we found Spud. Figured we'd start from there, you see. We found tracks where they'd gathered about fifty head and run them off to the north. Well, we'd knowed about those and figured them long gone so we didn't try to follow. Then yesterday evening we come on another bunch of tracks where they'd taken another fifty or sixty head. And those tracks was fresh, Richard. Whoever is doing it never quit just because Spud saw them. They're bold bastards, whoever they are."

"Did they take them out the same way?"

"Ayup. We followed that bunch this morning for about fifteen miles 'til we came to a place where someone moved a bunch of beeves lately. The ground was too beat down to tell even which way they might've turned there. They sure didn't cross straight ahead. So we come back here to see what you thought about it. I, uh, don't suppose your pa is back home yet?"

Richard shook his head. "No, I'm afraid not. And I just don't know . . . There are too few of us to go chasing after them now." He lapsed into an uncertain silence. The load of responsibility on him —for the ranch and for the hands—was heavy for a youngster.

"Are you open for a suggestion?" Hart asked quietly.

"Of course."

"Maybe the best thing to do for right now is see to it that there aren't any more stolen. If they're after horses—and God only knows why they'd want them—maybe the thing to do would be to gather the whole herd and move them in close where they can be watched. There's enough grass in a five-mile circle around this place to carry them for a while anyhow. We could hold them in a loose herd and move them a little each day. At least they'd be here when your pa gets back."

Richard considered it. After he saw a brief nod of assent from Wynn he said, "All right, we'll try it." He smiled. "Though how three men are going to gather and trail five hundred head of horses I don't know."

"There's no reason I can't help," Hart said. "I can't find them for you, but I can damn sure move them once they're located. And listen, we'd best carry a remuda along with us. Short strings anyway. From what I've seen of your pa's new horse herd they're all silly as hell. I wouldn't count on using any of them unless you want to take the time to break a fresh mount every time you need one."

"He's right about that, Richard. I don't think those animals have ever been touched except by rope and iron," Wynn said. "You can ask Harry about that."

Grimes grinned and shook his head. Whatever he had experienced with the Box 11 geldings was not something he wanted to brag about.

"It will mean Twy will be alone here to care for Spud and that stallion," Richard said. He was beginning to have doubts.

"Ask her if you want," Hart said, "but I wouldn't think she'd be worried. And she's all the time messing with that stud horse. I don't think your pa has touched him in weeks."

"Really?" Richard stood. "I'll ask Twy, of course, but . . . I think you can be ready to leave before first light. We'll pack on horses and not fool with the wagon. Count on a week or so of supplies, all right?"

After he was gone Grimes sighed. "I suppose we'll have to keep carrying these guns."

"Damn right you will," Wynn said. He sounded as if he hoped they would get a chance to use them.

XX

They were a half dozen miles from the headquarters by dawn, each leading a spare horse and with two pack horses to carry the food and the gear they would need for a week without sight of a roof or walls. Except for Hart, each of the men was armed, and Hart had strapped a long-bladed fighting knife on his belt.

They spent a half day riding to the far side of the broken horse range before starting the gather. They would work their way back, picking up the small bands of scattered horses as they came to them and pushing them as a growing herd toward the relative safety of the grass close to headquarters.

Richard proved to be as familiar with the V-Slash-4 range as was Wynn, more at home on these farther, less often worked horse areas than Grimes. Between them Richard and Wynn knew the watering places and the hidden, grassy coverts where free running horses could likely be found. On the hilly far fringes of the range the two men also knew a few closed draws where the gather could easily be confined overnight by a single rider. By the time they reached flatter country the herd would have become accustomed to close grouping and would not be so difficult to hold.

The first afternoon they pulled in thirty-seven head, Hart taking over the job of herding them and the other men scattering to find the animals and bring them under Hart's control. That night they pushed the small herd into a three-sided hollow and built their fire at its mouth. There was little graze to be found in the hollow, which was to their advantage. The next day the horses would be more interested in eating than in running.

"We'll split the nighthawk duties four ways," Richard said. He had taken charge of the work from the first, and Early Wynn seemed glad to be relieved of the responsibility. "Wynn, you can take the first watch. Gotch, you've had it pretty easy today so you can split your sleep and take the next. I'm the youngest and should be the most resilient, so I will take the third. Which leaves the dawn watch for you, Harry. You'll want to be careful, though. They should be hungry and restless by then." Grimes nodded.

Richard rocked back on his heels. He fingered the butt of his revolver and a half embarrassed, half amused smile twitched at the corners of his mouth. "What I am wondering is, does anyone think we should guard the camp also?"

"Oh, hell no, Richard," Wynn scoffed. "We ain't playing out some penny dreadful, you know. All we have to worry about here is maybe falling off our horses. Nobody's going to bother us, and once we get them in close nobody's going to bother the livestock." He snorted. "A body would think you believe everything you read in those eastern noose-papers. Don't worry about it."

Richard looked relieved. "That was my opinion to begin with, but I thought we all should have an opportunity to express our views. I don't want anyone to feel he is being put in danger against his will. Harry? Gotch? No objections to sleeping through except for the herding? All right then. Grab yourself something to eat, Early, and get to work. The rest of us will be here if you need us."

By the end of the third day they had a hundred seventy-odd head in the herd, and Harry Grimes had to begin staying with them to help Hart bunch and move them. Richard and Wynn continued to do the harder work of locating the horses and forcing them into the larger herd since they were more likely to know the grazing areas than Grimes.

They followed a serpentine route through the less and less broken country, trying to cover as much territory as they could so they would miss as few animals as possible. They all knew they could not hope to get a completely clean sweep of the range, not if they had three times as many riders and twice as long to do the work. With the ever-moving habits of grazing animals there would always be a few outlaws that would escape any roundup no matter how carefully it could be made.

At night Richard and Early Wynn would argue with good humor—but vigorous defense of their own views—which route should be followed the next day. Part of the time each man would be stubbornly supporting the same route but using different landmark names, Richard using old place names and Wynn using names coined by hands who had worked the area while Richard was away. Neither would confess the similarities when they occurred, but it was obvious to all four when it happened.

By the fifth night, with roughly four hundred head to hold on nearly flat country, they had to double up on nighthawking. One man could not hold the herd alone. That also cut their sleep in half.

Late on the sixth day Wynn came back to the herd at a hard run and without a fresh gather running before him. He pulled up near Hart. "Which way'd the boy go?"

Hart pointed in the direction he had last seen Richard. "What's up?" Wynn was obviously in a state of agitation.

"The sonsabitches are hitting us again," Wynn yelled over his shoulder as he spurred his horse away. "I seen 'em myself."

Grimes had seen Wynn's unusual action. He rode around the grazing herd to join Hart. The horses were accustomed to being together now. There had been little need to press the edges of the herd that day. Hart told him what Wynn had said.

"We might could get those horses back," Grimes said.

"Uh huh. Let's get Richard and Early some spare horses ready for when they get back here. Theirs ought to be about used up by then. Early's especially. He was blowing like a north wind when he came through here."

Grimes captured the fresh horses and hobbled them outside the herd. The two men sat their animals and waited, growing increasingly anxious as the time lengthened to more than an hour with no sign of either Richard or Wynn returning. They began to fidget as the long shadows melted away into twilight. The herd began to loosen as the uncontrolled horses stepped from mouthful to mouthful of grass.

"Damn!" Hart exclaimed.

Grimes was equally worried. "Surely they wouldn't have gone straight after them, just the two of them."

"I can't think of any other reason for them to still be out."

Grimes cursed and squeezed the horn of his saddle like he was trying to throttle the neck of an unseen horse thief. He took a deep breath and loosened his muscles. In a matter of fact voice he said, "I'd best get on the other side of the herd. We can circle them and put them back together."

"Uh huh. We can count on circling on through the night, I guess. Or until they get back to us. And listen, Harry. I can't see you across there so I'll go ahead and start circling to the right. You move to the left. That way we'll pass every so often. We just might wanta keep in touch tonight."

"Yeah. Dammit." Grimes turned his horse to the left. They might have a long night ahead of them, and the uncertainty made it all the worse.

They were still circling the herd, tired and worried, at dawn. They changed horses without speaking; and Hart stayed on the ground to build a fire and put coffee on to boil. They ate in silence also and, since the horses seemed content for the time being, hunkered by the fire to wait and drink coffee. They did not look at each other.

It was several hours into daylight when Grimes

came to his feet and said he could see a dust to the north. "It could be them, Gotch."

"Not just two horses it couldn't be."

"Well, I'm gonna go see."

"Okay, but you stay ready to turn and run if you have to. If it comes to that don't bother trying to get back here. Just fire some shots to warn me and run like hell. I'll scatter these horses and line out for home too."

"Sure hope it's them," Grimes said. He ran to his horse and was spurring the animal before he was fully seated.

Hart looked at the opened packs on the ground beside him and decided against repacking the camp clutter. If the dust was made by Richard and Wynn they would be wanting something to eat. If it was not, Hart did not intend to drag any pack horses behind him on his run for the headquarters. He poured himself more coffee and sat down to wait.

The dust moved close enough that he could see it, and soon dark, blurred shapes took form at the base of the reddish yellow cloud. He had heard no signal from Grimes. It must be all right. Hart released a tightly kept breath that he had been holding without realizing it.

It was Richard and Wynn, pushing a herd of horses that contained more than a hundred head. Richard and Grimes were doing all the herd work when Hart could see them. Wynn was trailing slowly behind. They drove the horses through and let them mingle with the larger herd that Hart and Grimes had held through the night.

Hart was weary, his eyes gritty and feeling swollen from lack of sleep, but he came fully awake when Wynn came near. The foreman's shirt and vest were splotched with dark brown stains that had to be dried blood. Hart was helping him off his horse when the others rode to the fire.

Wynn was undaunted even if he was hurt. He grinned broadly. "Got ever' one of those horses back." His voice was steady enough but he leaned heavily on Hart and accepted his help to a seat on the ground by the fire. Richard and Grimes joined them.

"Don't just play with that coffeepot," Hart demanded. "*Tell* us, dammit." He got a cup and filled it for Wynn.

Richard blew on his coffee and took a slow, deliberately teasing sip before he spoke. "Well, now. Early saw them, of course, told you and came to find me. It was already late, and we felt Harry would be needed with the herd in any case." He grinned. "So we went after them. We caught up with them just south of Beartrack Rock."

Grimes nodded. Hart had no idea where they meant.

"There were three of them, just as Spud told us. They had to be the same men. It was nearly dark, so we didn't stop to plan any good strategy. We pulled our guns and rode straight in. They saw us and started the shooting, and we fired back."

"Didn't hit any of the bastards, though," Wynn complained.

"They broke and ran. We started to follow, but one of them caught Wynn along the ribs. It knocked him out of the saddle, and I thought sure he was a dead man."

"Turned out they just pinked me, but that damn

bullet felt like a good smith's hammer when it hit," Wynn said with a chuckle. "Scairt me proper, I don't mind telling you."

"The horses weren't too excited by the shooting," Richard said, "and this complete fool here insisted that I gather them back together. Early couldn't do any hard riding, of course, and I couldn't drive them alone at night, so we held them until we could see what they were doing and started them back this morning."

Wynn was in a good humor in spite of his wound. "You boys should've seen the pup. I never seen a boy be in three places at once before, but I swear he had to do it this morning. All I could do was tail along in the drag. Ol' Richard had to ride swing, flank, and point all by his lonesome. Funny as hell from where I was sitting." He laughed and winced at the dart of pain from a bruised or possibly broken rib. "The boy did a good job for all that. I don't think he lost more than a dozen head the whole way back here."

Hart began preparing a breakfast for them. Neither would have eaten in more than twenty-four hours, and they should be even more exhausted than Grimes and himself.

"Did you recognize any of them?" Grimes asked.

"Nope," Wynn said. "Not that we got all that close or was paying all that much attention at the time. But I'd have to say I never seen any of them before." His voice trailed. "Except . . . maybe one fella. I never got a close look and then only saw his back, but . . . there was something about him, the way he sat his horse or something, that puts it in my mind that I've seen him before. Maybe just passed him on the street in town or some such thing. Nobody I know anyhow."

Wynn's shoulders slumped and the animation left his features when he quit talking. His face was gray and haggard from combined shock and fatigue. Yet Hart knew that when the time came for them to move, Wynn would have to be helped into his saddle but he would be there. He would fork his horse and be upright when they started, and he would still be there when they ended.

"What now, Richard?" Hart asked.

"We have no choice. Home."

Grimes nodded. "With what you brought in this morning and what they've already stolen, there can't be very much left out here anyway, and most of those will be our own yearlings and two-year-olds. We already have most of the Box II geldings."

"That's what Early says too. We can start back this morning, drive them straight for home. We'll sleep in our own beds tonight." Richard's face tightened. "And in the future we will be riding a guard on those animals. Whoever these people are, they started the shooting. From now on it will be our privilege to fire the first shots any time they are seen. We will carry rifles as well as revolvers and will aim for their horses. I would very much like to have a talk with one of those gentlemen."

Grimes offered no argument now about the need to carry a gun.

XXI

"Are you done being mad at me?" Hart asked.

"Huh? Oh. I ... guess I am." Twyla was propped against the stud's fence. Her chin rested on her crossed forearms over the top rail. One booted foot was placed on the bottom rail. In a man the posture would have seemed normal, but in her long skirted housedress Twyla looked awkward and unladylike. It occurred to Hart that she probably would not have cared had she bothered to think about it. She did not seem to spend much time worrying about what was or was not ladylike.

Hart got the impression she did not particularly care to remember the cause of her anger, so he changed the subject. If she did not want to discuss her future hopes he would let it slide. "How is your hospital getting along?"

"Spud seems to be getting better. He's pretty comfortable now, or says he is, and he is eating anything that doesn't take much chewing. He says he hopes he never sees another bowl of soup as long as he lives. I can't really blame him."

"Soon as he gets back to the bunkhouse I'll try to make us some good, old-fashioned soup."

She laughed. "You're even nastier than I thought."

"And Early?"

"Him! He's impossible. He let us tape him up and went back to the old house. He insists he's going to ride out with Richard and Grimes tomorrow. He won't listen to a thing I say."

"Can't fault the man for that," Hart said blandly.

"You're as bad as he is."

"Maybe worse," he agreed.

"Are you going to work Gray Lad this morning?"

"Yeah, I better if I don't want him to start losing what he's learned so far. He's had way too much of a layoff as it is."

"I hope he busts your butt for you," she said lightly.

"And I thought your hospital was already full."

"It'd be worth it," she declared.

"Vindictive damned woman, aren't you?"

"For pure mean, hey-boy, I can match you pound for pound, any day of the week and any way you want to call it."

"B'God, I think you could, too. No wonder Indians turn their captives over to the women when they really want them tortured."

"Do they really?"

"Uh huh."

She seemed quite satisfied by the idea. She thought a moment and said, "I'll bet they could put some fear into the criminals of this country if they would forget all that silly jail business and turn them loose in a room full of women." She sounded half serious.

"That'd sure cut down on the lawbreaking population," he said, "but the idea scares hell out of me." He rubbed his neck and stifled a yawn. He still was not caught up on his sleep. "Well, I better see how that boy of yours is going to work today."

"I'll be right here cheering for his side," she said.

"Don't I know it." He went to get the saddle and bosal.

The big horse was tractable when he mounted. It barely made an effort to unseat him and quickly subsided. He looked at her and grinned.

"I can still hope," she called.

He began working on the horse's response to commands, using his own weight and the position of the animal's head to change its direction. It had to move where he wanted it or lose its balance. When he pulled the saddle and turned the horse loose in its pen it had not even worked up a good sweat.

"You sure aren't much for whip and spur," she said when he lugged the old saddle to the rails.

"I thought I told you before, I use them when I need them but it ain't a habit. Anyway, nobody'll ever have to bloody that horse. He just don't need it." He threw the saddle over the fence and crawled between the rails.

"How about a cup of coffee," she invited.

"Sure. I'll put this stuff away and join you."

She had two cups and a moist, heavy, freshly baked pound cake on the table when he joined her.

"I just checked on Spud," she said. "He's sound

asleep. He's still sleeping an awful lot. I don't know if that's a good sign or not."

"Don't look to me for an opinion either." He nodded toward the cake. "You're getting mighty fancy these days."

"It's Richard's favorite. And I'll tell you what. It's awfully nice to have someone around here to cook for again. Daddy's gone most of the time these days, and when he is home he hardly pays any attention to what I put on his plate. I think I could serve him stewed horse apples and he wouldn't notice."

"If he asked for seconds you'd have to worry."

She cut him a thick slice of the cake. It was the first he had tasted in several years, and he wondered anew at how she managed to make a supply of special treats so far from town or transportation. They had no ice house—no place to cut any and the winters often open and fairly mild—yet there had to have been a large amount of unspoiled butter used in the cake. She could not have used the lard they had in the cookhouse for frying and for the more common pies. He complimented her and savored every mouthful of the delicacy.

"More?" she asked when he had finished.

He wanted more but shook his head. Richard and the others would want some too. It was supposed to be Richard's cake, after all.

"You haven't heard anything from your pa?"

"Not a word. Hell, hey-boy, we don't even know where he went. It isn't like him to go *any*where, much less to just leave like that. I know whatever he's doing must be important, but . . ."

"Yeah. But. I wish there was something we

could do to help, but I sure don't know what it would be."

"Me neither. I'm glad Richard is here, though. Daddy has always been in his best humor when Richard is home. Always before, anyhow." She sighed. "I don't know why Daddy keeps insisting that Richard should go off and study all those silly things in school that don't have a thing to do with ranching. It isn't like Richard wants to do anything except this or to be anything but a cowman. He's happiest when he's home, too. I could tell that from his letters even if he wasn't willing to admit it."

"Your pa must have some reason for it."

"Oh, I'm sure he does. I just wish I knew what it could be."

Hart finished his coffee and left. He was beginning to wonder how many problems Titus Venable's V-Slash-4 was wrapped in.

Richard and Grimes reported no sign of the quick-to-shoot horse thieves, but when Wynn declared himself ready to get back on a horse, Grimes began riding at night and sleeping through the day. They were taking no more chances than were strictly necessary.

One evening after Richard had returned to the house a thought occurred to Hart. He asked Wynn, "Say, Early, you boys have been watching those horses real close. Is there any chance your thieving friends might be slipping around behind you, stealing cattle?"

The foreman snorted. "Not much, I'll tell you. Hell, man, they're scattered so thin it wouldn't hardly be worth the trouble it'd take to put together a herd big enough to bother stealing."

"That thin? I thought this place was pretty well grassed. Everything I've seen has looked real good."

"It is, too. Good grass everywhere you look. Nosirree, boy, it ain't the grass." He began to look angry. "Ti told me not to be talking about this, like it wasn't anybody else's business, and I guess it ain't, but you been through as much as the rest of us lately, and you've stuck with the brand. I figure you have a right to know. Dammit, Gotch, the last couple years Ti has been selling heifers along with his steers. Right now we couldn't put a really good market herd together if we tried to ship the cows too. *That's* why they're scattered thin. There just aren't hardly any more of them out there." Wynn prodded Grimes with his elbow. "Is that the truth, or ain't it?"

The cowboy looked uncomfortable. Business talk was out of his line. He could describe in detail the condition of the beeves that were his responsibility, but the number of them was the boss's affair, not his. Still, he reluctantly nodded and said, "There's few enough of them and hard to find, all right."

"Lordy," Hart said. There had to be more troubles here than he could have guessed if Venable had been selling heifers.

Steers were what a cowman sold. Beef on the hoof to feed the people crammed into the eastern cities, beef on government contract to feed soldiers or meet treaty obligations. But always beef. The cows stayed on the home range to produce more beef for future sales, self-maintaining machines that with careful husbandry would drop calves to become saleable steers or growing heifers.

And the heifers. They were the cowman's hope for the future. Tomorrow's cows and the only way he could hope to increase his herd and therefore his livelihood. No cowman would dream of selling his heifers unless his grass was jammed beyond its capacity. And Titus Venable's grass was nearly empty. For him to sell his heifers and leave his grass uneaten was unthinkable.

Grimes mumbled something and left the table. He snatched his hat from the wall peg and hurried through the door. He did not like this kind of talk or the thoughts it led to. He knew as well as anyone that a man does not sell his heifers.

Hart and Wynn looked at each other briefly and lowered their eyes. They understood Grimes's departure.

Titus Venable returned home two days later. He rode into the yard at dusk just as the men were gathering for supper.

They watched him come in, slouched low in his saddle, his shoulders slumped. He did not speak to them or look their way. They thought he looked older than when he left.

An hour later Richard joined them in the cookhouse. "Dad would like to see you boys over at the house," he said.

"What's up, Richard?" Wynn said.

Richard looked as puzzled as they were. "I'm damned if I know, Early. We told him all that's been going on here, and all he did was nod his head. It was like it didn't really matter to him. He ate his supper and went into the office for a while.

When he came out he said he wanted to talk to us, everybody, up in Spud's room so we could all hear it at the same time. But what it is about . . . I have no idea."

"We'll know soon enough," Hart said.

They trooped out behind Richard and walked in silence to the main house. Four pairs of booted feet made a thumping clatter on the narrow staircase that seemed overloud and somehow out of place at this moment.

They shouldered their way into Spud's tiny room and stood awkwardly against the wall. Each of them, even Richard, felt compelled to remove his hat and hold it self-consciously before him.

Spud was lying on the canopied bed, his arms still strapped to the splints. Hart realized that Twyla would have had to feed him every mouthful of food or sip of fluid Spud had had since he was injured. He had not thought about that before. Spud's beating must have been taking quite a toll from her too.

The girl was seated at the bedside. She looked tired and worried.

Venable was seated against the wall opposite the men, near the foot of the bed. He could face the entire room from there.

The ranch owner was haggard. If Twyla looked tired, her father looked like still-breathing death. His cheeks were drawn and his complexion muddy. Dark circles gave his eyes an unhealthy vacancy. Short months before he had been a vigorous man in the prime of his maturity. Now he looked twenty years older than the first time Hart had seen him.

Venable sat with his head down, his eyes not

meeting any of them. He cleared his throat weakly.

"My dear friends," he began in a thin, old man's voice. He cleared his throat again and restarted in a stronger voice. "My dear friends and family. There are some things I want to tell you."

XXII

"I am afraid that we . . . are in . . . no, dammit, I am afraid that *I* . . . have placed the V-Slash-4 in trouble. It's a long story. The result very simply is that my children and I can expect to lose our home. You who have worked for us—with us, really—so loyally will lose your jobs. I am afraid I cannot even . . . pay you what I already owe you." His chin sank even lower. He looked utterly miserable, utterly dejected.

Of the others, neither Hart nor Early Wynn showed their feelings. Harry Grimes was disappointed. Only Spud gave an indication of anger. He glared openly at Venable.

Both of Venable's children sat or stood immobile, breathing so shallowly the movement could not be seen. Each of them seemed intent on betraying no emotion for public view. That effort was assisted by a deep and disbelieving sense of shock. It was too sudden, entirely too overwhelming for them to assimilate the impact of their father's words. For the men it was only a job lost and a quantity of money. For Richard and Twyla it was the end of the comfortable world they had known.

Hart looked at Twyla. He could see little of what she was feeling, only a fraction of it leaked through her defenses to be reflected on her face, but he was able to guess at least some of it. He kept recalling the conversation they had had less than two weeks before. What she had asked of life—and what she had *expected*—was to live out her days at this ranch, tending only her father and her brother and her horses. She had been asking for peace if not joy. Now she would have neither.

Spud began to whisper curses at Venable. That, even more than what her father had said, bled the color from Twyla's face. Wynn cut the man off before Hart could react. The foreman leaned forward and took Spud roughly by the front of his nightshirt. "Shut up, you son of a bitch," Wynn hissed. "These people've been good to you." Spud lay sullen but quiet after Wynn released him.

"He has the right, Early," Venable said softly. There was no life in his voice.

"He does not," Wynn protested. Grimes shook his head as well.

"None of us has that right," Hart said. "We know better than to think anything that's happened would ever have been deliberate." Twyla gave him a brief, grateful look. He went on, "But I think we would like to know what did happen."

"Morbid curiosity, Hart?" Venable's lips twisted into a grimace that he intended as a bitter and accusatory smile. He owed Hart the most money and felt toward him the greatest guilt, had singled him out as a target on which to vent his resentment.

"Daddy!" It was Twyla who came to Hart's defense.

"That we *are* entitled to, Dad," Richard said.

Venable twisted his hands in his lap. He did not know how to begin. Falteringly at first and then with increasing speed until the confession poured from him, Venable told them:

"More than ... two years ago, closer to three now it was, I ... met a lady. A very exciting lady. Very pretty. Just thirty-two." Bitterness and perhaps remembered, distant joys tugged at his mouth. "She liked me. So much older ... but she liked me. We began ... seeing each other. A *thing* you young people might call it. I wanted to marry her. Bring her here as my wife. That was when I built this house, you see." He shuddered.

"She told me she was ... legally married already. A prominent man. Separated now but still legally married to him. Couldn't get a divorce. I ... wanted her to. I would have married her even so. She said it was impossible. I didn't care. I wanted her anyway. On any terms. Any conditions. She ... *allowed* me to build a house for her. Near town. And to support her. She likes ... nice things. I wanted her to have them. I began to spend a good bit of money. More than we could afford. That didn't seem so important at the time. We could make it up later." He looked at Wynn. "We started selling more cattle than the herd could stand. Which meant less beef to sell the next time. A circle now coming to its last stages, eh, Early?"

Wynn bobbed his head mutely. Venable continued to knead his fingers. His eyes fell.

"I had some money in the bank. It is long since gone now. I owe ... Richard's school. I owe

Mary's school more." He barked out a short, depreciating laugh. "I'm giving them a grand start in polite society, I know. Send them to the very best of schools. As deadbeats. They can make all sorts of useful social contacts that way."

"Dad . . ."

"No, it's all right, Son. You don't have to say it. I already know. At least . . . I have been blessed with fine and loyal children. You are all I could have wanted you to be and much, much more." He looked at the two who were in the room, looked closely at each of them and smiled. "You can't possibly know how much comfort that knowledge has given me of late. Without that, without you two and Mary, I would have nothing."

He looked at Richard and chuckled. "You begin to see now, Son, why I wanted you to prepare for a career in business." He barked out the ugly laugh again. "At first it was because I expected the ranch to be left in . . . her hands. Later the need became even more urgent. And I am truly sorry, my son.

"At any rate, I went through what I could afford and went right on spending. I knew it was an impossible situation. I tried to cut back, tried to spend less. She still wanted all the nice things. I tried to explain the situation to her. Tried to tell her I couldn't afford to continue. She . . . became cold. Withdrawn from me. Just in little ways at first. Then . . . in others. She began to talk of moving to St. Louis. She said she had relatives there. She could live with them. Be close to nice places. Do gay things. She missed the theater, she said, and the fine dinners and the dances. Maybe she should go back at least for a visit. It would be fun, she said."

Venable rocked back in his chair. He threw his head back and laughed into the ceiling with bitter mirth. "Oh, boys, she did have me hooked. Solid as a fish with your bait clear down in its gullet. I swear she did." His face gradually fell and became grim again. He did not seem to notice it, but now he was looking at the men. He did not look toward his daughter.

"I didn't want her to go, boys. Wouldn't let her go. I told her not to worry about the money. It would work out somehow. I promised her that. *Promised* it.

"That seemed to help. It really did. She was . . . nice to me again. And she seemed to be really trying to cut down on her spending, even after I'd promised we would work it out. I . . . I really thought that was wonderful of her, for her to be so considerate. I really did.

"It didn't get any better, of course. There wasn't any way it could by then. I finally told her about it. She was very . . . understanding. Very warm. She wanted to be helpful. She said she knew a gentleman, the husband of an old friend, who might help. She said she would write to him. He returned a letter, and we corresponded last winter. He had several ideas. He said he was an investor himself and might be able to work out something that would profit us both.

"We met a few months ago. He came here, and we reached a business agreement. He said he was a dealer in many things. He wanted to take a more active interest in livestock, buying on speculation, hoping to resell at a profit. He wanted to deal more in horses especially.

"He bought our mares and weanlings. It was his

people you delivered them to, Early. But he said he knew that was not the kind of help ... she ... and I needed. We ... I ... needed something that would turn a good profit without stripping the ranch of its breeding stock. Not that there was much of anything here to strip by that time. And of course he was right. I did need a quick profit.

"He said he had just paid six-fifty a head for six hundred head of good geldings. He was a businessman. He would not sell them to me at cost. But I needed a high profit and he didn't. He would sell me the horses at seven dollars, and I could take the profit he expected to make by selling them to the Army. It sounded wonderful. I was very grateful to him. So was she. We agreed on what a fine and generous friend he was. Can you imagine that? I was really grateful to him.

"But I didn't have the cash to buy the horses. Forty-two hundred dollars. The money he'd paid me for the mares was already gone, for the hands and for ... her. For other things to keep the place going. She agreed I could sell him the house—her house—and rent it back from him. He was trying to help, after all. The rest I borrowed. Put up everything we had left at that point to secure the loan.

"There wasn't anything to worry about, of course. I would get those six hundred horses and sell them to the Army and make a fat profit and everything would be just fine."

Venable sucked in a deep breath and held it for a long time. "The only thing is, the Remount Service isn't buying any more horses this year. The bottom's fallen clean out of the horse market. And

I still owe the money. The spring herd wasn't anywhere near enough to cover that.

"I thought maybe I could carry those horses over until the market comes back. Pay interest in the meantime but still take a profit on them. Bad as they turned out to be, they should be worth something eventually. Not Army prices, of course. There's not a one of them that meets the remount specifications for size or color—or something. Always some reason they would be rejected. My guess is . . . that those are some government contractor's rejects that he'd normally have sold for hair and hide value. Not that I will ever know.

"Anyway, I thought if we could carry them over we could still do something with them. Something, anyway.

"Well, the past couple weeks I've been trying to get a loan to get us through until next summer. Just until there is a market for horses again, you see. The bank in town already has paper on me, of course." He laughed. "Or they did. *He* bought the note from them. I . . . tried to find a loan elsewhere. Went as far as Chicago. I've dealt with some of those stockyard buyers for years and years. I thought they would vouch for me with their banks. They wouldn't. The word is already out and spreading further. Nobody there would hold my paper. They . . . looked like something smelled bad when I tried to explain to them." He spread his hands. "So that's it, boys. No money. No credit. No prospects. No ranch. End of the V-Slash-4." Venable slumped in his chair with his eyes downcast.

"Why would somebody be stealing horses,

though?" Wynn asked. "Is there some connection there that I don't see?"

"I expect so," Venable said tiredly. "I can't prove it, of course, but it likely is a form of insurance. Make damn sure I can't use those horses at the last minute to pull something out. Then he'll have everything. Absolutely everything."

"They sure took you to the cleaners, Ti," Wynn said with sympathy.

"Hell, Early, they haven't hardly begun yet." If anything, Venable sounded more tired than ever, without hope or even interest now that the story was out. It was as if having told it he could now withdraw from it. His voice was a monotone. "The note I signed, the one he holds now, carries the ranch itself as part of the collateral." He chuckled in the same flat monotone. "They not only took me and took it all, they had me paying for the privilege of them doing it to me."

"And your . . . friend, Dad? What about her?"

"In the same house." His face contorted briefly. He dragged it back under control. "With him."

"Oh, my God."

"I'm sorry, Richard. Truly."

"I know."

Hart looked at Twyla. She was as still as if she were carved from stone except for her hands. They were twisting and kneading in her lap much the same way her father had been doing throughout most of his explanation. Wet tear-tracks streaked her face but were ignored. Hart wondered if she even knew she was crying. She had to have been listening, aware of all that was said, yet Hart had the impression one of them could fire a revolver in the small room and get no reaction from her. It was understandable, he decided. She had just seen the end of the world. And she could not even look forward here to the release of Judgment.

Quietly the three hired men turned and filed out the door. They tried to make no noise as they descended the staircase and let themselves out.

XXIII

Twyla came to Hart the next morning. Her manner was hesitant, almost shy. It was most unlike her, but he reflected that nothing was quite the same now as it had been.

On the surface, however, things were little changed. Grimes had not ridden a guard circle the night before, but after breakfast he and Wynn had self-consciously brushed at their jeans and taken their hats from the pegs. "Might as well go look at them horses," Wynn had said. The two of them caught horses and rode out to work. They knew they would not be paid for it, but the habit of work was strong in them. And the V-Slash-4 animals still needed tending.

Hart had not seen Richard that morning. Nor had he heard Venable ride out again. He suspected that Titus Venable's day-long absences were ended now.

Twyla stood uncertainly in the doorway of his kitchen. "May I . . . come in?"

"That's kind of a dumb question, isn't it? I mean, it *is* your kitchen."

"For a few more months," she said. "Then it won't be."

"Look . . ."

"No. Please. It's all right. And I'd rather not talk about it if you don't mind."

"Sure. Uh, would you like some coffee? It's my turn to offer some, you know."

She smiled. "I think I'd like that, hey-boy." She dragged a pair of tall stools next to the kitchen-center work table and waited for him to bring the coffee. He could not remember how she took hers and was sorry he could not.

"I'd like to ask a favor of you, hey-boy. If you don't need to leave today, that is. If you plan on going right away, well, just say so."

"Hell, I got no place to go and nothing to do. If there's something I can do . . . why not? If I can, anyway."

"I . . . Richard doesn't know much about driving." She giggled. "Smart as he is, he never *has* been able to hitch a team right. And you never saw anybody with worse hands than him when it comes to handling driving reins." She launched into a long story about Richard's troubles with a team of mules when he was a boy. Hart listened with half an ear and wondered why she was working so hard to put off asking the favor of him.

"Anyway," she said, "he's no help at all with such things. And . . . I'd really kind of like him to stay close to Daddy for a while. That's the real reason, I guess."

"Your pa's taking this pretty hard, isn't he?"

"He sat in his office all night last night. I don't know if he got any sleep. I doubt it. He's still there. Not doing anything. He's just sitting there."

There was not much Hart could have said to comfort her. He waited for her to choose her own time to go ahead. Finally she did.

"The thing is . . . Oh, *hell*, hey-boy. I just hate to ask you to keep on doing for us. We owe you for all that horse breaking and for your wages and I don't know what else. I just hate to pile a favor on top of all that."

He shrugged. "If I don't want to do it, I'll say so. Fair enough?"

"That's fair. Well, what it is, Spud wants to leave today. The quicker the better, he says. We don't have any way to get him and his things to town."

"For cryin' out loud, girl. Is that all you want?" He laughed. "You prob'ly wouldn't believe some of the things I was getting ready to hear you ask for. Of course I'll drive him in. My word, that's no bother at all."

From the relief on her face he might have just agreed to extend her father's loans by another month or longer. She rose and said, "I'll go tell him."

"Fine. If you like I'll pack his gear and find his saddle. Grimes hung it somewhere around here when we brought that horse in. I sure didn't think Spud was in any shape to travel, though. Sure didn't."

"The truth is that he's not. But he insists. He just keeps cussing Daddy and saying how poorly we've used him." She sounded as upset about Spud's ingratitude as about her father's problems.

"His choice, I suppose. A man is always entitled to make a damn fool of himself if that's what he really wants to do."

"Don't I know it," she said bitterly.

"Hey now. I didn't intend for that to have two cutting edges on it. Honest. I never even thought about . . . that . . . or I wouldn't have said it."

"Okay. Nothing meant, nothing taken."

"Good. Now you go on and get Richard to dress that idiot and kick him down the stairs. I'll have the wagon and his gear in front of the house directly, and you can be shut of him."

She nodded and gave him a small smile.

Hart went to the bunkhouse—the first time he had ever had occasion to enter the building—and found Spud's gear easily enough. There were only two bunks being used so he had a fifty-fifty chance of being right even if he guessed. As it was he prowled through the first bunk area he came to until he found a shirt he recognized as belonging to Harry Grimes. He went to the other bunk and packed everything he found there.

It did not take long. A cowhand has few personal possessions. A bedroll. A canvas warbag more than large enough to hold a change of work clothes and a set of town clothing. A smaller bag containing a razor and a pair of dress spurs. A bundle of tobacco cards bearing pictures of amply endowed women. That was all Spud owned. No change of socks or underwear, Hart noticed. Nor any chaps. Not that they were needed in open country like this, but still it was odd. Hart hoped he was not overlooking anything.

Hart carried the bedroll and warbag to the wagon and found Spud's saddle where he would least have expected it, hanging clean and freshly oiled on a rack in the saddle shed. Grimes must have taken the time do that for him. If Spud owned his own bridle and bit Hart did not know where they might be so he took only the saddle. He hitched the team and drove the wagon around to the front of the house.

Spud and Richard were waiting on the front stoop.

"You took your damned time," Spud grumbled. He looked like a scarecrow come to life with his splint-straight arms held slightly angled out to each side. Richard helped him down the house steps and onto the wagon seat. Spud could not have managed it on his own, and Hart would not have helped him. Spud's complaints after all the care he had received from Twyla gave Hart a place to focus his frustrations.

Ignoring Spud, Hart asked, "Do you need anything while I'm in town?"

"I'll see," Richard said. He went inside and returned almost immediately. "Twy says we don't need anything. But I don't know how far ahead she plans for her shopping to last. How are your supplies over at the cookhouse?"

"I can't really say that I've paid much attention, but it's been a long time since Brown bought supplies. I sure haven't got anything since he left on the market drive, and that's been a spell."

Richard dug into his pocket and pulled out a light collection of coins. He counted it. He had twenty-three dollars. Hart felt positive it was all the money Richard had to his name. The youngster held back three dollars and gave Hart the rest.

"Stock up as far as this will go while you're in there. Cheap stuff that spreads far. You know what I mean. Dried beans. Rice. That sort of thing."

"Sure."

Richard at least was thinking clearly, Hart thought. He seemed to be taking it better than anyone else, perhaps because much of his closeness with both ranch and family was a result more of memory than of recent association. He had been away at school for several years.

"Hurry up with this crap, will you?" Spud complained. "I wanta get to town."

Hart turned on him. He grabbed the front of the man's shirt and shook him with no regard for any lingering, invalid pains. "Shut your mouth you ungrateful son of a bitch or I'll rip that ear back off your head."

"I don't have to take that from you nor anybody else. Damn it, that's twice in as many days that one of you bastards has called me that, and if my arms weren't . . ."

"If your arms weren't busted already I'd bust them myself. Now shut your face. Take that time to think about just *why* people keep telling you your mother's itches are caused by fleas."

Richard looked apologetically up at Spud on the wagon seat. "Look, man, I . . ."

"Aw, don't worry about it," Hart said. "He ain't worth it." He picked up the contact with the team and drove away before Richard had a chance to demean himself.

Spud sat in sullen silence beside him, nursing injured pride. A few miles down the road he began to fidget on the seat. He clamped his jaw firmly shut and sweat began to roll down his forehead. With his arms in splints he could not reach it to wipe it off. Finally, after they had covered perhaps half the distance to town, Spud could stand it no longer. "Stop the damn wagon, will you?"

Hart had been watching Spud's growing discomfort. His answer was cheerful, almost eager. "Glad to," he said. He lightly reined the team to a halt.

"I gotta take a leak," Spud said.

"Go right ahead. I'll wait for you."

"Now *look*, dammit."

"Yeah?"

"You know I can't get up and down by myself. Can't get at my damn fly buttons neither. You'll have to help me."

Hart laughed. "I *have* to do that, do I?" He shoved his wavering eyes close to Spud's sweating face and leered happily. "Somehow, Spud old fellow, I just don't think that is something I *have* to do." He faced forward again and took up the reins. "Getting off?"

"No," Spud said. He was in misery.

Hart drove on at a more brisk and bouncing pace. Spud's wriggling became increasingly more pronounced for the next few miles until suddenly his face flushed dark red with acute embarrassment. A wet stain spread across his jeans and down his left leg. "You *bastard*," he moaned.

"Uh huh." Hart sounded as if he thoroughly agreed. And liked it.

The wagon bumped on at a more normal speed the rest of the way into town. Hart stopped outside the freight office, piled Spud's gear on the already cluttered loading dock and motioned Spud out of the wagon.

"How'm I supposed to get down?" Spud asked with self pity lacing his tone of voice.

"Jump. Fall. It don't make any difference to me. The wagon's going over to Perce's store. If you're still on it when I start back, I'll throw you off."

"You don't give a man much, do you?"

"Just exactly what he asks for, and I don't much care what that is."

Spud stood and teetered uncertainly in the wagon box for a moment. He jumped and landed heavily, but upright, on the platform. Hart climbed into the driving box and pulled away without looking back.

At the mercantile he found that the word was clearly out. Perce had been friendly the several times Hart had seen him before. The man still was cordial, but he eyed the wagon with the V-Slash-4 painted on its side and said, "I can't give you credit. Sorry."

"You'll take cash, won't you?"

Perce smiled and said, "You just bet I will. Say, uh, maybe the things I've been hearing aren't true?" He quite openly put it as a question. Hart thought he sounded concerned as well as curious, perhaps even for more than business reasons.

"That kinda depends on what you've heard, doesn't it?"

The man did not try to duck, his expression was still open and full of concern. "The people in town are saying that the V-4 is about to go under. I, uh . . . I'd be happy to hear it isn't so."

"I'm damned if I'll lie to you," Hart told him. "It could happen. But don't go counting the Venables out yet, Perce. The old man's been awful poorly used by some sonavabitch, but they can't bury him until he's dead. And that ain't quite yet."

Perce nodded. "I'll put the word around that that's so. And, uh, if you need anything on tick, well, go ahead and load it out. Ti's given me a lot of business in the years past. By God, I don't see why I shouldn't trust the man now."

"That's mighty kind of you, Perce, and I'll tell him what you offered. But I was told to pay cash for what I take." He grinned. "That'll be little enough, but we'd rather do it that way just the same."

"Good for Ti. The others are going to hear about *that* too."

They loaded out hundred pound sacks of dried beans and a quantity of pickling salts to preserve fresh meat—Hart realized their days of being wasteful and unthinking with fresh beef were ended—and when they were done had nearly a full wagon load in exchange for Richard's twenty dollars. Hart suspected Perce was being deliberately generous to them in his pricing, but it was his right to do so if he wished. Hart did not argue.

When they were done Hart thanked the storekeeper and drove on without stopping for a beer or other relaxation. The few dollars he had in his pocket might be needed for something more important later.

Spud's gear was still on the freight dock, but Spud was nowhere in sight when Hart drove past. Hart was still angry with Spud. He had expected the man to show more loyalty to the brand he rode for than Spud had been willing to give. When he thought about it Hart decided he had been surprised by both Spud and Harry Grimes. Spud had given less and Grimes far more than Hart would have guessed.

People, he thought. Sometimes you just couldn't tell about them ahead of time.

XXIV

"I'll tell Dad about it. I know it will please him," Richard said when Hart related what Perce had told him. "You know, that was awfully decent of him, wasn't it?"

"Uh huh. You still have some friends in town, anyway."

Richard seemed to take some measure of cheer from that.

They unloaded the wagon into the pantry in the Venable home. The load took up all the available storage space, with the huge burlap sacks crowding the floor as well.

"At least no one is going to starve for a spell," Hart said.

"No, and listen, Gotch, we talked about this today and with so few of us here it would be pointless for us to continue dividing the cooking. There is room for us all in our kitchen. Twy will take over the cooking."

"Does she know that?" Hart asked skeptically.

"She is the one who insisted," Richard said with a laugh. "She has to cook for us anyway. Three more mouths won't even be noticed."

"What about your pa? He might not want me at your family table, you know."

"It will be all right with him, I can assure you." From the tone of Richard's voice and the set of his jaw Hart wondered if it had already become an issue among the members of the family. Still, it was their business, and Hart guessed that Richard and Twyla would be maintaining their pride in the future by doing as much of the ranch work themselves as they could possibly manage.

"All right," Hart said. "It will damn sure please Wynn and Grimes anyhow. I don't claim to be any kind of a cook, and I think they'd agree with that."

"They do," Richard said with a laugh. "In fact, I would say they are delighted."

"Cain't blame them. So am I."

The family members were quiet during the meal. Wynn and Grimes tried to cover their silence by talking at great length about the good condition of the grass. Their efforts did not help; they only emphasized how few animals there were to graze it. Hart told them all again what Perce had said. That seemed to go over better.

When they had exchanged their plates for last cups of coffee, Venable spoke to the men.

"Boys, I guess I must thank you all over again for helping us today. It was fine of you." He went so far as to meet Hart's eyes when he said it. The old man was trying, Hart realized. "I, we all, appreciate it. But you know what the situation is. We don't want to hold you back from anything else.

You needn't feel there is any obligation for you to remain. You know I can't pay you for your help."

"If you want us off the place you can say so, Ti," Wynn told him. "Otherwise, me anyway, I guess I'll stick as long as you need me. I been here—what?—five years now? A little longer can't hurt."

Grimes looked uncomfortable. He shrugged his shoulders. "Nobody's hiring this time of year anyway. If you're still feedin' us there's no reason I can't hang around 'til the fall work opens up anyhow. Won't be any paying jobs until then, an' I don't mind working for my eats."

Twyla looked at Hart.

"I'll be here," he said simply.

Venable looked down at his cup. His shoulders shook ever so slightly. When finally he looked up again his face was stern and rigid but his eyes were still damply misted. "Thanks, boys," he said in a tight voice.

"How long until your note is due?" Hart intruded. "If you don't mind my asking."

Venable sighed. "No reason you shouldn't. Not quite three months now. The tenth day of October. Interest and principal are due then."

"That isn't as bad as it might be, Ti," Wynn said hopefully. "Something might turn up before then. The horse market could open up. Something. You never know."

"Thank you, Early, but I wouldn't count on that if I were you. Believe me. I have racked my brain looking for a way out. I don't see one."

"Well, a man can hope, Ti. He can always do that."

"Yes. Not much else. But we can always do that."

Grimes appeared to be concentrating on something. He raised his head with a look of comprehension. "Damn!" he said. "Excuse me, miss. We missed the celebrations on the Fourth, didn't we?"

Twyla laughed. "You sure did. You were out chasing horses on the Fourth."

Grimes snapped his fingers. "I sure had been looking forward to that. I sure love those horse races."

Grimes' disappointment over something as trivial as having missed a public celebration lightened the mood in the room. They were all feeling better as they left the table and drifted toward their separate quarters. They were on a ranch where every hand had a whole building all to himself, Hart realized with wry amusement. No pay but a whole building all to yourself for sleeping purposes. And good food, too. He could still say he had held worse jobs before this one.

Twyla caught up with him near the cookhouse. Her face was indistinct in the darkness.

"Could I talk with you for a minute, hey-boy?" She sounded excited.

"Sure. Say, I'll bet you need a hand with those dishes, don't you?"

"That isn't what I wanted."

"Oh hell, I didn't mean it was. C'mon. I'll walk back with you. You can wash and talk at the same time, can't you?"

"Of course," she said cheerfully.

"That works out fine. I can dry and listen, both at the same time."

"Amazing."

They walked back to the house side by side. Hart

was aware of the soft air of the summer evening and of the whir and chirp and drone of insects around them. He was going to regret having to leave this place. He decided he liked it better than anyplace he had worked before. He could even tolerate Twyla. She wasn't all *that* unpretty really. Those eyes of hers. Feisty little thing though, he thought with a grin.

Hart carried in fresh buckets of water while she filled her wash basin from the reservoir in the range and shaved soap chips into it.

"There's a dish towel hanging on the back of the pantry door," she told him.

He got it and stood to his post by the rinse water tub. He could hear someone moving around upstairs. She began to wash.

"I've been thinking," she said.

"Uh huh?"

"About what Harry Grimes said at supper."

"About missing all that hoo-rahing and speech-making? So what!"

"No, not the speeches. About the horse races. Hey-boy, we've got one really good race horse here. Gray Lad." Her excitement showed all the more, and she scrubbed at the dishes all the harder. "I was thinking . . . he might be the answer to our troubles. Hey-boy, I'll just bet that big, gray bastard can run like the wind."

Hart threw back his head and laughed. She looked offended. "Hey, I'm sorry," he said quickly. "You're thinking, girl. You're trying. I'll give you that. But it wouldn't work. I wish it would, but you'd best put that out of your mind."

"I don't know why it wouldn't," she said indignantly. "You just don't like the idea because a woman came up with it."

"Hell, even you know better than that. Neither me nor your pa nor anyone else would let this place be ruined just because you were the one to come up with an idea for keeping it. Looka here now." He dried his hands and took her elbow and pulled her to one of the kitchen chairs. He turned another around and straddled it, facing her.

"There's lots of reasons it wouldn't work," he explained. "First, you don't *know* if the horse is really fast, and there's no other animal on the place good enough to try him against so you could find out for sure, with the kind of competition a real running horse would give. Also, he isn't trained to run. To run a horse for big money he's got to be trained for it. He has to really know what he's doing. That can be done with any horse that has the heart to run, but it takes time.

"And he isn't in shape to run. Hard as he looks and feels on the outside, he's been paddling around in that little corral with long feet and no hard work to do for I don't know how long. He's too soft. For real speed a horse has to be conditioned for it. That takes even *more* time. A lot of it.

"And you don't have a rider. For big money races you want a real little fella that doesn't weigh hardly anything but that knows what he's doing. If you could find a rider you'd still have to hire him. And pay him, win or lose. That takes money.

"And you'd have to find someone to run him against. There's no celebrations coming up soon. No public races. So you'd have to find a match race against somebody with a really good horse and confidence enough to back him. What's worse, your gray horse *looks* fast. He probably is, or would be if he was ready for it, but he just plain looks like a sprinting horse. That means about the only opponent you could find for a match race would be someone who makes his living running a really fast horse that he keeps trained and fit. That's putting your boy against the wall right from the start, because somebody that makes his living from running horses knows pretty much what he can win and what he can't or he couldn't manage to stay in the game.

"And finally, maybe most important, in a match race like that you got to have money to start with or you can't make any even if your horse does win. If you want to win a couple thousand dollars you got to have a couple thousand of your own that you can put up and be willing to lose, just in case your horse don't win." He shook his head. "I'm sorry, girl. I really am. But it just wouldn't work."

She gave him a weak, false smile. With an attempt at lightness she tossed her head and said, "It was a thought, anyway."

"It was that. Come on, now. Let's finish those dishes." He stood.

"Damn it all, hey-boy. There must be *some*thing I can do. I can't just stand here and wash a bunch of damn dishes and wait for the ax to fall."

"Of course not, but while we're all trying to think of something that will help, we'll just go on with the regular stuff. Like washing dishes."

She stood up with a long drawn sigh. "I suppose so." She returned to the wash basin and went back to work. "Thanks for telling me, anyway."

"Sure. And I really do wish it could've worked."

When he was alone in his room again Hart lay awake for a long time, staring at the ceiling and thinking. He had never before really considered how a man might go about getting together a large sum of money in a hurry. He had at times pondered the ways a man might slowly build a future for himself. Everyone was entitled to such dreams as those, he thought. Venable's problem was something else entirely.

He lay awake through much of the night, and the same thought kept coming back to him time and time again: The key to any solution, if ever one was to be found, had to lie in that herd of Remount-rejected geldings. They were really all Venable owned free and clear. If they could not pull him out of it, he would go under and take the V-Slash-4 with him.

A vague notion kept tickling the back of his mind, and every time he tried to grasp it it wiggled free, as elusive as a lizard on a flat rock. Near dawn he drifted into sleep. He awakened half an hour later and forced back the smile that kept trying to creep onto his face. It was too soon for that.

At breakfast he announced he would be gone for a few days. He would need a sack of food to carry along. The others assumed he had decided to move on until he said, "I'll be gone two days. Three at the most. And you people guard them horses 'til I get back, hear?"

Wynn and Grimes and Richard nodded. That, guarding the horses, was about all they had been doing of late. That was about all there was left to do on the place.

Hart was saddled and gone a half hour later. He would not say where he was going. Twyla noted with an unexpected measure of relief that he was riding one of the ranch geldings. His bay mare was still grazing in the horse trap.

XXV

Hart returned the afternoon of the third day. He was wearing a broad, satisfied grin but—although the others did not notice it—no spurs. He had spent what he had left in his pocket and had had to sell his spurs in order to complete what he had started. Twyla and Richard were at home. Their father had decided to ride with Wynn for the day. Grimes was asleep in the bunkhouse. He was still riding nighthawk.

"You look pleased with yourself," Twyla said.

"Uh huh. Very."

"You must have a good reason then."

"I do."

"Are you going to tell us about it?"

"Uh huh. This evening. When everybody's here."

"Oh, come on now. Tell us. Give us a hint anyway." Hart's mood was contagious. She had caught it and was nearly jumping up and down in her eagerness to be told. Almost literally jumping up and down. She kept bouncing onto her toes and rocking back on her heels. "Please tell us. Please!"

"Later," was all he would say. Throughout the afternoon he sat in their kitchen drinking coffee and enjoying her efforts to wheedle the information out of him. It did not work but he did not discourage her attempts.

They ate earlier than normal that evening. Twyla had the meal ready so early she insisted that Richard ride out and call Wynn and their father in before everything was ruined. Both Richard and Hart knew that the things she had prepared would have stayed warm in the oven without harm, but Richard did not argue with his sister. He saddled a horse and rode. Hart woke Grimes.

As soon as they were all at the table Twyla renewed her attack on Hart.

"After supper, dammit," Hart said finally. He was becoming annoyed. She caught his tone of voice and subsided. Only when they were cooling their coffee would he speak again.

"How much exactly do we need to pay off that note come October?" he asked. None of them still on the place thought his use of the word "we" out of place.

Venable knew the answer to that readily enough. The figure had been on his mind constantly for weeks. "With interest," he said, "two thousand four hundred fifty-six dollars. Exactly."

"Uh huh," Hart said. He fingered his chin and grinned. The others were totally silent. Their attention was wholly concentrated on him. Hart dipped two fingers into his vest pocket and pulled out a folded square of flimsy paper. He tossed the paper onto the table in front of Venable. "Read it," he invited.

Venable unfolded the paper with trembling fingers, guarding himself against hope while he did so. He read the paper and his eyes came alight with sudden joy. He started to rise, thought better of it and dropped to his knees beside the table. He was shaking. A moment later he climbed back into his chair.

"For God's sake, what *is* it?" Twyla cried. Richard was more direct. He grabbed the paper and read it himself.

"*Mister* Hart, here," Venable said, "has found a buyer for our horses. Any number up to four hundred head." With glee he added, "At twenty dollars a head. Twenty dollars. That is eight thousand dollars."

"Where?" Richard asked. "The telegram doesn't say where they're to be delivered, but I see it's signed by a man in San Antonio."

"Uh huh," Hart said. "He's a buyer at the big horse market there, but the horses are to be delivered to the nearest railhead. They pay transportation from there."

Richard sighed. Wynn and Grimes were grinning. Twyla was too exhilarated to know what to do. She sat quivering, looking from one to another around the table.

"There is a condition," Hart said quietly.

Venable's face fell. "What is it you want?" he asked dully. The look he gave Hart was no longer one of gratitude. He clearly thought Hart was going to keep him in a wringer but transfer the hand on the crank from the note holder to himself.

Hart laughed. "Not what you're thinking," he said, "but it won't be a real easy condition to meet. We'll have to do a bit of work."

"If that's all it takes . . ." Richard said.

"What is your condition, young man?" Venable asked.

"Not mine," Hart said. "The thing is . . . the thing is, I sold your horses as being broke to harness. I sold them as light harness stock."

"What!"

"Oh my," Wynn said softly.

"That's what I said," Hart told them happily. "The damned Army ruined the market for saddle horses, but I kinda got to thinking about that. And Early sold that stumblebum spotted stallion of his for a hundred dollars as a fancy harness horse." He grinned. "Well, the biggest market for driving horses in the whole damn world, I guess, is down at San Antone. There's always buyers there from the east. Some they even ship out to Europe and such places. So . . . I sent a few telegrams. Nothing has hurt that market. The remount don't affect them at all. So I sold 'em those four hundred head as green broke light harness horses. For, well, delivery trucks, hansoms, that sort of thing."

"But damn it all, man, don't you realize," Venable moaned, "as soon as the buyer found out those horses aren't broken the deal would be off anyway. Even if I'd deliver a horse on a lie like that —and by God I will not," he slammed a fist on the table, "I would have to return every penny of what he paid. Why, that would do no more than give the ranch to this, uh," he looked at the paper again, "this William Marcus. No sir, I will not be a party to that."

"Oh, I wasn't lyin' to him," Hart said mildly. "By the time those animals walk up the chutes they'll be broke to harness. *That* is what I meant when I said we'd have a bit of work to do first."

"A bit of work," Wynn said. "My, oh my. Four hundred head of unbroke horses. And five of us to break them, every one of them, in—say—two months time. To give us time to get to the railhead with them, that's what it would have to be."

"Eighty head apiece," Richard said. "That's more than a horse a day per person. And none of us knowing a thing about how to break a horse to harness, I'll wager."

"Oh, I've done it before," Wynn said. "Ti prob'ly has too, haven't you, Ti? It takes about a week to break your average horse, right? So you figure we have eight weeks, five people. Forty head at twenty dollars. That'd be . . . eight hundred dollars. Would that help, Ti?"

The old man shook his head. "No. I'm afraid it would not even postpone things. But of course it would allow me to pay you boys what I owe you. We can do that much at any rate."

"I'm willing," Grimes said.

"We all are," Richard added. He smiled at Hart. "It seems your idea was a good one after all, Gotch."

Hart turned to Twyla and asked, "Girl, have you ever noticed how easy these fellas give up?" He laughed. He was enjoying this even if no one else was. "Boys, boys, now you fellas listen to me, you hear? Now I promised that Mr. Marcus four hundred head of harness horses, and that is just what he's going to get. Every last one of them. And they *will* be ready to work in light harness." He smiled. "The four of you are going to do the breaking. With a little guidance from me. Meantime I'll be doing some gentling after you do the real breaking work." He chuckled. "You fellas might not realize it yet, but you're each of you going to break two horses a day. I figure that oughta work out just about right."

The others looked at him as if they thought he was a bit light in the head.

Twyla stood. "I have some berries I picked yesterday. If you gentlemen will wait, I will bake a pie. I think we need a . . . a celebration for this. Don't you?"

"No, ma'am," Grimes said, "but I'll be happy to eat your pie."

At breakfast Hart was still in high humor, full of confidence and eager to get started. The men had had time to think about Hart's idea overnight. They had even less confidence than they had shown the night before.

"Dammit, man, you know we couldn't begin to handle all those horses ourselves," Venable said. "We couldn't do the job with three times as many people, and we have no money to pay you much less a regular crew. I say it can't be done, Hart."

Richard put another slab of meat on his plate and said, "I believe I know what he is doing, Dad, and I think it is a very kind and thoughtful thing too."

Venable's eyebrows went up in curiosity. So did Hart's, but with amusement. "What?" both asked at the same time.

Richard looked at Hart and smiled sadly. "Dad, I believe he's trying to keep us busy, give us hope and keep us so busy we won't have time to worry right up until the loss has become a fact. Then we will be busy coping with our new situation so we still won't have time to worry. As I said, it is a generous thought."

Venable nodded wisely. Hart laughed.

"If I'd thought of something like that I just might've done it," Hart said, "but I guess I ain't as bright as you. I never would've thought of doing that."

"Hart, I just don't see that any five men could break four hundred horses in two months time," Venable said. "Now that's all there is to it. Maybe Richard's right and maybe he's not, but I don't see that your idea could ever work. Early?"

The foreman looked at Hart and hesitated. Reluctantly he admitted, "It don't seem possible for a fact."

"Grimes?"

Harry Grimes was taken by surprise. He expected to listen, not talk. "Don't ask me," he pleaded. "I don't know 'bout any of this, one way or another."

"Well now, it sure looks like you fellas have cooled down considerable since last night," Hart said. "That's up to you, of course, but I'll tell you one thing that's as straight as anything you ever heard. No, I'll tell you two things. The first is that we *can* ready those horses and deliver them in time. The second is this. We won't even begin to get the job done if we all aren't willing to work our butts off every day between now and then. And that means starting right now. If you aren't all willing to tear into this and to stay with it, well, it'll never get done. And I do mean *all* of us."

They were as depressed this morning as they had been since Venable's talk with them. Hart could tell they were not willing to make the attempt.

They had no real hope the idea could work. Why bother trying?

Twyla shoved her chair angrily away from the table. She stalked across the room to the oven, took a sheet of biscuits out and clattered it onto the table top with a crash that made them all jump.

"There, dammit," she declared. "Sit there and stuff your faces. You can choke it down for the next couple months like a bunch of boar hogs at a trough. I'll just stay here and cook for you, all right? That will be *so* much easier than trying to do something about it, don't you agree? Is that what you want?" She marched around the table and flung herself back into her chair. "Don't just sit there. Eat up, you lazy hogs."

"What brought that on, Twy?" Richard asked. He looked hurt. The rest, including Hart, looked embarrassed.

"Dear brother," she said sweetly, a faint dusting of sugar over bile, "has it occurred to you, or to any of you," she swept the table with her eyes, "that none of you has asked the most obvious question of all? Well, has it?"

"Twy, you don't know what you're talking about here. We know more about this than you do, I promise. Dad and Early do, anyway."

"Bullshit," she said. "I still say none of you has bothered to ask him the first and most important question of them all."

"What are you talking about, Twy? What the hell question do you mean?"

"I mean, stupid, that no one has bothered to ask the one thing that would let you make up your own pig-stupid minds. I mean, no one has bothered to ask how he intends to do it. You keep saying it can't be done. Why, you don't even know really what it is he wants you to do."

Richard was unimpressed. He rolled his eyes and threw his hands in the air. "All right. All right, Twy. I will please you. We all will please you. *Any*thing to please you, by all means." He turned to Hart. "Would you tell us, sir, how in hell you intend for us to break four hundred horses in the next two months?" Richard sat back in his chair and folded his arms.

Hart told them.

While he talked the men began to sit forward in their chairs. They took quick, furtive looks toward each other, sheepishly at first and then with growing interest. When he was done they coughed into their fists and shifted in their chairs.

"It . . . might just work that way," Wynn said slowly.

"It could be worth a try," Richard said.

"What do you want us to do?" Venable asked.

"Hammer and saw first," Hart said. "Then the horses." They reached for their hats.

XXVI

He had them working as a team, Venable and Wynn raising a racket with heavy hammers, Richard and himself maintaining a steady, rasping grind with a pair of bucksaws. Harry Grimes shuttled to and from the farthest corral on horseback. Grimes was tearing the corral rails down, roping them into bundles and dragging them in to make do for the lumber they needed. He had already worn out one rope from the friction between timber and soil and would soon need another.

"You're getting ahead of us, Harry," Hart told him. "Why don't you give Ti a hand with that cross bracing."

"Sure," he said eagerly. Grimes felt he had been given the easiest and the least skilled job and he resented it, even though he could do most of it from horseback. Normally he would not consent to do any work that did not require a horse. Now he was more than willing to use hammer and nails with the others.

Richard straightened and leaned backward to

ease the strain caused by so much bending. "I've been thinking," he announced.

"It's about time, boy," his father said without looking up from his work.

"No, I'm serious, Dad. I've been thinking about those horses."

"Yes?"

"We can't guard them and break them too. That is where we are most vulnerable."

Venable stopped pounding. "Yes." The others took a breather as well. Richard had their attention.

"If they raid the horse herd while we are busy with the breaking they could still ruin us. We have to deliver a large herd if we are to win, and as tight as our schedule is already they would not even have to take the horses to defeat us. Scattering them would probably be enough for them." He looked at the others and got a round of nods.

Richard grinned. "What I was thinking was, you could go to this man who holds your note and let him know he's won."

"What?" Titus Venable sounded upset.

"That's right. Oh, you wouldn't want to tell him right out that he had won. That might just make him suspicious. But you *could* go cuss him out. Really yell and carry on. You know. Call him everything you can think of. Cuss him for ruining you. Let it slip out that you gathered the horses and tried to sell them, but there's no market any more. Accuse him of knowing that before he ever sold you the horses. He probably did anyway, though we'll never know. Anyway, that would explain us rounding them up and running his horsethieves away. The big thing though, Dad, before you stomp out in a huff you should swear and be damned that he won't walk onto your property one day before October tenth. That way we can hole up here like we're hiding our faces from the world, and he won't think a thing about it. And I'm betting he won't bother to pay any more to keep a crew of tame thieves around if he doesn't think he needs them." Richard chuckled. "He'll figure he will be getting the horses back soon enough anyway so why pay someone to steal them for him."

"Sounds awful good to me," Hart said.

"It could work," Venable said. He laughed. "I'll go in town tomorrow while you boys move the horses in close. By Jove, I'm going to have fun doing it too. I can cuss him right and left—been wanting to do that anyway—and it will all be for the good."

They resumed their attack on the cut wood, each of them in high spirits and growing more confident as they worked.

By evening they were finished with their construction projects. The results were unbeautiful by the most charitable estimation. Built of used timbers and posts and rails and oddments of milled lumber, with whatever had come to hand, they had assembled four blocky, ungainly and immensely heavy sleds on the order of the stoneboats used in other parts of the country to haul rocks out of plowed fields.

The sleds were flat bottomed and had no runners. Their entire weight would drag the ground. They were nearly as wide as they were long, making them virtually impossible to tip over. To add even more weight to them the men piled them full of dirt and as much scrap iron as they could find. At the front of each sled was chained a massive, jury-rigged doubletree capable of withstanding the most violent plunges of even a heavy draft horse.

They ate well that night, the flavor of their meal enchanced by peals of laughter and repeated jokes about each other's clumsiness with carpenter's tools. They were more tired than after twice as many hours working in the saddle. Their hands were raw and sore. No one seemed to mind.

Twyla capped the evening with a surprise. She had baked dried apple pies while they worked. They finished two of her pies and made a start on the last one before they declared themselves tickfull. Even then they were reluctant to break the mood by leaving the table. They stayed and drank coffee and eventually moved only when Venable remembered a bottle of long-aged corn whiskey in his office. It was late when they sought their beds.

The next day Venable rode toward town while the other men took their time about moving the horse herd to the flats immediately surrounding the ranch headquarters. There would be enough grass within sight of the buildings to last for the little time they would have need of it. The stand would take years to recover afterward, after such heavy grazing, but theirs was an all-or-nothing gamble. If it failed the grass would not be their worry. If it succeeded the damage would be a small price to pay for the victory.

In the afternoon Hart worked the gray stud while the others stood at the rail to offer their criticism and none-too-gentle comments. It would be the last chance he would have to work with the horse for some time, he knew, and he did it for the sheer pleasure of it.

All of them were relaxed. They did little that might be considered work. Grimes wandered along the fence rails collecting splinter-lodged tail hairs that he would sort by color and save for a horsehair belt he wanted to braid. Richard sprawled in the shade with a book. Wynn entered his house in broad daylight—probably the first time he had done so in months—and lay down for a rest—probably the first time he had ever done so. They were gathering their strength for the work to come.

When Venable returned they gathered eagerly around him. They were careful to do it outside of Twyla's hearing.

"What'd he say, Ti?"

"Read it back to us."

"Don't just stand there grinning, dammit. *Tell* us."

Venable coughed into his fist. He removed his hat and examined the sweatband. He replaced the hat and looked at them. "Boys," he said, "I was not polite to that man today." He sounded quite proud of himself.

"I found him at home," Venable said. "The, uh, lady was out. She missed my performance. Pity. I think she would have enjoyed it.

"Anyway, I didn't even knock politely at the door. I barged right in. Found him sitting in an armchair with his feet propped up and a decanter of wine at his elbow and a newspaper in his lap. The very picture of a gentleman. His name is Jones, by the way. Paul G. Jones. A true gentleman, P.G. Jones." Venable's eyes were aglow with pleasure.

"Mr. Jones was not alarmed by my presence. He seemed to be enjoying it. I, of course, was steaming mad. I wouldn't be surprised if there was smoke curling out of my ears. I really had myself worked up from thinking about what I would tell him. Spent the whole ride in thinking about that.

"Boys, I started out by calling that poor Mr. Jones a son of a bitch. I suggested his mother had bedded with a donkey before she whelped him and therefore he was half an ass as well. I elaborated on that at some length. I suggested he himself was a Sodomite and a procurer. The lady's reputation suffered as well. My comments were not kind to her. I expressed suspicion about her parentage and compared it with his own."

Venable laughed. He looked younger, almost the same as when Hart first met him. "Boys, Mr. Jones did not even get angry. He listened and nodded his head, and he smiled and smiled and smiled. It was like seeing a snake smile. I expected to see his tongue start flicking out any time there. Forked, of course.

"I began to get warmed up to it. Really mad. I was sweating. He said he was concerned about my health. He hoped I wouldn't have a heart attack. I returned to my original subject and repeated what I thought of him as an individual. I repeated what I had already said and added a few last-minute thoughts as well.

"I returned to the subject of the lady. I listed every item I could remember giving her and informed him of the value of each." Venable smiled grimly. "I don't know what their deal is or how long it's been going on—somehow I think he was brought into the game late, when the easy pickings were already gone and she wanted help to make the kill—but, by God, boys, I hope she was holding something out on him. If she was, he knows about it now for damn sure.

"Anyway, I went on like that for a while. It took a fair amount of time, you understand. Then I started on the dealings I'd had with him. I told him how much I had trusted him." Venable was breathing heavily. The recitation, now and with Jones, was not as easy for him as he wanted to believe. He had not been acting out a false role.

"I told him about honor and discussed his lack of it. I was downright abusive about it, but he did not seem to mind a bit. He is undoubtedly the most complete sonuvabitch I have ever met.

"I reminded him of the mares I had sold to him. I complained about their loss, went into some detail about their quality and the quality of the foals they had produced. I discussed the value of those foals and the profits I would lose by not having the mares.

"From there we moved on to the geldings I bought from him. I reminded him of what he had represented them to be and that I had taken him at his word. I described for him the condition and the quality of the horses that had been delivered to me. I contrasted the difference between what was promised and what was received. I reminded him of my opinion of him and suggested the horses could never be sold to the Remount Service because they were already rejects."

Venable was puffing. He was genuinely angry now.

"The miserable bastard sat there and smiled at

me and agreed that they were indeed rejects that he had bought at four dollars the head. He laughed about it and offered me a glass of wine for medicinal purposes. He said he didn't want me to drop dead on his rug. I, uh, told him I could if I wanted to. I bought and paid for that rug the same as everything else in the house. We discussed the house and its contents for the second time.

"Then, boys, I started talking about the mortgage I put on the place to buy those horses. I screamed and hollered some. I told him he knew good and well I didn't have cattle to sell to pay off that note. I told him how much I had been counting on a profit from those horses. I told him without that I would lose everything I had built here. I told him about the children and their schools and said they would be ruined also.

"I told him I knew he had bought my paper from the bank. We talked about his lack of ethical standards. The discussion was quite loud at that point. He looked to be quite pleased with himself."

The tension in Venable began to ease. He was returning to the safer ground that had been his reason for confronting Jones with the tirade.

"I told him we tried to sell the horses, boys. I told him I thought he had had warning that the horse market was going to blow up. He smiled. I complained about the lack of time. I said if we could get through until next summer we could weather it out somehow. He just smiled and shook his head.

"I told him again what I thought of him and came up with a few more additions to the list. He seemed to appreciate some of the points I made.

He offered a toast to me with his wine glass, and I knocked it out of his hand. He laughed. Sonuvabitch never even flinched.

"I ranted some more. I told him he and his horses could drop dead for all I cared but he was by God *not* going to set foot on my land one day before October tenth and if he did I'd blow his head off. I told him I'd use his blood to make a pudding and buy some hogs to feed it to." Venable breathed out heavily. "Boys, that man seemed awful happy when he finally got around to throwing me out. And, boys, I still had a couple dollars in my pocket. I stopped in town and got us a bottle. What do you say we have a little nip after supper? I think I could use one."

XXVII

Hart dropped a loop over the head of the first of the four hundred geldings. The animal reared against the pull of the rope and slashed the air with its forefeet.

Hart kicked the big-boned horse he had chosen for his roping. It was a yellow horse—a color he did not favor in a horse—but it was tall and stout and had the weight and strength he wanted. He charged toward the Box 11 gelding hauling in slack with both hands and pulling his dallies until he had the half-wild gelding snubbed so tight to his saddle horn that its burr-matted mane pressed against his leg. It was snubbed too close to be able to fight him or his horse.

By main strength the palomino hauled the stiff-legged, protesting Box 11 horse with it. The lighter animal had to follow or have its neck broken. Hart led the gelding out of the small enclosure where they had penned the first day's cut of eight horses. He took it to the massively heavy sled and used the palomino's force to shove the gelding more or less into position along the thick log that served as a tongue for the sled.

Harry Grimes approached the gelding from the front, and it panicked. It tried to rear and fight despite its confinement and the presence of the placid yellow horse beside it.

Hart reached into his pocket and pulled out a long pair of pliers. He waited until the gelding's head was nearly still before he leaned forward. He took a fold of the gelding's ear in the jaws of the pliers and clamped down hard. The horse tried once to pull away. The pain increased. It did not try to move its head a second time.

"All yours, Harry. 'Til this sonuvabitch's ear gets numb anyhow."

"Plenty of time," Grimes said.

The cowhand moved to the terrified animal and stroked its neck and sides. He picked up a set of heavy harness and draped it awkwardly over the horse. Before they were done Hart knew those movements would be deft from much practice.

Grimes sorted the straps and breeching into their proper places and buckled the harness into place. They had had to punch new holes in the leathers so the big-horse harness could be drawn snug on a saddle-weight gelding. Grimes fumbled with the straps and apologized for taking so long.

"No problem, Harry," Hart assured him.

"Do you want some help?" Richard offered. He and the other two men were near, watching the first hitching with interest.

"Leave him be, Richard," Hart said. "We got to learn to do it this way or we'll never get it all done."

Grimes picked up the log chains they were using for traces and hooked them to the tugs. He forced a driving bit into the gelding's mouth and buckled the bridle behind its ears. With a long piece of cloth provided by Twyla he blindfolded the horse before he straightened out the reins.

A short chain bolted to a thick wooden bar about the size of an ax handle formed a twitch. Grimes put his hand through the chain and let the twitch dangle from his wrist. With the same hand he grabbed the upper lip of the gelding and pulled the soft flesh away from the horse's teeth.

With his free hand he pushed the chain forward until it was over the twist of lip he was holding. He rotated the handle of the twitch until the chain tightened and bit into the horse's sensitive lip.

"Okay, I've got him," Grimes said.

Hart released his plier hold on the horse's ear and removed his rope. Because of the bridle—and Grimes being virtually attached to the animal's muzzle now—he had to pull his rope through the honda and rethread it in order to remove it from the gelding's neck. Hart turned the palomino away. Blindfolded and twitched, the gelding was not going anywhere now.

As soon as Hart was clear Twyla stepped forward with a bucket and small brush. In large, bold figures she painted 1L on the ribs of the gelding.

Left side of the first team. The buyer would be able to match the teams and driving positions when the horses were delivered.

Hart returned to the pen and chose a second horse as alike the first in size and color as they could conveniently find. He roped the animal and battled with it as he had had to fight the other. Perhaps foolishly he hoped the two horses would get along. From now until one of them died they would be paired side by side.

The palomino did its job, and Hart took up his dallies. It took more time to get the second horse under control for he had to snub it on the left side of his saddle. Being right-handed he had always worked a rope to that side, and the change felt unnatural to him. That, too, would be modified by practice in the weeks to come.

He dragged the gelding out finally and shoved it into place against the sled tongue.

Twyla edged near and painted a 1R on its ribs, then placed her bucket and brush aside and took a position beside Grimes. "All set," she said.

Grimes nodded and transferred the twitch handle to her. By then Hart had his pliers clamped on the ear of the second horse.

Grimes made slightly quicker work of the harnessing this time although he cursed under his breath, hoping Twyla would not hear. He bridled the horse and draped the reins. Finally he hooked in the chains.

"Take your chair, Harry," Wynn called to him.

Grimes shook his head nervously. He climbed onto the massive sled to which the new team was now hitched. He nested himself into the load of dirt mounded on the sled and shifted his buttocks until he was comfortable. He sorted his reins and took a wrap with them on his wrists, then braced his boots firmly on the front timbers of the sled. "Ready enough," he called.

Hart nodded to Twyla. She reached up with her free hand and removed the blindfold from the first horse. It rolled its eyes wildly. Its team partner was trying to pull away from Hart's pliers.

"Don't you forget now, girl," Hart said. "Stand over to the side an' when I count three you run like hell."

"Don't worry about me. I won't be anywhere near when you come to the end of that word."

He grinned at her. "Okay, Harry. One... two... *three*!"

Twyla let go of her hold on the twitch. She ducked and ran. At the same moment Hart released his grip with the pliers and hauled the palomino into a spinning turn to the other side.

It took the newly partnered horses several seconds to realize they were free. When they did they squealed and reared. They began to kick and buck when they felt the restraints of harness and chain.

The near-side horse tangled its legs in the chains and fell. The off horse tried to clamp its teeth into the neck of the downed animal. The first horse scrambled up only to find that the tongue and the chains kept it from turning on its partner. Both horses bugled their rage and tried to fling themselves away from whatever this danger might be. Dust flew into a thick haze around them.

On the sled Grimes was being jounced from side to side as the horses' efforts jarred the tons of dead weight behind them. Grimes was grinning. "Jump, you sons of bitches," he cried. He had forgotten about Twyla.

The other men were laughing and waving their hats at the already frantic horses. Grimes picked up a driving whip and popped it like a pistol shot in the air over the horses' backs. "Go, you idjits," he yelled.

The off horse remembered it could run. It tried to do so and was brought up short by the tremendous weight it was chained to. The charge was enough to slew the heavy sled sideways and to knock the near horse to its knees. The off horse rolled its eyes and squealed.

More dust was flung into the air as the near animal scrambled to its feet despite the jerk and sway of repeated lunges by its partner. Behind them Grimes caught his balance long enough to crack the whip again.

Both horses flung themselves against their breast straps. The power in their haunches pulled the sled into a lurching slide. Grimes' head was snapped back and he cut off a yell in mid-bellow. He snapped the whip again.

With the inertia of the sled overcome, the team unknowingly began to work together. They threw their weight into their harness. With each drive of their muscles Grimes was jerked backward anew. The sled began to pick up speed. It grated over hard earth and gravel.

The team became aware of the frightening thing that was following them. Their instinct was to run away from it. They quit lunging and began to pull in earnest in their attempt to outrun the sled.

Grimes no longer was feeling the head-snapping

lurches. Now he was being bounced and flung as the sled was drawn over irregularities in the ground.

The weight of the sled did not allow the horses to gain much speed but it did not limit the amount of effort they could put into their escape attempt. They pulled with all the strength they had, and the limitations imposed by harness and chains and tongue forced them to pull together. They would quickly learn by harsh experience that one could not turn away from the other without the balance of both being destroyed.

Dust billowed behind the sliding sled. Between bounces Harry Grimes yelled and popped his whip. Behind him the other men shouted encouragement, and Twyla picked up Grimes' twitch from where it had fallen.

Shortly, when the team's first terror had been sweated out of them and their initial burst of energy and resentment were drained away, Grimes would begin applying control with his reins. The team would already have begun to learn about pulling together. Soon they would learn to turn together. By the end of a day pulling the sled they would be lathered as if with soap and exhausted to the point of muscle tremors. They would also have learned enough to be considered green-broken to harness.

Hart stood in his stirrups and watched Grimes careen out of sight around the far side of the corrals.

"You can't miss knowing where he is," Wynn laughed. "Just look for flying dirt in the sky. Harry'll be under it."

"You bet," Hart said with a grin. "Okay, gentlemen. Who's the next in line?"

"They're mine," Richard claimed.

"Wait right there then. I'll bring one to you." He turned the palomino away and jogged toward the pen and the horses waiting there to be molded into teams.

XXVIII

The work was wildly exhilarating, but it was not easy. The end of each day found their shoulders sore from hauling against heavy reins, legs sore through calves and thighs from constant bracing against their sleds, necks stiff and aching from the unending lurch and jolt of the teams. More bruises and sores accumulated from the occasional lapses of wariness that could lead to a cowkick smacking into a man's thigh or a forefoot raking his side.

The drivers each had to break their two horses per day, eight head of marketable horses being made each day, fifty days to assemble the herd.

Each day when the last new team was hitched and moving Hart shifted his saddle from the palomino he came to value for its calm strength and rode from one to another of the four sleds, hazing the teams when necessary to help teach them to turn, using his free horse to control the fractious hitches, climbing onto one sled or another to help when a team was not responding to rein pressure, taking more idle moments to choose and pen the eight color matched horses that would be broken the next day.

Twyla helped them with the harnessing each morning before she was free to do her breakfast dishes and get on with her other work. She also kept their tally book showing the number of teams broken, with a description of each.

Twice they had to work far into the night to repair sled bottoms abraded dangerously thin by the constant friction of being pulled over hard ground.

Once Twyla had to make a hurried trip into town and use her savings to buy replacement chain. She gave more of her money to Perce Ditwell for him to buy a bottle of whiskey she could take back as a present for the men. She kept the bottle hidden until the end of the fiftieth long day, until the four-hundredth green-broken horse had been released from its harness and turned out with the now large herd that bore bold, black numbers on their sides from 1L to 200R.

"Well I will be double damned, boys," Venable said reverently when the last horse was free and its harness draped over the sled for a final time. "It's hard to believe. But, by God, we did it. Every last one of them."

"A drive to the railhead, a telegram and that's it," Richard said.

The others looked at him uneasily. It seemed, suddenly, to be too near, too easy now to be believed. Their whole effort could be wasted now if the herd were stolen or scattered. That possibility, in the wake of all they had done, struck them all seemingly at the same time, and they shifted from one foot to another and resolved not to speak of it

THE NAME IS HART

lest admission of the potential should call it down on them as fact. They turned quietly, without the jubilation they had expected to feel, and filed toward the house.

Twyla met them at the door. They might be overwhelmed and made fearful by the nearness of success, but she was not. She fairly bounced with pleasure, as if it was all she could do to keep her feet in contact with the floor.

"Come in, come in, your supper's ready," she bubbled happily.

"Let me guess what it is," her father teased. For more than a month they had lived on beans and rice and biscuits and what little she had been able to take from her ill-tended garden. Venable and Richard had long since quit teasing her about her garden. In other years it had been one of her major responsibilities and one of her major joys. This year she had had little time for it. They had run out of beef more than a month earlier and had not been willing to take time to find and slaughter a fresh animal.

They came into the comfortable kitchen that now had a homey feeling for each of them and hung their hats on the specific pegs now reserved for each man by force of habit. They went to certain chairs in the same manner and sat quietly. Twyla was humming a gay tune. It intruded on their mood rather than lightening it.

So cheerful herself that she was genuinely unaware of their mood, Twyla set the meal before them.

"Where in the devil did you find all this?" her father asked in amazement.

"I've been hiding and hoarding things for ages," she said with pleasure when she saw their eyes widen.

One bowl was mounded with corned beef. Another held a few, a very few, potatoes. Most of the potatoes she tried to save had spoiled. There was late squash, sliced and fried with onions. She had baked loaves of yeast bread. She put onto the table sliced tomatoes—there were only a few survivors from the overgrown garden—and four kinds of pickles, several flavors of homemade jam. The miracle of the meal was her cake. A tall, moist, pale orange colored cake iced with real sugar frosting. She refused to tell them what it was—she thought they might not admit to liking squash cake—and they ate it anyway and praised her extravagantly.

"I feel better than I did a while ago," Hart said when they were done.

"I don't suppose you hid away any last bit of coffee?" Richard asked.

"Oh, Richard. I'm so sorry. I used it up before I thought."

She looked distressed, and Richard quickly smiled to chase away any hint of complaint the question might have left. "Then I'll have another piece of that cake, Twy. Just a tiny one, though. I'm about to bust."

"If you each have another tiny piece I won't be bothered with leftovers," she said. They each had another piece.

They finished and sat back in their chairs with contented discomfort. Twyla capped it all by producing the whiskey bottle she had been hiding from them.

"Shall we leave in the morning, boys?" Venable asked the room at large.

"The sooner the better," Wynn said.

"And wear your guns, boys," Venable warned. "We go armed, and if we have to we use them. We don't wait to talk if we see somebody coming. We shoot and run."

"How about you, Gotch?" Richard asked. "You might need a gun."

"I told you before, I wouldn't know how to use one."

"You could make noise with it, scare hell out of them if nothing else," Richard argued.

"Hell, boy, there'd be just as much chance of me hitting one of you fellas as one of them. No. A better chance. You'd be closer. I still say I'm better off without one."

Richard shrugged. "I can't force you to wear one."

"No, and you'll be safer if I don't. Besides, I've got along without one this far."

Harry Grimes smiled. "I can remember a day when I wished you'd been wearing one. Seems a long time ago now." He paused. "Look, Gotch. . . in case I don't get around to mentioning it again. . . if you'll take it, I guess I'll give you an apology for trying to hoorah you that time."

"I guess I will, Harry, if you'll take mine for being so hard with you."

"Done," Grimes said. He seemed relieved about it, as if he felt there might not be another opportunity for such talk between them.

The horses were easy to drive now. They had

been held in a fairly close herd for several months and were well accustomed to each other. Hart noticed that a number of the team pairs traveled together by choice even though they had been in harness together only one day. Those would be the best working teams among them, he guessed.

The animals stretched out into a loose oval much more compact and much easier for a few men to manage than cattle would have been. Driven cattle string themselves out nearly into a single-file column. The horses stayed more tightly bunched.

Richard, on the other drag position, reined sharply to the left to head a would-be bunch quitter that wanted to sneak out the back way. Richard allowed the impetus of his mount's charge to carry into a lope toward Hart.

"I feel better now that we're moving," he said. He was smiling.

"We all do. You could feel it at the table this morning."

Richard swung in knee to knee with him. "You're a strange one, Hart. If you don't mind my saying so. Would you allow a personal question?"

"If I don't want to answer it I guess I can say so out loud."

"You seem to be an educated man. Whatever are you doing," he grinned, "or more accurately, whatever *were* you doing as a hey-boy?"

Hart tipped his head back and startled the stragglers forward with loud laughter. "Sonny boy, did you ever figure that one wrong. I never had a day's formal schooling in my life. Everybody figured I couldn't see anything so there wasn't no point in me going to school. Oh, I can read and do figures.

My ma taught me that herself. But educated? Huh-uh, boy. Not by a long shot."

"All right, not educated. You've got a brain, anyhow, and you don't mind using it. And you still haven't answered my question."

"That's easy. It was the only work I could get. But I don't reckon I'll keep on working for wages all my life. That mare I've got back at your place is carrying the start of a whole horse herd, Richard. I'll make it one of these days."

"One horse at a time if you have to?"

"Uh huh. If I have to do it that way, I will."

Richard's smile returned. "Good. I'm betting you'll do it."

"Uh huh. And I know your eyes are a helluva lot better than mine, but it sure looks to me like your bunch quitter is trying it again."

"That little bastard." Richard spurred his horse after the culprit and chased him back into the herd.

The horses traveled much more quickly than cattle. After the first day's drive Venable checked the few visible landmarks to judge how far they had come. He and Wynn estimated another four days would put them at the railhead.

On the third they splashed across the Arkansas River. It was low this late in the year. They walked their mounts across without getting their saddles wet.

"Sure is different than the last time we saw it, eh, Harry?"

"You bet. It was bank-full then. We had to swim across. Lost some cattle, too."

"Eleven head," Wynn said. "Once their horns went under that brown water we never saw 'em again. Couldn't even find one to butcher."

"The old Santa Fe Trail is around here somewhere, isn't it?" Hart asked.

"Of course. We crossed it the other side of the river. Didn't you see it?"

"Damn! No, I didn't see it." He was disappointed. He had heard much about the road. It no longer carried any real traffic—the railroad had sent it into the past save for a few families too poor to move except under their own power and for local traffic—but the beaten ruts should still be clearly visible even to his eyes. Riding in the drag with his attention on the horses' backsides he had ridden over the trail without ever knowing it. "At least I can say I crossed it."

"That wouldn't be a lie. Come on, boys, let's move them. We can be there late tomorrow."

They pushed the horses on, across short, brown grass that looked dry and withered and worthless yet which would support grazing animals by the tens of thousands. The country was mostly flat and featureless, even the river bed lost to view by the time they were a mile beyond it.

Late in the afternoon Hart saw Richard snatch his horse's mouth—unusual for Richard—and wheel to face back the way they had come. "What is it?" he called.

"Troubles, Hart. Coming hard."

Hart looked but he could see nothing. The horizon to him was no more than an indistinct merging of blue with brown from above and below. He could not begin to see anything moving there.

Richard spurred around the herd, yelling to pull the others back. They gathered in the drag, placing themselves between the horses and their pursuers, still invisible to Hart.

"We'll have to fight them here, boys," Venable said.

"No," Richard snapped. He pulled his carbine from the boot slung under his right leg. "*We* won't fight them here, Dad. Early and Harry and I will make a stand here. You and Gotch are going to push these horses on just as hard as two men can take them. It's three guns to three, and by God I give you my word those sons of unnatural bitches won't ride past us."

Grimes, so full of complaint before about the annoying weight of his revolver, laid a carbine across his saddle and calmly added a sixth cartridge to the cylinder of his pistol. The greater safety of having the hammer rest on an empty chamber was not important now. Grimes appeared totally unconcerned. Wynn looked anxious. He wanted to get something back for the scrape across the ribs he had suffered earlier.

"That's foolish, Son. We'll all fight them, and then we'll all take the herd on in."

"No, sir." Richard's voice was level and controlled. It was also firmly adamant. "Shooting close to that herd could scatter them all to hell and gone. We'd never get them all back together."

It was the plain truth, and they all knew it. "All right," Venable said. "But I'll be the one who stays here. You ride with Hart, Son."

"No, sir." He was calmly matter of fact. "You're the only one who has authority to sign the bill of sale tomorrow."

"Lord God, why didn't I think of that before?"

Venable moaned. He turned his back to the men who were riding after them. "Come on, Hart. Let's run 'em."

The two men took no time to shape the herd but pushed it gradually into a hard gallop that they were barely able to control.

They were perhaps a mile and a half away when they heard the first shots behind them.

XXIX

"I have to go back and see what happened to them. They should have caught up with us by now." Venable's face was drawn and gray in the early morning light. A heavy beard stubble made him look worse.

"I can't take these horses in alone, Mr. Venable, and you can't waste what those boys did—maybe still are doing—back there." Hart did not lightly call a man mister, but he did not mind doing it now. With his only son somewhere behind them the man needed all the gentling he could get.

"They could be back there wounded, needing help," Venable protested weakly. "They could. . ."

Hart's patience snapped. He too had had a long night. "Shut up, damn you. We both know what *could* have happened back there. We don't know what *did* happen. And right now we can't take the time to find out. Now get over there where you belong and help me move your horses. We can't be too awful far now."

They hit the spur tracks about mid-morning and turned the sluggish horses west toward the railhead. The animals were thirsty and tired. Hart and Venable had continued to keep them drifting slowly on during the night. Since the two of them had had to remain awake and moving themselves anyway—both to keep the herd together and to guard them in case one or more of the thieves got past Richard and the others—they kept the herd moving as well.

The railhead came finally into view on the horizon. The acres of stockyard pens beckoned welcomely to them, and it was with relief that they accepted the help of some depot loafers to drive the tired horses into the maze of corrals. Theirs were the only animals there at this time of year.

"Thank God," Venable breathed.

Hart could easily guess what he was thinking. He took the older man by the sleeve. "Not yet. You have to make out the paperwork in the railroad office. I'll wire Marcus in San Antonio. He can send the shipping instructions and authorize your bank draft. And, Mr. Venable... You aren't going *any*where until you have that bank draft in your hand, dammit. Until you sign for that thing and carry it back we haven't accomplished a thing." He hesitated. "And neither have they. I don't know what they had to do to get us here, but whatever they paid you and me ain't going to waste it. Sir."

Venable sighted heavily. "You're right, I suppose, damn you. Damn Jones. Damn every stinking one of them." He climbed painfully down from his saddle. He had not been out of that saddle since they crossed the Arkansas, now many miles behind them.

The telegraph office was in a small room off the depot platform. Hart sent the wire to Marcus—collect, he was flat broke—and joined Venable in the railroad office. The V-Slash-4 owner was making out a bill of sale in Marcus's favor, care of the rail agent. It was a moment he had waited for and worked for for months and had hoped toward for far longer, yet he could not smile. His concern for Richard was too strong. The pen shook in his hand. He signed his name to the document and stood.

"Now we wait," he told Hart.

"I don't suppose you have money for a bath and shave and maybe a meal to pass the time?" Hart asked hopefully.

Venable shook his head. "Sorry."

"I didn't expect you to, but I had to ask. I sure do smell bad." He grinned. "So do you." He got no response from Venable.

They returned to their pack horses, and Hart prepared a meal of sorts—boiled beans—while Venable stood on the stockyard rails and stared down their back trail in desperate hope of seeing three figures approach. His hope was in vain.

The bank draft authorization from Marcus did not arrive until the town's lone bank had closed for the day. Hart thought the old man would collapse from nervous exhaustion before the bank opened the next morning. He spent the evening in an unsuccessful attempt to cajole and then to bully any of the bank's officers to reopen for emergency business. They refused to be convinced.

In the morning Venable was pacing in front of the bank's door well before it was opened. As soon as it did he bolted inside and slammed the telegraph message down with all the power in his fist. "Now, you lazy son of a bitch. Pay me," he bellowed.

He took four hundred dollars in cash and gave it to Hart. "Buy us two fresh horses ready to do some running, Gotch, while this lump of molasses makes out the draft for the rest."

Hart left Venable fuming at the bank clerk. The town's livery had five decent horses for sale, and Hart bought four of them. Riding in relays they would be able to move faster. The pack horses and the mounts they had ridden on the drive could be turned loose. The livery man had not wanted to take them on trade in the hard-used condition they were in. Or perhaps, Hart thought with amusement, the man assumed they were stolen. Hart *did* look rough and hurried.

It was dark when they reached the site of the gunbattle, and again Hart worried that Venable would keel over with his heart burst in his impatience for the daylight that would allow a search. Hart considered rapping the old man over the head to knock him out or at least to quiet him. It was with regret that he decided against it.

In the morning they learned little. They found one body, a man neither of them had ever seen before. One horse was dead also. The tracks of another animal led back down the trail they had followed from the V-Slash-4. Four other sets of hoofprints led off at an angle.

"But whose are they?" Venable cried. "Our boys chasing them or the other way around? That lone horse could've been one of them running to tell Jones. It could've been a loose horse." He went white. "It could've been a runaway with a wounded man in the saddle. Oh, God," he beseeched. "Don't let it have been Richard. 'Cause I've got to follow those other four horses."

Hart gripped his shoulder. "No, sir, Mr. Venable. Do you recall what day this is?"

"I don't *care* what day this is."

Hart shook him roughly. "Well, I do. And Richard. And Twyla. And the rest. Mister, if we don't head back right now we might blow the whole thing. Mister, you and me are heading for your bank before we ruin every damn thing. Do you understand me? Richard might be dead, yes. Twyla isn't. You've got to protect her, man, before you start grieving for a son you may still have. Now we are getting back on those horses, and we are heading straight for home. Right.... damn... now!"

He shoved Venable toward the horses.

The ride back was fast but not fast enough to outrun the old man's fears. They reached the bank on October ninth. The transaction there, after all they had done to make it possible, was anticlimactic. Venable made a deposit into his own account and had the bank certify a deposit into Jones's account as well. Legally the note was satisfied and Venable need have no more fear of Paul G. Jones.

"I suppose that takes care of the son of a bitch," Venable said, but there was neither heat nor satisfaction in his voice. His fears were of what Jones might already have caused, not what he might still do.

Venable led the way disspiritedly toward the ranch. It was late when they arrived, but lamps were lighted throughout the big house. No light showed in any of the other buildings. Twyla must have been afraid alone there in the dark, they decided.

"I'll take the horses," Hart said. "You go on inside."

"Would you bring my bedroll in, Gotch? It has my razor in it. And . . . thanks."

"Sure."

Venable clumped slowly up the steps to the front stoop and went inside. Hart took the four horses to the pens, unsaddled and turned them all free for a well-earned rest. He unstrapped his bedroll and Venable's from behind their cantles and carried them toward the kitchen door he was now so used to using at the house. For some reason he was not comfortable using the front door. It implied a formality he did not feel with the easy familiarity of the kitchen entry.

Achingly tired, he stepped inside, hung his hat on the peg he had come to regard as his own and laid the bedrolls on Twyla's table.

From the front of the house he heard voices. The words were indistinct. But Venable's voice was angry. Another voice responded. Hart was sure he had never heard it before.

Alarmed, he eased toward the hall door. He was careful to make no noise.

The hall and foyer were empty. The voices came from Titus Venable's office. Hart slipped forward, grateful for the runner of rag rug someone had placed in the hallway. The rug muffled the fall of his boot heels.

He crept to the doorway. It was open, which made it more difficult for him to look in without being seen. At least now he could hear the voices more clearly.

"And I tell *you*," Venable was saying loudly, "I have already been to town. The money has been paid into your account. Your note has no force now."

A cool, smooth, male voice responded. "And I told *you* already that I have a cash buyer for this property, sir, and I do not intend to lose that money. Now that is all there is to it. Although I do thank you for the contribution you placed into my account. That was very thoughful of you."

"I don't care what you want, you son of a mangy coyote bitch. You took me for plenty. All right. I don't know any legal way to get that back, and I admit I was stupid enough that maybe I deserve to be taken like that. But no more. Do you hear? No more."

The other voice answered, "Oh, there will be more, Mr. Venable. I told you I have a buyer. I, uh, accepted a substantial option payment already. I do not propose to return it."

"No."

"I believe you can be persuaded, sir. This daughter of yours, now. Attractive as a fence post, of course, but you are probably fond of her. An accident might happen to her if you don't cooperate with me, sir." The voice was calm and assured. "It might happen now. Or in a week. Even a month. I assure you it will happen if you do not agree to, uh, help me in this business transaction, sir." The man chuckled. "After all, we have been partners before. I really think we should continue a little while longer."

"You wouldn't dare."

"Of course I would. It would be no bother at all, believe me. A hundred dollars to the right man would do nicely. And a hundred dollars is nothing to the sales price I have put before my British investor friends." He laughed. "Those gentlemen have the most astounding concept of land values. Simply unbelievable."

Hart risked a look past the doorframe. Venable and Twyla were in the chairs by the stove. The other man, P.G. Jones it would be, was facing them. Hart could not be sure but from the angle of the man's right arm he must have had a gun in his hand.

Hart backed away from the door. He bent to remove his boots. For the first time he wished he had a revolver in his hand. Or a shotgun. But all the guns he knew about on the V-Slash-4 were in that room with Jones and the Venables.

Sock-footed and silent, Hart slid into the room. Twyla was facing directly toward him. She had to see him there, but her eyes never flickered. Hart sidestepped away from the doorway to place himself more squarely behind Jones. He moved forward, praying there would be no creak of a loose floorboard to give him away.

He positioned himself behind Jones's right shoulder. The man was holding a small, nickeled pistol. The gun was pointed toward Twyla.

There was nothing to gain by waiting, Hart realized. He swept his right hand up under Jones's wrist. A reflexive jerk on the trigger sent a bullet smashing into the ceiling. The report in the confinement of the room was astoundingly loud from so small a gun. Broken plaster and white, powdery dust sifted down on them. The stink of exploded black powder was strong.

Hart continued to sweep Jones's arm up and over. Jones's body lagged behind the speed of his arm, and Hart felt the shoulder separate. Jones screamed as the pain lanced through him. The gun fell harmlessly to the floor. Hart kicked it aside. He dropped Jones heavily onto the floor.

The man writhed in pain for several moments. When he regained control of himself Hart, Venable and Twyla were standing over him. He came painfully to a sitting position. To Hart he said, "You haven't changed a thing." The pain made his voice brittle but otherwise he remained calm.

"You're probably right," Hart said. "You could still threaten that girl there, couldn't you?"

"Exactly," Jones said. He was able to emphasize it with a tight smile. He felt himself still in control of the situation.

Hart turned to Twyla. "Would you please go cook something for your pa and me while he does some thinking? It's been a long time since we've had a chance to eat."

She gave him an odd look and opened her mouth as if to speak. She closed her mouth again and nodded. She left the room.

"Ti, why don't you go tell her what you'd like for your supper."

"All right, Gotch. I suppose . . . it's best."

Jones's eyes widened. Venable walked away.

Hart bent over Jones.

Moments later he joined Venable and Twyla in the kitchen. They were seated at the table.

"It's a shame," Hart said. "That poor fellow who was visiting. When he went to get up off the floor he slipped. Fell down and broke his neck, I do believe."

XXX

When Twyla was done crying—though whether from relief or guilt they could not tell—Venable put his head in his hands. "Now if Richard is just all right."

"Oh, Daddy. I haven't told you. I'm so sorry. Richard is all right. He's just fine. They came back last night. They'd... been in a gunfight with Jones's men. They killed one and thought they killed another, but his horse bolted so they weren't sure. The one healthy one tried to run. They were afraid he might still try to scatter the horses so they chased him.

"It must have been an awfully long chase. They finally caught up with him and he turned to fight. They know they wounded him at the least, but he ... shot Harry. He got away. The man, I mean. And Harry needed help. The closest place they could take him by then was back here, so they headed home. They got in last night.

"Daddy. Harry's dead. He died in the bed in Mary's room. We ... buried him this morning.

Then Richard and Early rode back looking for you. But they're all right. Both of them are all right."

"We can be thankful for that much, anyway, I suppose," Venable said. "And Richard..."

"Damn shame you already put that money into his bank account," Hart said.

"What? Oh." Venable waved his hand to brush aside the question of the money. "No shame about that at all. If I hadn't, she would have found some way to get the place. No, sir. The only shame here is Harry Grimes."

"I never meant that wasn't."

"We know that." Venable stood. "Daughter, do you think you really could put something on the fire for us? Hart was telling the truth about us being hungry. Meantime we'd best carry that... thing outside. We can take it into town in the morning. Damned if I feel like doing it now."

"Sure, Daddy, though there isn't much to offer."

"We can change that while we're in town tomorrow. That's a promise."

The county sheriff accepted without comment or apparent suspicion an explanation that Jones had come out to deliver a satisfaction of his note, took a spill from his horse and broke his neck.

Richard and Wynn returned four days later. Their horses had been ridden nearly to death and probably would never be right again. They had been all the way to the railhead and back. They did not know Venable and Hart had made it through with the horses. The herd had already been shipped, and no one they talked with at the depot knew anything about them. They had not thought to ask at the telegraph office or the bank.

"It's going to be one helluva uphill fight to get the place built up and paying again," Wynn said when they had eaten and rested.

"It will," Venable agreed. "But I think we'll make it. We have cash enough left over to buy some cows and mares and to carry us until next year. We still have a hundred head or so of those geldings we should be able to sell then. We'll make it through, Early. And I guarantee you've got a job here for life. That goes for you too, Gotch. And of course you both have pay coming."

"The pay I'll take," Hart said, "less whatever I owe you for a stud fee. But. . . I think I'll be moving south in a day or two. I thank you just the same."

Venable looked surprised, but he accepted Hart's decision. Richard actively tried without success to talk him out of it.

Later Hart drifted outside to lean against the stud pen rails and admire the big gray horse. He was going to miss that animal. And his room. And more.

Light footsteps crunched in the gravel behind him. He did not have to turn to know who it was. "Pull up a rail and join me," he invited.

Twyla propped herself against the top rail and held her hand out. The gray came to her and snuffled in her palm. "Why wouldn't you at least give Richard a reason why you're going?"

"Personal reasons," he said.

"That could mean anything."

"Uh huh."

"You haven't given up your dreams, have you?"

"Not the least bit."

"Well, I'm glad about that anyway." She hesitated. "You know, hey-boy, if you stayed here you could breed your mare back to Gray Lad next year."

He grinned at her. "Hart, ma'am. The name is Hart." She ignored him.

Twyla drew in a deep breath. "If I tell you something, you wouldn't... Well, shit, what difference would it make anyway? I won't be seeing you again anyhow, will I? So I can say anything I please."

"Try to be ladylike in your language, though."

Her mood did not lighten at the jibe. "What I was going to say was that I've been doing some thinking about what you said. The thing that made me so mad. About *my* dreams, I mean."

"Uh huh."

"It's a funny thing, but I was starting to, well to let myself dream a little too that... maybe someday I might find a man for myself. Somebody who might find some use for me as a ... as a woman." She snorted. "I guess Jones had me pegged right, didn't he? Pretty as a fence post, that's me."

He turned on her. "Don't you say that, girl," he growled. "Don't you *never* say a thing like that again, you hear? Do you hear me?"

"Get your damned hand off me, hey-boy. And I'll say what I please. It's only the truth, anyway."

"I told you not to say that, dammit. Why ... why, you're a fine looking girl, you idiot thing. Any man would be proud to have you. Any man with half a brain would be."

"I've never met one who would," she said. "I thought I did once. Not too long ago. Right here on this ranch. But he had dreams of his own, and they didn't include me."

"Well, the man's a fool then. That's all. A fool."

Twyla took in several long breaths. She squared her shoulders and tried to swallow away the obstruction in her throat. She turned to look into his bouncing eyes. "Fool," she said.

It took a moment to sink in. "Are you. . .? No, that couldn't be. Couldn't be." He shook his head.

She tried to hide the wash of incredibly deep hurt that spread through her. With pretended lightness she said, "See what I mean? That's what I knew you'd say." She turned and ran toward the house.

Hart was beside her within two steps. He grabbed her by the shoulders and swung her roughly to face him. "What I was saying no about was believing you could've meant what I thought you said there. No woman could look on me with any favor. Hell, I know that. 'Specially any woman that knows about the seed I carry in me."

"I could," she said. "And you don't know you'll have daughters. You might end up surrounded by sons. Mean little bastards, every one of them."

"You couldn't be serious."

"I am. Tell me something, though. Why were you fixing to leave?"

He dropped his eyes but raised them again before he spoke. "When that sonuvabitch Jones was saying he'd have you hurt, when he said that untrue thing about you not being pretty. . . it tore at my gut. More than I thought anything could. Then later, well, knowing the kind of thoughts I was getting, knowing you wouldn't want anything to do with me, well I just didn't want to be staying around here close to you but not. . . *close*. If you know what I mean."

"You. . . I swear you can't have even half a brain

to think a thing like that. No wonder you're fool enough to say you'd have me. You did say that, didn't you?"

"Uh huh. I think I did." He grinned. "There's a condition, though."

"Yes?"

"You gotta scrub my floor, woman. You owe me that. And you gotta kiss old Fancy on the nose."

"Before I even kiss you the first time?"

"Maybe not quite that soon."

"I swear you are an idiot, hey-boy." She swayed toward him, into his arms.

Into the softness of her lips he murmured, "Hart, ma'am. The name is Hart."

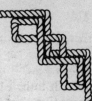

*Blazing heroic adventures
of the gunfighters of the WILD WEST
by Spur Award-winning author*

LEWIS B. PATTEN

____ **GIANT ON HORSEBACK**	0-441-28816-2/$2.50
____ **THE GUN OF JESSE HAND**	0-441-30797-3/$2.50
____ **THE RUTHLESS RANGE**	0-441-74181-9/$2.50
____ **THE STAR AND THE GUN**	0-441-77955-7/$2.50

Available at your local bookstore or return this form to:

 CHARTER
*THE BERKLEY PUBLISHING GROUP, Dept. B
390 Murray Hill Parkway, East Rutherford, NJ 07073*

Please send me the titles checked above. I enclose _____. Include $1.00 for postage and handling if one book is ordered; add 25¢ per book for two or more not to exceed $1.75. CA, IL, NJ, NY, PA, and TN residents please add sales tax. Prices subject to change without notice and may be higher in Canada. Do not send cash.

NAME_____

ADDRESS_____

CITY_____STATE/ZIP_____

(Allow six weeks for delivery.)

Powerful Western Adventure from

ELMER KELTON

Winner of the Spur Award and the Western Writers of America Award for Best Western Novel

__0-441-05090-5	**BARBED WIRE**	$2.50
__0-441-06364-0	**BITTER TRAIL**	$2.50
__0-441-15266-X	**DONOVAN**	$2.50
__0-441-34337-6	**HOT IRON**	$2.50
__0-441-76068-6	**SHADOW OF A STAR**	$2.50

Available at your local bookstore or return this form to:

 CHARTER
THE BERKLEY PUBLISHING GROUP, Dept. B
390 Murray Hill Parkway, East Rutherford, NJ 07073

Please send me the titles checked above. I enclose _____. Include $1.00 for postage and handling if one book is ordered; add 25¢ per book for two or more not to exceed $1.75. CA, IL, NJ, NY, PA, and TN residents please add sales tax. Prices subject to change without notice and may be higher in Canada.

NAME_____
ADDRESS_____
CITY_____ STATE/ZIP_____
(Allow six weeks for delivery.)

The Biggest, Boldest, Fastest-Selling Titles in Western Adventure!

CHARTER'S MOST WANTED LIST

Merle Constiner
_81721-1	TOP GUN FROM THE DAKOTAS	$2.50
_24927-2	THE FOURTH GUNMAN	$2.50

Giles A. Lutz
_34286-8	THE HONYOCKER	$2.50
_88852-6	THE WILD QUARRY	$2.50

Will C. Knott
_29758-7	THE GOLDEN MOUNTAIN	$2.25
_71146-4	RED SKIES OVER WYOMING	$2.25

Benjamin Capps
_74920-8	SAM CHANCE	$2.50
_82139-1	THE TRAIL TO OGALLALA	$2.50
_88549-7	THE WHITE MAN'S ROAD	$2.50

Available at your local bookstore or return this form to:

BERKLEY
*THE BERKLEY PUBLISHING GROUP, Dept. B
390 Murray Hill Parkway, East Rutherford, NJ 07073*

Please send me the titles checked above. I enclose _____. Include $1.00 for postage and handling if one book is ordered; add 25¢ per book for two or more not to exceed $1.75. CA, IL, NJ, NY, PA, and TN residents please add sales tax. Prices subject to change without notice and may be higher in Canada. Do not send cash.

NAME_____
ADDRESS_____
CITY_____ STATE/ZIP_____

(Allow six weeks for delivery.)